TEXAS
THUNDER

TEXAS THUNDER

KIMBERLY RAYE

St. Martin's Paperbacks

This is a work of fiction. All of the characters, organizations, and events portrayed in this novel are either products of the author's imagination or are used fictitiously.

TEXAS THUNDER

Copyright © 2015 by Kimberly Raye.
Excerpt from *Red-Hot Texas Nights* copyright © 2016 by Kimberly Raye.

For information address St. Martin's Press, 175 Fifth Avenue, New York, NY 10010.

ISBN: 978-1-250-06395-3

Printed in the United States of America

St. Martin's Paperbacks edition / September 2015

St. Martin's Paperbacks are published by St. Martin's Press, 175 Fifth Avenue, New York, NY 10010.

10 9 8 7 6 5 4 3 2 1

This book is dedicated to my BFF
Debbie Villanueva Dimas,
For always listening when I whine/
bitch/complain/cry,
You always know the right thing to
say and for that I am forever grateful,
You're the best!

ACKNOWLEDGMENTS

Being a writer is the best job in the world, but it can be tough at times because it's just you and the computer. I would like to say an extra special thank-you to those people who help make this job a little less lonely. To my wonderful agent Natasha Kern, for always being the voice of reason and encouragement. To my editor Holly Ingraham, for helping me wade through all the crap—i.e., the dreaded rough draft—to get to the really good stuff. And to my husband Curt Groff, for being my real life cowboy and introducing me to the wonders of a small Texas town. Y'all are the best!!!

And to the wonderful people at Hill Country Distillers in Comfort, Texas. Many thanks for patiently answering all of my questions, no matter how trivial, and for introducing me to some of the best moonshine I've ever tasted. Who needs a margarita when you've got a Moonshine Mule?

PROLOGUE

Some men were good at drinking whiskey, and some men were good at making whiskey. And a select few were even good at both.

James Harlin Tucker had always been convinced that he fell into the third category.

But as he stood in the small shed in the dead of a hot Texas night and sampled his latest batch, he wasn't so all-fired sure.

He swirled the god-awful swig around in his mouth for a few long seconds just to be fair before giving in to his gag reflex and spitting the vile stuff into the dirt.

"Horse piss," he muttered. That's what it tasted like. And the smell? Holy mother of Jesus. He wrinkled his nose and wondered what the hell had happened to the sweet scent of apples he'd been shooting for.

Lord knew he'd used a good half a bucket of Miss Maribel's prize-winning Pink Ladies. And some cinnamon, too. And cardamom. And a handful of other ingredients he'd been playing around with over the past few years.

He sniffed the jar of liquor and grimaced.

Not that it was a poor effort. Hell, no. It was pretty damned decent for the average Joe.

But he wasn't some run-of-the-mill bootlegger. He was

a Tucker, for damn sake. He had shine running through his veins. Any Tucker worth his salt could mix up a decent-tasting batch of liquor in his sleep.

And a direct descendant of Archibald Tucker himself? *The* greatest moonshiner in Texas history?

Why, James ought to be cranking out some top-of-the-line, Grade A hooch with his eyes closed, his bunions cryin', a crick in his neck, and both hands tied behind his back.

No problem at all *if* he'd had more than half of his grandfather's famous recipe.

He wiped at his bleary eyes. His gaze shifted to the old, yellowed sheet of crinkly paper that sat on a nearby tabletop, the edges frayed, the first five ingredients nearly faded.

And the last five?

Gone as all get out.

Ripped away by Archibald's sworn enemy and bona fide sumbitch—Elijah G. Sawyer.

Once upon a time, Archibald and Elijah G. had been friends, as well as business partners. They'd cooked up the best home brew in the Lone Star state until Elijah had screwed Archibald royally. He'd tried to cut Archibald out of the profits and so the two men had come to blows. The fight had ended with the men dividing the recipe right down the middle, and then they'd gone their separate ways.

And while Archibald had surely known each step by heart, he'd refused to write them down or use any of the ingredients that Elijah had contributed.

"I don't need that double-crossing Sawyer. Never did and never will. I can make my own shine with my own fix-ins. Damn straight, I can."

And he'd done just that.

He'd come up with a brand-new mix that didn't have

anything to do with that sneaky rat-bastard Elijah G. Sawyer. A decent white lightning that had earned Archibald a fair living for the rest of his life. *Decent.* But nowhere near the mother lode he'd pocketed in the beginning when he and Elijah had been running their 160-proof corn liquor.

The original Texas Thunder, as folks had called it, had made Archibald enough money at the tender age of eighteen to buy a two-thousand-acre spread and build a fancy house smack dab in the middle. The two-story colonial had been James's grandmama's pride and joy, right up until she and Archibald had died on the front porch in a standoff with revenuers some thirty-odd years later.

That day stirred in James Harlin's memory—the shouting, the cussing, the shooting—but he pushed it aside and sucked it up the way any man with an ounce of backbone would do. He'd never been one for tears.

Not back when he'd been a wet-behind-the-ears six-year-old hiding under the front porch, bullets flying overhead and his grandmama crying something fierce above him.

And sure as hell not now, at the ripe old age of eighty-six, the house falling down around him, the land overgrown and desperate for some TLC. Tears were useless. They didn't put food in your belly. Or settle a massive tax debt with the Rebel Savings & Loan. Or silence the whispers of a conscience he'd spent a lifetime trying to ignore.

Only a good jar of shine did all that.

It also sent him straight to Hell the morning after, but that fact never figured in the night before when James was drowning his troubles. He didn't worry over the bone-splitting headache or the nausea or the goddamn exhaustion that was sure to follow the next day. Instead, he focused on the magical cure-all of a *really* good buzz.

He wasn't the only one, either.

Many a customer had driven from clear across the state for a measly sup of the legendary Texas Thunder. They'd paid through the nose for it, too.

And so James had abandoned his granddad's so-so mix and the piss-poor amount of change he now made selling the occasional jar to the locals, to re-create the original shine.

That's why he was here in the pitch black of a sweltering July night, workin' his ass off when he should be kicked back in his recliner, his window unit blowing full blast, watching that fella Jimmy Fallon on the color TV.

He needed money.

Real money.

And he knew just the fella willing to pay hand over fist should James manage to nail down the original recipe.

He folded the worn paper, set it on the windowsill near the radio, and walked across the dirt floor of the small shack that sat deep in a tangle of trees a good ways behind the main house. It wasn't nearly the covert setup he'd had back in the day when he'd been running hundreds of gallons and had his livelihood stashed miles away, deep in the oak and cedar maze that lined the nearby creek, a dozen booby traps set up along the way to ward off intruders. A man had had to be careful back then. No, he was only running ten-gallon batches now, the bare minimum to keep a little change in his pocket and a sliver of hope in his chest while he perfected his recipe.

A single bulb hummed overhead, generating just enough glow to push back the shadows and illuminate the ancient pot still that stood center stage. An old transistor radio sat in the corner, tuned to the only AM country station still in existence. George Jones crackled over the air waves, crooning about good times and stubborn women. James started to whistle.

Not that he was a huge fan, mind you. The Possum didn't hold a candle to his all-time favorite—the legendary Hank Williams Sr. But James had to respect a man who knew how to put away a bottle of whiskey, and the Possum had guzzled more than his fair share, that was for damn sure.

James hobbled over to the small shelf where he'd left the notebook he'd used to pencil in the ingredients for this last run. Sliding on his bifocals, he eyed the list. He scribbled a few corrections to the final product—no cardamom, a pinch more cinnamon—before turning back to the ten-gallon mash bucket to start working his next batch. He was on the right track. He could feel it. It was just a matter of fine-tuning now. Tweaking.

He was just about to add his sweet feed and his honey—a full pint instead of a half—when he heard the noise above the slow whine of George's electric guitar.

The creak of wood. The click of metal. The rush of propane. The sizzle of a flame.

"Who the hell—" He turned just as the lid blew off the still and sent him spiraling backward. Glass cracked. Fire rumbled. The floor shook. The fumes rushed at him, burning his nose and punching him hard in the chest.

James gasped for air and tried to keep his legs beneath him as he floundered against the far wall, but it was useless. The blackness was too strong, too suffocating. It pressed him down like a giant hand and snuffed out his air. His knees buckled and he slid to the floor.

He blinked his watery eyes and tried to focus on the shapes moving in front of him—a hand here, a leg there, an arm to his right, a face just above his . . .

Smoke crowded around him and his vision went blurry. His lungs burned. The shadows closed in.

And then everything went pitch black as James Harlin Tucker drew his very last breath.

CHAPTER 1

Callie Tucker had never thought very highly of the Senior Women's Quilting Circle. In her opinion, there'd always been way too much gossip and not nearly enough quilting.

Par for the course in a small town like Rebel, Texas, where everyone knew their neighbor's business and tongues wagged faster than a flag during a Gulf Coast hurricane. Still, like them or not, she had to give the busybodies their due. They might not be able to keep their mouths shut, but they certainly knew their way around a funeral.

"Put the macaroni salad on the left side." Ernestine Mabrey pointed to a six-foot table draped in a white linen tablecloth. Eight more flanked the back recreation room of the First Presbyterian Church where eighty-six-year-old James Harlin Tucker had just been memorialized in front of his closest friends and family, and a few not-so-close folks who'd shown up for the free food and gossip.

Callie was still trying to wrap her head around the truth as she stood in the corner and watched Ernestine, the queen bee of the quilting circle, fuss over everything from casseroles to an influx of cakes and pies. It seemed most everyone had dropped off *something*.

Not that James Tucker had been beloved by an entire community. More like half.

That's the way it was in Rebel, a town divided for over a hundred years since Archibald Tucker had had the mother of all falling outs with his best buddy, Elijah Sawyer, back during the turn of the twentieth century. They'd been friends, business partners, and the masterminds behind the hottest selling moonshine back in the day.

Until the fight.

A legendary knock-down drag-out that had been mentioned in more than one local history book and even a few crying country songs.

The fight had gone down in the middle of town, in front of family and friends and several lawmen who'd been powerless to stop the inevitable.

The two men had beat each other to a pulp before going their separate ways, both intent on making a go at the business on their own. And while each had cooked up some halfway decent bootleg during the Prohibition era, none of it had ever compared to the ever-popular Texas Thunder that had made the two men famous.

A recipe that had been severed all those years ago, right along with their friendship.

The town had been divided, as well, as the Sawyers sided with their kin and the Tuckers sided with theirs.

It had stayed that way over the years as the descendants of the two men had kept up the fighting and the animosity, and given Texas its own bloody version of the Hatfields and the McCoys.

Things had calmed down over the years and the shotguns, for the most part, had retired to the closets, but the hatred and mistrust were both still alive and well. The rift was big as ever.

At the same time, there were always a handful of

Sawyers—mostly second and third cousins and a few distant aunts and uncles—who weren't above paying respects to a lowly Tucker via a tuna surprise casserole or a three bean salad if it afforded the opportunity to nose around and pick up all the juicy details.

Like whether James's oldest granddaughter had been able to scrape together enough cash to purchase a decent casket spray instead of the plastic daisies the church loaned out to those needier families. Or if she'd bought a new dress instead of relying on the hand-me-down black number she'd pulled out of her mother's closet after the woman had passed ten years ago.

Callie tugged at the too-tight skirt and tried for a deep, calming breath. But her mom had been a full size smaller than Callie under the best of circumstances. Since finding Grandpa James burned to a crisp four days ago hadn't been one of Callie's finer moments, the dress fit even tighter.

Callie was a stress eater, which explained why she'd gained forty pounds after her parents had died in that car crash ten years ago. Sure, she'd managed to shed three quarters of the weight over time, but the remaining ten pounds—give or take a few—had dug in their heels and were fiercely standing their ground. Proof that she would never, ever be a svelte size 5, no matter how hard she tried, and people did like to talk.

"Thanks for all of your help," Callie told Ernestine as the woman unwrapped a chocolate cake and positioned it next to Sue Anderson's homemade pecan divinity.

Ernestine shrugged her bony shoulders. "It's our Christian duty, even when it comes to a man like your granddaddy. Why, I can't believe you girls put up with him all these years. And then to know that he turned around and stabbed you in the back just like that." Ernestine's gaze collided with Callie's. "Why, you must be crushed. Absolutely, positively *crushed*."

"I'm fine. Really." Or she had been before Ernestine had reminded her of what a mess her grandfather had left behind. A truth she'd been doing her best to bury while she went through the motions today. "I know he didn't do it on purpose. Gramps had a gambling addiction."

"There you go defending him." The old woman snorted. "But vengeance is mine sayeth the Lord, and He did get the last word." She pointed a finger heavenward. "Your granddaddy finally got what was coming to him. He surely did." She shook her head before her gaze snagged on a nearby table. "Heavens to Betsy, not *there,*" Ernestine screeched when one of the quilters tried to put a platter of fried chicken next to a sweet potato pie. "That goes on the meat table." She pointed. "Next to the ham. Here, let me show you." Ernestine whisked away, rushing toward the opposite side of the room and leaving Callie to her own temptation.

Her stomach hollowed out and she fought the urge to reach for a cookie from a nearby platter that one of the women had just freed from a tangle of Saran wrap.

The town had enough to talk about, what with her grandfather's death and his backstabbing ways—namely the imminent foreclosure on their property.

Thirty days.

That's what the letter had said. She and her sisters had all of thirty measly days to come up with the taxes due to the bank, or find another place to live. Taxes Callie had thought she'd paid when she'd handed over every last dime in her savings account to James over six months ago.

The certified letter had come just yesterday, delivered to her doorstep in between a lime Jell-O mold from the Senior Women's Book Club and a sausage surprise casserole from the high school booster club.

One down, twenty-nine to go.

"I just want you to know," came the familiar male voice, "that I'm real sorry about James."

Callie turned just as her boss came up next to her. Les Haverty was the owner and head Realtor of Haverty's Real Estate, the second biggest real estate firm in town. He was in his late forties, with thinning brown hair, a cheap beige suit, and a car salesman mentality that made Callie want to run straight home into a shower. Not that Les was dishonest. He just laid it on thick when it came to selling. Still, despite the pile of BS, he was actually a decent person.

"He was a good man," Les added. "And he sure made a good moonshine." As if he'd realized what he'd just said, he added, "Of course, I never bought any from him myself. But I hear the fellas talk down at the lodge, and he definitely whipped up a good product. Not as good as the original Texas Thunder, mind you, but close. Real close."

She'd started working part-time for Les six years ago, answering phones and keeping track of his listings, and never once had he complained when she'd come in late thanks to one of her granddad's all-night benders. Or when she'd had to take an extra half hour at lunch to check up on her sisters. He even worked around her school schedule, though he'd made it clear that if she had half a brain, she'd be taking real estate classes instead of attending the local junior college. Overall, Les was an easygoing guy. Except when it came to his archenemy Tanner Sawyer, founder of the number-one-ranked Sawyer Realty.

Tanner had stolen more than one listing out from under Les, who'd countered with a flurry of promotional products, including fourteen cases of *Les Is More!* koozies and five hundred rolls of *Do It with Les!* preprinted toilet paper—two-ply.

Surprisingly enough, the promo—including a heartfelt commercial with Les offering free turkeys to anyone who posted a Haverty Real Estate sign in their yard—had actually worked. Les was now running neck-and-neck with Tanner for year-to-date sales. Another biggie and he was sure to slide right past his nemesis, straight into first place.

"I just want you to know you can take as much time as you need." Les clapped Callie on the shoulder in a gesture that was meant to be friendly but came off more awkward. While Les was an easygoing guy, he wasn't a touchy-feely person. Especially since he had an overpossessive wife named Selma who watched him like a hawk. He glanced around to make sure no one had seen the shoulder clap before he added, "No need to rush back to work tomorrow, even though we do have that big open house scheduled over at the Bachman place. I barely beat Tanner Sawyer out of that listing and I'm strapped to pull off a smooth open house. But don't you worry, I can handle it all myself. I can pick up some crab dip at the Piggly Wiggly and maybe a cracker and cheese tray and some ginger ale." He shrugged his narrow shoulders. "Granted, it won't be nearly as good as your ham and cheese pinwheels and that tiki torch punch that you make, but I'll make do. I'll greet the customers. And hand out all the freebies. And talk up the features. And field the offers. And work the numbers." He seemed to realize the enormity of what he was saying. "Then again, it might be good just to climb right back on that horse. You know, put in a few hours just to get your mind off of things.

I hear distraction is good for the grief process." Hope lit his gaze and he gave her his most persuasive smile. "I'll even pay time and a half to help with funeral expenses."

"I'll be there."

She had to be. Haverty Real Estate was her only source of income at the moment and while it wasn't nearly enough to reconcile her debt, she needed all the help she could get.

"Fan-friggin'-tastic." Les sighed as if the weight of the world had lifted off his shoulders. But then he caught sight of his wife, who stood across the room with a few ladies from the local bridge club, a frown on her face as if she'd glimpsed the shoulder clap. His shoulders slumped again. "But only if you're sure."

"I'll be there by eight."

He grinned again. "And don't forget to pick up the new chip clips I had printed up over at the Print-N-Go. I've got a whole box of them back at the office. I'd swing by myself, but I have to drop Selma at her yoga class and it's clear on the other side of town."

"I'll pick up the chip clips. And the water bottles," she added when he started to open his mouth. "And I'll even grab a few rolls of the toilet paper."

"Atta girl. Oh, and don't forget the pinwheels and punch." He glanced around. "And maybe bring some of these leftovers, too. I bet those pigs in a blanket would go over way better than a crab dip." Les headed for Selma, pausing only to wave at Loyd Vickers who, rumor had it, was this close to retiring and putting his pharmacy up for sale so he and the wife could move down to Port Aransas and fish their days away. While Haverty's didn't specialize in commercial properties, Les was always looking to make his next buck.

Callie turned her attention back to the dessert table and

a mouthwatering tray of peanut butter blossoms. Her stomach hollowed out and her hands trembled.

"Who knew they made so many different kinds of egg salad?" The question came from the young woman who waltzed up next to Callie, effectively distracting her from a temporary fall from grace. "I thought one was bad, but we've got six." She gave a shudder. "If I didn't hate funerals before, I'd definitely have ammunition now."

At twenty-one, Jenna Tucker was Callie's youngest sister. With her blond hair and green eyes, she looked like all the Tuckers who'd come before her. Even more, with her bossy manner and ballsy attitude, she acted like a Tucker.

At least that's what their granddaddy had always said.

"Why, that gal's the spitting image of my daddy, she is. She's got his eyes and his mouth. She's a ballbuster if I ever seen one."

A good thing to Grandpa James, who'd always had a good chuckle over Jenna's bold ways. A bad thing to Callie, who'd been the one dealing with all of the messes caused by said ways.

With their parents gone and their grandfather too old to take care of himself, much less anyone else, Callie had been the one trudging to the principal's office whenever Jenna had called someone a name or picked a fight or set fire to the boys' locker room.

Not that her little sister had been a bad kid. She'd just never taken any crap. Not from the Sawyers. Not from well-meaning school officials. Not from anyone. She'd never had to because she'd been young.

Free.

Meanwhile, Callie had been the one stuck making the meals and washing the clothes and apologizing for every one of her sister's transgressions. She'd looked after everyone, including their grandfather.

Gone.

"You might not like egg salad, but I'm sure there are a lot of people here who do." Callie motioned to the influx of bodies pushing through the double glass doors and crowding around the food tables. "It sure is a big turnout."

"For one reason only. You know half these folks didn't even speak to Granddad, don't you? They're just here so they can get to all the dirt. And when they realize there's nothing to dig, they'll just make up something." Jenna motioned to their sister, Brandy, who stood in a nearby line behind Pastor Harris, waiting to get a cup of punch.

Their middle sister had the same Tucker good looks, but she also had an overabundance of curves that put her right up there with Kim Kardashian.

"I'm sure tongues are wagging right now," Jenna went on, "because Brandy is standing too close to the good reverend. And flirting shamelessly."

"She's doing no such thing."

"You know that, and I know that. But by the time this thing is over rumor will have it that she jumped him just as he was about to reach for a cup of sherbet shebang and humped him like a rabbit in high heat." She shook her head. "You know how this town is."

Boy, did Callie ever.

Which was exactly why she'd always wanted out. She'd hated the whole small-town life where everybody knew everybody's business, and if they didn't, they eagerly made something up. She'd wanted the bright lights of a big city like Houston or Dallas or Austin, and she'd been well on her way. She'd worked her buns off in high school, making straight As while serving as the editor of the *Rebel*

High Gazette, president of the photography club, head photographer for the yearbook, and producer of the school's daily five-minute newscast—and all to land herself a journalism and broadcasting scholarship. Her hard work had paid off and she'd earned a full ride to the University of Texas in Austin. Then her parents had died just weeks before her high school graduation and she'd had no choice but to forfeit the scholarship.

She'd put her dreams of one day traveling the world as an investigative reporter or burning up the television screen as a hotshot news anchor on hold to take care of her family and work part-time for Les while she went after the ever-practical marketing degree at Travis Junior College. James had been seventy-six at the time and in no condition to care for two young girls. Even more, he hadn't wanted to. He'd been too busy drinking and playing cards and cursing the Sawyers for his losing streak and his piss-poor lot in life.

They'd caused all his trouble. And killed the family's moonshine business. And stolen his beloved Texas Thunder recipe. And sullied the family name. To hear James Tucker tell it, the Sawyers had been responsible for every evil thing to come along in the past few decades, including the floods of '92, global warming, and every cast member of *Jersey Shore.*

While Callie wasn't fool enough to lay blame on a handful of individuals for the world's problems, she did blame the Sawyer clan for one thing—the car accident that had killed her folks.

She swallowed against the sudden tightness in her throat. The past was the past. Over and done with. Time to move on.

Which was exactly what she intended to do. Her gramps was dead. Her sisters were all grown up. If ever the moment had arrived for Callie to start thinking about herself and her own future, it was now.

Or so she'd thought until she'd opened that notice from the bank.

She swallowed the lump in her throat and fought down a wave of anxiety.

"I know what you're thinking and don't." Jenna eyed her. "You go for even one chocolate-chip cookie and the entire town will have you signing up for a lap band before the day's over."

"I'm not going to eat a cookie."

If she was going to fall from grace, it was going to be with something much more substantial. Sweeter. More satisfying.

"Same deal if you go for a piece of pie," Jenna added, as if reading her thoughts.

"Would you stop it? I'm not going to stuff my face with pie." No, she was going to stuff her face with a cupcake—a big, fat, chocolate cupcake with lots of rich crème filling—and she was doing it in private. "Cover for me, would you? I've got some things to do in the kitchen."

"Sure you do," Jenna's voice followed. "Don't take too long. The reverend wants us back in the sanctuary after lunch to say a farewell prayer before they take the casket to the cemetery. Sort of a private moment just for the immediate family."

"Ten minutes," Callie told Jenna. "That's all I need."

CHAPTER 2

In the back parking lot of the church, Callie headed for the beat-up '69 Ford pickup truck that sat near the end of the first row.

It was a far cry from her mother's late-model green Oldsmobile, but she'd been in a hurry that morning to get her grandfather's only suit to the church and so she'd left the car for her sisters.

The truck was the one and only thing her grandfather had owned outright. A rusted-out pile of blue metal that should have died a long, long time ago. Even so, it cranked right up every time because despite being old and beat to hell, it was at least reliable.

Unlike the man who'd driven it for the past forty-odd years.

She ignored the strange tightening in her chest and turned the key. The engine crackled to life like a two-pack-a-day smoker clearing her throat. The ancient eight-track tape player mounted under the dash fired up and the smooth, country twang of Hank Williams Sr. filled the small cab.

Back in the day, Hank had been hell on wheels, which explained why Callie's granddaddy had always liked him so much. She and her sisters had learned the words to "Honky

Tonk Blues" long before the Lord's Prayer. No wonder Pastor Harris had been more than a little surprised when Callie had asked him to conduct an actual church service.

Her hands tightened on the steering wheel and she blinked against the heat behind her eyes. Tears were a wasted emotion. That's what James had told her when her parents had died. He'd taken the news of his only son's death with a somber shake of his head, followed by a forty-eight-hour drinking binge during which he'd sang and cussed and even slobbered a little.

But no tears.

He hadn't even cried when he'd lost his beloved wife, Rose. At least that's what Callie's mom had told her. She couldn't remember herself because she'd been only two at the time, but the story wasn't all that hard to buy. James had always been as prickly as the fields of cacti that lined the nearby interstate.

He'd been a hateful, mean SOB who'd never done anything for anybody other than himself. Even taking in his granddaughters had been self-serving. He'd needed someone to cook and clean and look after him whenever he drank himself into a stupor, and Callie had been right there. Ready, willing, and able at seventeen to get the job done if it meant keeping her younger sisters out of foster care.

That's why she'd forfeited her dreams for the time being and put up with James for so long. Not because he was family and she had some misguided sense of loyalty to him.

She'd sacrificed for her sisters. So that they could stick together and see their own dreams realized.

Mission accomplished. Jenna had graduated high school early—while she was hell on wheels, she was as smart as a whip—and finished her bachelor's in animal husbandry. She'd just landed an internship at a local veterinary office while she did her medical training. Brandy had opened up a small bakery in the heart of Rebel. While they were both just starting out, Callie knew her sisters would be just fine on their own.

They could make it without her now.

If she could figure a way out of the mess that James had made and keep a roof over their heads. Jenna was barely making anything as a first-year animal med student and Brandy had stuffed every bit of cash she had into Sweet Somethings. Both women needed a place to stay and time to get on their feet, and Callie had to give it to them if she ever meant to get out of this town.

But first things first . . .

She was just about to shift the truck into reverse and head for the nearest convenience store when she caught the movement in her rearview mirror. She turned in time to see a shiny black pickup trimmed in shimmering chrome rumble into the parking lot.

The monster engine vibrated the ground, temporarily drowning out Hank's familiar whine. Tires crunched gravel as the truck swung into an empty spot. The engine died. Metal groaned as the door pushed open and a man climbed out. Dressed in faded jeans, a soft white T-shirt, and dusty brown cowboy boots, he looked like any of the ranch hands that called Rebel home.

At the same time, there was something oddly familiar about him.

Wranglers caressed his firm thighs, cupped his crotch, and outlined his long legs. The warm breeze flattened his T-shirt against his strong, muscular chest. Several days' growth of beard darkened a strong jaw and cheeks, drawing attention to a firm mouth. A pair of Costa del Mar sunglasses hid his eyes. A straw Resistol sat atop his short, dark hair.

He pulled off the cowboy hat and left it on the front dash of his truck. Slowly he removed the sunglasses from the bridge of his nose and hooked them on the front pocket of his tee. He turned his head just enough and his blue eyes sparkled in the sunlight.

Her breath caught and her heart stopped because this wasn't just some random working man come to pay his respects. He was the owner of the biggest spread in the county.

Her first love.

Her most hated enemy.

The one and only Brett Sawyer.

CHAPTER 3

No freakin' way.

Callie blinked. Once. Twice. But he didn't disappear.

He simply stood there in the bright light of day, sunshine spilling down around him, making him seem that much darker and more dangerous.

She licked her suddenly dry lips.

Brett had been gone for the past ten years, having only recently returned to Rebel a few weeks ago when his own grandfather had taken a turn for the worse thanks to a bad case of Alzheimer's. With his father deceased, his mother remarried and living far, far away, and his only sibling—a younger sister named Karen—away at college, there'd been no one to look after Archibald "Pappy" Sawyer once he'd become a danger to himself, and so Brett had come home to take care of his pappy and the fifty-thousand-acre spread that stretched clear across two county lines.

Too little, too late, or so everyone said.

The disease had taken its toll quickly and Pappy could barely remember his name most days, much less his only grandson. A shame since the man had doted on Brett once upon a time. He'd been at every rodeo his grandson had competed in back in high school and he'd sat front row at graduation. He'd even thrown Brett a huge going-away party when his grandson had announced to everyone that he was leaving for the PBR circuit and a career in pro–bull riding.

Brett had certainly done the man proud. He'd made a name for himself over the past decade, and even won a few championships.

Callie could still remember Pappy's face on the front page of the *Rebel Yell* beneath an announcement that his pride and joy had snagged himself a buckle.

Her gaze went to the not-so-shiny metal plate at Brett's trim waist. Far from the coveted PBR trophy, but then he'd never been the type to waltz around and brag. He'd always been too busy working his ass off to pay much attention to the fact that he stood to inherit the largest cattle spread in the state of Texas. Too focused.

Unlike the Tuckers, the Sawyers had given up the moonshine business when Prohibition ended and demand for the product had taken a nosedive. They'd taken all that money they'd stashed during the prosperous years and put it into something much more legitimate—cattle.

They'd hit pay dirt.

They now owned practically the entire county, and quite a bit of the adjoining ones, and controlled nearly all of the prime beef industry in Central Texas.

All the more reason Brett Sawyer shouldn't be here right now. He was a busy man.

Even more, he was a Sawyer. *The* Sawyer.

A direct descendant of Elijah Sawyer, Callie's own great-great-grandfather's most hated enemy.

No, he definitely shouldn't be here.

She watched as he leaned in and pulled a lush, overflowing plant from the passenger seat of his pickup. Closing the door with his hip, he strode toward the sanctuary even though the entire crowd had already shifted into the recreation hall. He'd missed the main event, but that truth didn't seem to slow him down.

Her gaze went to the push/pull of denim across his backside as he crossed the gravel parking lot and stepped onto the walkway.

He'd always had a great butt. And great abs. And ripped arms. And a perfect face.

He'd been the total package back in high school. Handsome. Rich. As wild as the summer was hot. He'd charmed more than one girl down to her skivvies out at Rebel Creek, that was for sure.

Not Callie, of course.

Contrary to popular belief, she hadn't gone skinny-dipping with Brett Sawyer and given up the goodies that fateful night after their senior prom.

He hadn't taken *her* virginity.

No, he'd taken something much more precious from her.

She drew a deep breath, trying to ease the tightening in her chest and watched as he reached the door. He paused. Turned. His gaze collided with hers. For a brief second, something flickered in his eyes, as if he'd seen her and read the direction of her thoughts.

But just as quickly, it was gone. He hauled open the white metal door and disappeared inside, leaving her to wonder if she'd just imagined the momentary connection.

Brett.

Here.

Now.

Crazy.

A wave of anxiety went through her and her hands trembled while Hank sang about lying eyes and cheating hearts. Her own heart stuttered and she killed the music. She should march inside and throw Mr. PBR out on his cocky ass. He had nerve showing his face on a day like this. It was one thing for the distant Sawyer relatives to crawl out of the woodwork to nose around, but this was different. This was ground zero when it came to the big explosion.

Brett had no business here.

At the same time, he was the last person she wanted to see up close and personal. Him, and every other funeral attendee who'd come out to get an earful of juicy gossip.

She eyed her reflection in the rearview mirror and noted the smudges beneath her green eyes. Her colorless cheeks. Her pale lips. She looked like hell and, even more, she felt like it. She was through making small talk and keeping up appearances.

She was tired.

Anxious.

Sad.

The last thought struck and she stiffened. Sure, she was sad. Sad she was stuck in such a shitty situation with zero money in the bank and the bills piling up. Sad that she had to worry about keeping a roof over everyone's head.

She certainly wasn't getting all misty over the old man's death. She'd seen it coming what with the way he drank and caroused and carried on as if he had nine lives.

Ernestine was right. No one could flip off the big guy upstairs that often and not pay the price eventually. James had simply gotten his due and, like always, it was her job to clean up his mess.

One last time.

Her throat closed around a sudden lump and she gunned the engine. Shoving the truck into reverse, she crunched gravel and pulled out of the parking lot.

And then she went in search of the biggest box of cupcakes she could find.

CHAPTER 4

She bought two boxes of cupcakes.

It wasn't Callie's finest moment, but she had a feeling she was going to need more before the day was over and she didn't want to make another run into town. That, and Brandy's bakery was closed today for the funeral, which meant Callie was stuck settling for the next best thing.

On her way past the drink cooler, she snagged two bottles of Diet Coke to balance out everything—the guilt, not the calories—and headed for the cashier. A few steps shy, she debated abandoning everything in her arms and heading for the door.

Ivy Earline Sawyer-Hilstead sat behind the counter at the Pac-n-Save, her bright red hair teased into a perfectly coiffed beehive and her cat eyeglasses hanging from a chain around her neck. She was just this side of seventy and determined to stay there judging by the assortment of cosmetics bulging the pockets of her blue smock.

Taking a deep breath, Callie braced herself and stepped forward. "Hey, there, Miss Ivy." She dumped her contents on the counter. "How are you today?"

"Hmph," the old woman snorted. She reached for the first box of cupcakes. Sliding on her glasses, she eyed the goodies and then keyed in the price on the ancient cash register. "Looks like somebody's got a craving." Questioning eyes rimmed in bright blue shadow stared through the thick lenses. "Had plenty of cravings of my own when I was pregnant with my first—"

"It's my book club," Callie blurted. "It's my turn to bring the snacks."

"Book club, huh?" Ivy eyed her. "And just which book club might that be? I know 'em all, sugar, on account of I usually work the night shift and it gets mighty boring around here at three a.m. Books help me pass the time. So which one you into? *Hunger Games*? *Fifty Shades of Grey*? *Eighty Psalms of Praise*?"

"*Hunger Games.*" Guilt welled, but she shoved it back down. Sure, she'd never read the book. But she had seen the movie on pay-per-view. Twice.

"*Hunger Games,* huh?" Ivy pursed her lips. "My daughter Louella leads that one and she insists on homemade snacks. She don't cotton to all those preservatives they use in this store-bought stuff. Why, she's liable to kick you out on your keister if you show up with this—"

"The other one," Callie blurted. "I forgot. It's the other one."

"Which one—"

"Listen, I don't mean to be rude, but I'm in a really big hurry. I've got to get back over to the church. For the funeral," she added, just in case Ivy had missed the front page of the *Rebel Yell,* which had detailed the fire and James's sudden demise.

The old woman looked as if she wanted to keep drilling, but if there was one thing that could kick nosey's ass in a small town like Rebel, it was the death of a loved one. "Mighty sorry for your loss," she murmured grudgingly before clamping her lips shut and reaching for the second box of cupcakes. "That granddaddy of yours sure could cook a mean moonshine. Not that I tasted even a sup myself," she rushed on, "but folks talk and I hear everything. 'Course it wasn't nearly as good as the original, but word is it ran a close second."

Close, but not quite there.

The story of James Harlin's life.

She'd heard the sentiment time and time again while growing up. James complaining about his lot in life. James complaining about the Sawyers. James warning her about the Sawyers. James cursing the Sawyers.

He'd nearly had a fit when Brett had shown up to take her to the prom that night. He'd even pulled out his shotgun, but luckily her father had taken it away before James had managed to do anything more than fire off a few warning shots.

Callie's father hadn't been too thrilled with her choice of escort, either. But he'd been a decent enough man to keep his thoughts to himself and let her make her own choices. He'd simply given her a hug, a concerned smile, and a "Be careful."

That had been the last thing he'd ever said to her.

". . . Earl over at the VFW Hall said your granddaddy was brewing up some really good stuff these past few months. Really good."

"I'm sure he would have been happy to hear that." Callie busied herself opening her wallet while Ivy finished ringing her up.

"Cain't say as I'm surprised about what happened though," the woman added as she handed over Callie's bags. While she might have quit prying, she wasn't about to give judgment a rest. "It's a wonder your granddaddy didn't blow himself up a long time ago. Those stills are unpredictable, ya know. That's why I never let my Robert get himself mixed up in any of that."

No, Robert hadn't done any cooking himself. Instead, he'd been one of James Harlin's biggest customers. At least that's what Callie had figured since she'd seen his old truck pull around back every Friday afternoon, along with a stream of other cars that had all paid her granddaddy a visit for their weekly fix of his brew. The sheriff had dropped by on occasion, as well, although for much different reasons. She'd gone to high school with Sheriff Hunter DeMassi. He'd been a grade above her, but in a small place like Rebel, everyone knew everyone. He was a good man and had tried on more than one occasion to shut James down. But Callie's granddaddy had been cooking far too long to get caught so easily. Every time Sheriff DeMassi had come sniffing around, he'd never managed to find any evidence. No liquor. No still. Nothing.

And so James had stayed under the radar.

"Why, my Robert was the picture of health," Ivy went on, "right up until the day he suffered a massive heart attack. Natural causes, of course." Her gaze collided with Callie's. "My Robert wasn't one to pollute his body. Not like that James. The man practically pickled himself." She waggled an arthritic finger. "I hope you and your sisters are smarter than that. It'd be a shame to see you all follow in that old coot's footsteps."

"We're definitely smarter," Callie mumbled as she took her bags.

"So I guess that means you won't be carrying on the family tradition?" Ivy tried to look nonchalant, but Callie didn't miss the sliver of hope that lit the old woman's eyes.

"No, we're all too busy with our own jobs to start brewing moonshine. Our own *legal* jobs."

"Happy to hear it," Ivy said even though she didn't look the least bit happy. "I always knew you girls were decent. Even for Tuckers."

Callie opened her mouth, but then thought better of it. Telling off a woman like Ivy accomplished little. The woman was old and set in her ways. Even more, she wasn't worth the extra cupcake it would take to calm down after Callie got into it.

"You take care," Ivy added, sliding the final bag across the counter.

"You, too." Callie turned and made it two steps before her phone rang. Shifting her bags to one arm, she shoved one hand inside her purse and rummaged for her cell.

"The reverend is asking for you," Brandy blurted the moment Callie managed to say hello. "He's got a golf game at two and he wants to pray with us before tee off."

"I'm on my way." She pushed through the glass doors. "Just sit tight and I—hmph!"

Her breath caught as she came up hard against a solid mass of warmth. Her heart stalled. Her phone took a dive for the floor. Her purse hit with a solid thunk. Her bags crashed and the contents scattered.

"I'm so sorry," she started. "I didn't see—"

The word *you* lodged behind the sudden lump that blocked her throat. Her head snapped up and her heart stalled.

Brett Sawyer's eyes were even bluer than Callie remembered. Deeper. More unnerving.

Especially up close.

They pulled her in and sucked her under like the cool, clear water that filled nearby Rebel Creek. Sensation washed over her body, lapping at her ultrasensitive skin, sneaking into every hot spot until she felt completely sub-merged and temporarily paralyzed and . . .

Uh oh.

The moment of doom struck and she stiffened, desperate to get a grip. "I—I should have been watching where I was going."

And how. Then she could have slinked out the back or hidden in the paper goods section—anything to avoid a face-to-face today of all days.

As if he read her thoughts, his brow wrinkled and he murmured, "Shouldn't you be over at the church?" His voice, so rich and husky, slid into her ears and prickled the hair on the nape of her neck. Her attention shifted to his mouth.

He'd always had great lips. Slightly full on the bottom. Sensuous even. Just right for kissing, or so she'd thought every time he'd folded himself into the desk next to her in freshman English.

"I needed a break. Too many people."

He nodded and she saw a glimmer of understanding in the deep blue depths of his eyes. As if he'd dealt with his own share of heartache.

As if.

Brett had no idea what it meant to sacrifice for someone else. He had money, a career, his freedom.

Especially his freedom.

She'd always envied that.

Then and now.

She pushed aside the notion. There was nothing to envy. She was *this* close. A heartbeat away from the rest of her life and nothing—not even a monstrous tax bill—was going to stand in her way. She had a portfolio she'd been building over the years, filled with all of the pictures she'd taken and all of the stories she'd written, and while most of it was out of date, she'd done a few recent pieces for the *Rebel Yell* in her free time. She'd covered Sam Hardy's retirement party last year and the local eighth grade car wash back in the fall. Hardly front-page news, but it still showed her skill. Enough to land an entry-level job at a bigger paper should she ever get around to sending out tear sheets and some zip drives.

She would. It was just a matter of time. Once she had everything under control here, she would get her work out to every major newspaper in the great state of Texas, and then it was *adios* Rebel.

"Listen," his deep voice slid into her ears. "I just want to say—"

"Brett Andrew Sawyer," Ivy's voice rang out, cutting him off midsentence. "Why, it's been ages since I've seen you!" She motioned to him. "Get on over here and give your great-aunt Ivy some sugar."

"Just a second," he called out as Callie took the momentary distraction to reach down and gather up her stuff. "Here, let me—"

"I've got it. Really." She snatched up her bags and purse and then scrambled for her cell before he could lend a hand. "You go on." She sidestepped him and pushed through the doorway. The bell tinkled in her wake, and just like that, the run-in was over.

Without her reciting the revenge speech she'd worked up a long, long time ago after he'd abandoned her down by the creek postprom and she'd been stuck making a two-mile trek to the nearest house in her first pair of sky-high pumps.

You blew it, buddy. Now you suck. Your truck sucks. Your dog even sucks.

But then she wasn't twenty pounds lighter, which she

most definitely was in her best revenge fantasy. Nor was she a prime-time anchor for CNN. And she certainly wasn't dressed to the nines in a killer red dress and three-inch heels.

No, now wasn't the time for The Speech, and so it was actually a blessing that she hadn't thought to lay into him.

She would have. She'd have given him the chewing out he so rightly deserved, the one she'd never had a chance to deliver, but he'd just been so . . . *close*. And she was so tired and, well, that alone explained everything.

That, and the fact that she hadn't had an actual date in two years. And sex? Well, that came in at a whopping six years.

Six years of deprivation could make any woman forget how much she hated someone, even when faced with said someone, who just happened to be the most conniving, coldhearted womanizer to ever walk the face of the earth.

Her mind traveled back to the church and the gigantic plant he'd pulled from his front seat.

Okay, so maybe he wasn't *that* coldhearted.

Before she could dwell on the unsettling thought, her phone buzzed. She hauled open the truck door, tossed her bags inside, and retrieved her cell.

"I'm climbing into the truck right now," she told Brandy when she finally managed to answer. "Be right there."

She hit the END button and settled behind the wheel. Keying the ignition, she let the engine idle and reached for a box of Hostess.

Cardboard ripped and paper crinkled and soon the first bite exploded in her mouth and . . . *ahh*. The morsel wasn't half as decadent as the jumbo chocolate nirvana cupcakes that her sister Brandy whipped up, but beggars couldn't be choosers.

Halfway into her chocolate fix, she glanced up to see the Pac-n-Save door swing open. Brett strolled out, a bottled water in one hand and his keys in the other. He crossed the parking lot, his strides long and sure, and hauled open the door of his pickup parked at a nearby gas pump. His gaze caught hers and she came so very close to flipping him off.

Really.

But for some reason, she didn't seem to have the energy. The cupcake was too good, soothing her anxiety and easing the anger and frustration she felt toward Brett Sawyer.

That, and there was just something about the way he looked at her, his blue eyes gleaming with an emotion achingly close to regret. As if he wanted to undo that one disastrous night even more than she did.

Impossible, of course. She'd lost everything that night. Her date. Her parents. Her future. *Done*.

The truth echoed in the heavy thud of her heart and she averted her gaze, concentrating instead on the scroll of text messages blinking on her phone.

Three from Brandy telling her to hurry the flip up. One from Jenna telling her that Eliza Louise Mills had brought yet another flipping/fudging/insert-your-favorite-F-word-here egg salad. And one from an unknown source sending prayers for her sudden loss.

She stared at the unknown number. An Austin area code. She couldn't recall anyone in Austin. At the same time, she knew at least a dozen Haverty clients who lived nearby, but had out-of-area cell numbers. Maybe one had heard about James's death.

The truck revved nearby, drawing her attention. She set the phone aside and turned up the volume on the ancient radio. A nearby AM station played a popular Florida Georgia Line song and she tried to concentrate on the thumping beat rather than the monstrous truck engine.

Black flashed in her peripheral vision and just like that, the noise faded and it was just sinfully cute Tyler singing about rolling his window down and cruising down some deserted back road. Relief washed through her and she drew a deep breath.

Stuffing the rest of the cupcake into her mouth, she gunned the old truck's engine and headed back to the church to power through what was quickly turning into the longest, most miserable day of her life.

CHAPTER 5

He'd ran smack dab into Callie Tucker.

Of all the shitty luck.

The truth echoed in Brett Sawyer's head as he turned onto FM 123 and sent his pickup gunning the twenty miles outside of town to his family's ranch.

Sure, he'd known there was a possibility of a face-to-face when he'd made the decision to pay his respects, but it had been a chance he'd been willing to take. Because it had been the right thing to do, and Brett had already spent way too much time doing the wrong thing where Callie Tucker was concerned.

Even so, he'd made sure to stop by well after the main service to avoid just such a situation.

Not because she'd been the last person he'd wanted to see.

Just the opposite.

The truth stuck in his head as his mind riffled back through the past, to all those afternoons in high school where he'd sat across from her while she'd attempted to teach him the ins and outs of senior calculus.

She'd failed the task, but she had accomplished one thing—she'd piqued his interest like no one else in this map-dot of a town.

Sure, he'd managed to forget her for the most part once he'd left, but when he least expected it, she crept up on him. Into his thoughts, his dreams.

She was the only one he'd actually had any desire to run into in the past two weeks since he'd been back at the Bootleg Bayou Ranch. He'd wanted to see her again. Talk to her. Touch her. He'd wanted it bad.

All the more reason he'd kept his distance.

Callie was the only woman who'd ever gotten under his skin, into his head, and shaken his precious control. She'd been the one thing he'd been forbidden way back when the world had handed him everything and so, naturally, she'd been the one thing he'd wanted most.

Then, he reminded himself.

Because he'd been a wet-behind-the-ears eighteen-year-old. Selfish. Entitled. Out of control.

Just like his old man.

No more.

He'd spent the past several years battling his impulses and perfecting his self-control. He'd learned the hard way that it took work and effort to make it in this world. And self-discipline. Lots and lots of self-discipline. Never again would his damnable urges win out over his good judgment. He wasn't his old man.

Wanna bet?

The doubt niggled at him, but he pushed it away. He hadn't come back to Rebel after all this time to face his own demons.

No, he'd come back to face his pappy's.

Brett tried to remember that all-important fact as he headed up the drive and pulled to a stop in front of the main house.

The place had been built back in the 1950s and still

stood as a shining example of his pappy's excessive taste. The house was a sprawling one-story that stretched clear across two acres. A porch wrapped from the back all the way to the massive double doors that sat in the middle of the front steps. But while the size and architecture were more than impressive, the house itself had seen better days. The trim was peeling. Several of the window screens were frayed and cut. A massive storm had sent a tree crashing into the far corner of the house and a gutter hung down, touching the ground near an overgrown flower bed.

It was nothing like the house he'd walked away from all of those years ago and he still marveled at how ten years could cause so much deterioration.

With the house and his grandfather.

Climbing out of the truck, he hit the decaying porch steps and headed inside. The place was big. Quiet. His pappy was probably taking his afternoon nap. He thought about looking in on the old man and stalled just shy of the door at the far end of the hallway. The door sat half open, the shadows inside still and overwhelmingly silent.

There was no Willie Nelson drifting from the CD player. No fishing show blaring on the TV. No crinkle of the newspaper. None of the sounds he remembered so well from his childhood.

Brett's mind shuffled through memories of the past night, of the man's agitation as he'd sat on his knees and dug through his closet looking for a pair of boots that had long since been tossed out.

Thirty years ago, as a matter of fact.

But to Pappy, the boots had been brand new and he'd been the fifty-year-old ready to get dressed up in them and take his wife out to dinner. A wife who'd been gone for the past twenty-nine years, lost to complications with pneumonia when she'd been only fifty-one.

But in Pappy's mind Brett's mawmaw had been alive and well and, damn, but he'd needed to find those boots.

That had gone on into the wee hours until Dolly, the cook/housekeeper who lived in the main house with Brett and his pappy, had managed to soothe the old man and get him back to bed.

Sleep. That always calmed him down and made him feel more like his old self. And after last night, Pappy needed all he could get.

Brett stalled a moment more before he turned on his heel and headed for the study. He found the ranch foreman waiting for him.

Pepper Goodman was a sixty-two-year-old Vietnam vet who'd been working at Bootleg Bayou since his discharge back in '72. Like most of the hands at the ranch, he'd been born and raised in Rebel. A descendant of the Sawyers, he was Brett's cousin four times removed and one of the few people besides Brett who actually cared that the ranch was headed straight to Hell.

Bootleg Bayou was Pepper's home and so he'd been busting his ass to help out over the past few months. He worked from sunup to sundown and then some, but it still wasn't enough.

"We're missing ten cows," Brett told Pepper as he looked over the ledger page for the hundredth time. An ancient system according to today's standard, but Pappy was old school and he'd resisted the automation craze. Even the laptop Brett had bought him for Christmas a few years back still sat in the original packaging in the back of the old man's closet.

"I don't need some hifalutin' machine to tell me how to do my business," Pappy had said. *"Why, I got all the computer I need right here,"* he'd tapped his temple. *"Up here in the old noggin'."*

But things had changed and Pappy's noggin' wasn't performing the way it once had. He was slower. Forgetful. *Sick.*

Brett swallowed against the sudden tightening in his throat and focused his attention on Pepper.

"According to this," he told the foreman, "they were branded last year and turned out along with the other three hundred and fifty-five, but they weren't rounded up for the sale this past week. That means they're still out there."

"Let's hope." Pepper shrugged. "That hurricane that blew in at Port Aransas sent a mess of weather our way about six months ago. Blew the roof off the barn and the debris even took out some of the hogs. Those cows could have gotten separated from the herd and caught in the weather."

"Maybe." And maybe they had a cattle thief among them.

The thought struck, but Brett pushed it aside. The ranch was in a sad state because of Pappy's poor business decisions.

Because of the Alzheimer's.

A man who had once documented every egg that had come out of the henhouse could barely write his own name now. Hell, forget writing, the man could barely *remember* his own name.

A complete one-eighty from the Pappy Sawyer he'd been just five years ago when he'd sat in the audience and watched Brett win his first gold buckle. He'd been lucid then. Coherent. Happy.

But then the symptoms had started. The moments of forgetfulness. The whispers of confusion. Pappy had written them off as old age, but then he'd gone for his physical two years ago and the doctor had delivered the diagnosis.

Not that Pappy had believed it.

"I don't care what that quack says. I feel fine. Ain't nothing wrong with me that a bottle of castor oil can't fix."

A teaspoon a day and he'd still taken a nosedive straight into Alzheimer's Hell. Most of the time, he was stuck in the past, searching for his boots or digging outside in a tomato garden that he'd abandoned four decades ago.

"Par for the course." That's what Doc Meyers had told Brett. *"Just be patient and understanding and know that it's probably going to get worse."*

Brett knew that, but he also knew that his pappy still had good days. Days where he walked and talked and acted like himself. And while Brett couldn't turn things around for his grandfather, he could turn things around for the old man's pride and joy—the ranch itself. So that on those good days, when Pappy was lucid and aware, he would know that everything was fine.

That his grandson had fixed everything instead of tearing it apart.

Then Brett could go back to his life with peace of mind because he'd done the one thing his father had never been able to do—the right thing.

That meant dealing with the endless pile of bills first and foremost. Even forking over every cent of his rodeo winnings—minus an overdue tuition bill for his sister, Karen—hadn't been enough to push Bootleg out of the red.

They needed to sell all three hundred and sixty-five cattle they had on hand in order to buy some time to find a permanent fix.

And once they were in the clear?

He wasn't sure. He only knew that he had to deal with the cattle first, then he could turn his attention to coming up with a solid plan for the future. One that included signing the pending contract with his new sponsor and getting his ass back on the circuit.

"No one's been out to the back forty in forever," he told Pepper. "They could be out there." Slim chance, but stranger things *had* happened.

The Cowboys had actually made it to the playoffs last year, despite their hellacious offense.

Ty Walker had been the first man to land a national title in the predominantly female-based sport of barrel racing.

And Brett Sawyer had finally settled his ass down, despite all speculation to the contrary.

Yep, much stranger things had happened.

"I guess they could be holed up somewhere." The foreman shrugged again. "But I still say we stop worrying about a few and focus on the shitload waiting to board the truck first. We've got a ton of work to do before the transport to the buyer in two days. They need to be weighed, tagged, logged in. With all of us working around the clock, we'll still be pushing it. We can worry about the last few once we get the majority taken care of."

But a few meant several thousand dollars, and Brett needed every penny, otherwise he was going to have to go into his grandfather's safe and sell off a couple of pieces of heirloom jewelry. His great-grandmother's bracelet. Or maybe a ring.

Maybe both.

He shook away the notion. He wasn't going into the safe if he could help it. Hell, he didn't even have the combination. His pappy had long since forgotten it and the only existing copy resided with Miles Cole, the family lawyer. The man had been out of town on a fishing trip the week that Brett had come home. While he'd been in the office the past few days, Brett had been too busy combing the ranch for cattle to actually stop by.

Not that it mattered. He wasn't going into the safe.

"Speaking of worry," Pepper added, "I sent one of the boys into town on a feed run today and old man Mills refused to load him up. He said our bill is past due and he needs a payment if we want any more grain. We're clean out," he added, his expression grave. "We can't do any more feedings without a delivery."

Brett glanced at his watch. It was just after four. "I can still get there before they close. I'll head in and see what I can do about getting a load. In the meantime, you gather up the boys and finish the roundup." Brett pushed to his feet. "When I get back, I'll head out and take a look around for the missing ten."

He was going to find those cows and get the ranch back on track. And he wasn't going to think about Callie Tucker and the way she'd smelled like fresh strawberry pie smothered in rich vanilla ice cream.

Or the disturbing fact that he was suddenly very, very hungry for both.

CHAPTER 6

The worst was almost over.

Callie held tight to the hope as she said yet another thank you to the last few lingering volunteers at the church and headed out to her truck, her arms overflowing with the monstrous plant that Brett Sawyer had delivered earlier that day.

Not that it was anything special.

No, it was just big. The few lingering volunteers—Betsy, Etsy, and Willamina Hammond—aka the Hammond triplets—weighed about two hundred pounds collectively and could barely wrestle a tea rose into the front seat, much less something larger. That had left Callie to deal with the monstrous ficus.

She adjusted her grip on the decorative planter and reached for the door handle. It was late afternoon and her gramps was now safely in the ground in the small cemetery that sat just outside of town. Tuckerville was a four-acre spread that dated back to the early 1800s where, as the name implied, nothing but Tuckers and a few marriage-related kin were laid to rest. While it wasn't half as fancy as Sawyer Hill, a picturesque landscape of rolling green grass dotted with carefully trimmed shrubs and lush flowers and fancy headstones, the grass was mowed every other week and the weeds pulled at least once a month. Most of all, Tuckerville was a free resting place to any member of the family bloodline.

And free was all that Callie could afford at the moment.

She jiggled the handle until it clicked and the door creaked open. All the leftovers had been Saran-wrapped and packed into the car with her sisters, while the house-plants had been loaded into the back of Callie's truck. The flowers—what few fresh bouquets there were—had been transferred to the grave to mark the spot until they withered and dried over the next few weeks in the blistering Texas heat. Pastor Harris had nailed his hole-in-one, or so the tweets floating around the church during cleanup had claimed, and Callie had made it the past few hours without eating an entire box of cupcakes.

Four. That was it.

Now all she had to do was pick up the stuff for the open house tomorrow and drop everything off at the Bachman place on her way home. The idea of getting her mind off of the day's events and onto work for a little while eased the anxiety knotting her muscles and she drew a deep breath.

Yep, the worst was over, all right.

"Callie Tucker?" The name rang out as she fed the plant onto the front seat and pushed it toward the passenger side before turning in time to see the man who climbed out of a beat-up green Ford Explorer.

He looked to be in his midtwenties, with dark brown hair that was spiked into the latest style and a clean-shaven face. He wore a white dress shirt, his collar unbuttoned and his sleeves rolled up to his elbows, and a pair of navy dress slacks. Polished dress shoes completed the urban professional look and told her he wasn't from anyplace nearby.

"Can I help you?"

"The name's Mark Edwards." The man thrust out his hand as he caught up to her, his dark brown eyes crinkling at the corners when he smiled. "Foggy Bottom Distillers. We're located just outside of Austin, about an hour from here."

"You're the one who sent me the text," she said as she remembered the Austin area code that had popped up on her phone.

He nodded. "Your grandpa gave me your number as backup in case I needed to reach him. We're business associates."

The admission sent off a burst of warning signals. "Listen, if you're here to score a few jars of his moonshine, I'm afraid it was all destroyed in the fire. Not that I'd sell it to you anyway because selling moonshine is illegal."

"I'm not trying to buy any moonshine." He held up both hands as if to say, 'Don't shoot.' "We make our own, or we're trying to. Right now we only manufacture one product. Foggy Bottom Brew is our trademark whiskey." Hope glimmered in his eyes. "Maybe you've heard of it?"

She shook her head. "I can't say that I have."

His shoulders slumped. "Yeah, that's what I figured. But hey, it was worth a shot, right?" Frustration edged his expression. "My partner and I used to brew the stuff in college. When we graduated, we applied for our license and three years later, here we are. We're still fairly new to the game and the product didn't take off quite as well as expected. Not that we're giving up." Determination pushed his spine a little straighter. "It's only been six months since our launch and we've got a full marketing campaign we're going forward with. That should give us some good customer exposure. We're also trying to expand our product line." He plucked a card out of his shirt pocket and handed it to her. "I was hoping your grandfather might have mentioned us to you."

She shook her head. James had been a Wild Turkey man when it came to anything store-bought. That, or peach schnapps. "How exactly did you know my grandfather? Was he a customer?"

"No, no. I mean, I did give him a few samples of our stuff, but only as a courtesy. He was working for us."

"You must have the wrong person. My grandfather didn't have a job."

"It wasn't anything official. He was working on a recipe for us. See, we're interested in buying your family's Texas Thunder recipe."

"My family doesn't have a Texas Thunder recipe."

"No, but you've got half. It's the other half that James was working on. We know all about the big falling out with the Sawyers. Hell, it was in our Texas history book back in college. Big fight. Recipe split in half. Both men too stubborn to keep up with a good thing, so Texas Thunder just disappeared off the face of the earth. Until your granddaddy. He was trying to find the missing ingredients. He was close, too, according to the last message he left me a few days ago. He managed to nail down three more of the ingredients and the right combination of everything. He was pretty certain he was just two ingredients shy of hitting the jackpot."

Callie remembered all those nights James had spent out in the woods over the past few months. She'd assumed he'd been cooking his usual home brew and selling the jars on the side for drinking money. That, and downing a good bit of the product himself.

Instead, he'd been working on something bigger.

Something that could have benefited them all.

The thought struck and she pushed it right back out. James might have been motivated by a higher goal, but it had nothing to do with helping his family. He'd been completely self-serving his entire life.

"He was supposed to call me yesterday with an update," Mark went on. "When I didn't hear from him, I decided to drive out. I heard the news over at the diner on my way into town. I have to say, I was pretty stunned." He shook his head. "I just talked to him last week." He stared at the toe of his shoe and kicked at a few pieces of gravel. "I'm really sorry for your loss."

"Thanks." Awkward silence fell over them for several moments before Callie glanced inside the truck. "I've got a lot of leftovers to get home. I appreciate you driving out. If you paid him anything up front, I'm afraid I'm not in a position to pay you back—"

"No, no. He didn't owe us. We were only going to pay him for a finished recipe. He put all his own money into the research."

Correction—*her* money. The tax money.

Suddenly everything made a lot more sense—namely how he'd managed to go through three thousand dollars in such a short time. She'd figured he'd drank most of it, and gambled the rest of it away in some backroom card game over at the VFW Hall.

But she'd obviously been wrong.

A strange whisper of regret went through her and she steeled herself against the emotion. So what if she'd been wrong? It wasn't as if James had ever given her any reason to give him the benefit of the doubt. He'd still spent her hard-earned money and now she was stuck between a rock and a hard place. And the niche was getting tighter by the second.

"I really need to get going. Thanks for stopping by."

"Yeah, sure. Listen," he said, his hand touching her arm just as she moved to get into the truck. "I don't suppose you have any interest in picking up where he left off?"

"Why does everyone keep asking me that?"

His brows furrowed. "Did Lone Star Distillers call you? Because I know they might have offered more, but we're willing to add a royalty to each jar—"

"No." She shook her head. "That's not what I meant. I was talking about the people around here." She remembered the influx of cars over the past few weekends and the sudden rise in James's home brew's popularity. If he'd been that close to the original . . . No wonder so many seemed sad to say good-bye to the local hooch. "Folks are going to miss his shine, that's all."

"All the more reason for you to continue on with his research. He was close. Doesn't seem like too much work to finish it off."

To someone who knew what they were doing, but Callie had no clue how to cook moonshine. Sure, she knew the actual procedure. She'd heard her grandfather talk enough about it over the years. And her great-grandfather before him. But she'd never actually seen them in action. Her parents had always kept her far away from James and his shed, and after that she'd been too busy keeping house and taking care of everyone to bother poking around out in the woods. As for coming up with a recipe?

She had no idea where to start.

And even if she did, cooking moonshine was highly illegal. And deadly.

Today was proof of that.

Even so, her curiosity got the better of her. When Mark started to walk away, she couldn't help but ask, "How much money were you actually going to pay him?"

He paused midstride and glanced over his shoulder. "Ten thousand dollars."

"You're kidding, right?"

"That plus the royalty. But I guess it's a moot point now. Take care and again, I'm really sorry."

So was she.

Ten thousand dollars.

The staggering amount echoed in her head as she dropped his business card onto the dash of the ancient Ford and climbed inside. Gunning the engine, she headed a few streets over to the realty office that sat on the main strip through town. Les had called it a day and gone home after the funeral, and so the place was locked up tight.

Callie pulled up at the curb out front, unearthed her keys from the bottom of her purse, and walked inside to retrieve the promotional merchandise, as well as a stack of information sheets for the property.

James had been *this* close to *ten thousand dollars.*

She tried to wrap her head around the notion as she loaded everything into her truck, locked up the office, and headed for the Bachman place that sat just two streets over.

Ten thousand dollars would have solved all of their problems.

Then again, James had a way of turning every positive into a negative. Like the time he'd won five hundred dollars on a scratch-off. The money would have been plenty to pay for Lexi's graduation announcements and prom dress, not to mention a few past-due bills.

But before James could even make it home, he'd stopped

off at a local bar, drank a fifth of the money, and lost the rest on a game of dominoes.

On top of that, he'd gotten himself arrested for public intoxication. Not only had Callie had to pay for the graduation announcements and prom dress by getting a second job on the weekends at the local dry cleaners, but she'd had to bail James out of jail on top of everything.

No, ten thousand dollars in her granddad's hands would have just meant ten thousand chances for more trouble.

Truth be told, it was probably better that he hadn't found the rest of the recipe. Texas Thunder had been a joint effort between the Tuckers and Sawyers. Fifty-fifty. She couldn't imagine any of the Sawyers sitting idly by and letting James take full credit, and full profit, from the original recipe.

The Sawyers would never let the Tuckers take anything from them. They were always up for a fight. A challenge.

She knew that better than anyone.

She'd resisted Brett for so long, snubbing her nose at him because he'd been the enemy. Because her granddaddy, not to mention her own mother and father, would have had a fit if she'd dared admit the hots for a Sawyer. But then she'd been forced to tutor him after school because of a program she'd signed up for. The more time she'd spent with him, the more he'd flirted with her, the more she'd started to give in like every other girl at Rebel High. And when he'd asked her to prom, she'd thought that maybe, just maybe an entire town had been wrong. Maybe the Tuckers and the Sawyers could find some common ground.

Maybe they could even fall in love.

But while she'd had visions of uniting the town, Brett had merely been playing a game, proving to the world that he could have any girl he wanted—including a Tucker.

Especially a Tucker.

That's what had been floating around the entire school after that fateful night. That he'd lured her in, only to throw her back because, well, he was a Sawyer and no Sawyer would stoop low enough to fall for a Tucker.

Not that she'd believed the gossip.

Brett himself had pushed the truth home with his behavior. He'd gone from walking her to and from her locker, to having nothing at all to do with her virtually overnight.

He hadn't even said so much as "I'm sorry" when her folks had died that very night while on their way to pick her up after he'd abandoned her. They'd had a head-on collision with a couple of prom-goers who'd had too much trash-can punch, and while the kids had walked away without so much as a scratch, her parents hadn't been so lucky. They'd veered off the road, straight into a gully in order to avoid the drunk kids, and it had cost them both dearly.

It had cost Callie.

There hadn't been a night since that she didn't regret calling them for help. She'd blamed herself at first and then the drunk kids, and then the damned gully itself, and then she'd come to blame the real culprit—the one and only Brett Sawyer.

If he hadn't abandoned her, she never would have called her parents. He'd set the tragic set of events into motion and she'd vowed never to forget.

Or forgive.

He'd taken not only her parents that night, he'd taken her trust, her hope, her stupid pie-in-the-sky optimism.

She was no longer that naïve girl who actually thought that love could overcome a hundred years of hatred. Love didn't overcome anything. It made people weak.

Blind.

Not that she'd been blinded by anything close to love

when she'd handed over all that tax money to James. The man hadn't deserved her love. No, she'd given him the money because he'd been the deed holder and she'd been busy working and, well, all he'd had to do was drive to the bank and make that one payment.

But he'd failed her. Like always. And he'd been headed for more trouble this time with that stupid recipe. Luckily Fate had stepped in to lend Callie a hand and stop him.

Callie ignored the strange tightening in her chest and pulled into the driveway of the Bachman house. The engine grumbled into a few sputters and then went silent.

Her gaze went to the sprawling two-story with the large front porch edged with lush azalea bushes and fragrant Texas sage. The owners had made dozens of renovations to the spacious four bedrooms and three baths, as well as new landscaping around the large patio and pool out back. It was one of the nicer homes in Rebel with a key location on the corner of Main Street and Yellow Rose. Everything was within walking distance, from the pharmacy to the feed store. For that reason alone it should draw an offer quickly, or so she hoped. The quicker the house sold, the more amicable Les would be when she threw herself on his mercy and begged for a pay advance. Or a loan. She hadn't decided which. She just knew she had to do *something*.

The clock was ticking, after all.

She drew a deep breath, tucked a wayward strand of hair behind her ear, and did what she always did when she was stressed to her limits and so dangerously close to breaking—she sucked it up and went to work.

Just keep driving.

That's what Brett Sawyer told himself when he turned the corner off Main Street and spotted the familiar blue pickup parked in front of the corner house. But then he saw Callie standing near the truck bed, struggling with a large box, and he couldn't help himself.

For better or worse, he hit the brakes and pulled into the driveway.

CHAPTER 7

Brett's headlights sliced through the dusky shadows of sunset as he pulled up behind Callie's truck and killed the engine. She turned and eyes as green as the lush pastureland behind his house caught his. Something twisted in his stomach.

That same something he'd felt back at the store when he'd run into her. And back in school when he'd slid into the desk across from hers every afternoon for tutoring. And when he'd glanced across the lunchroom to catch her looking at him.

Killing the engine, he slid out of the truck, his boots hitting the pavement with a loud *thunk*. With each step, his chest got a little tighter until he caught himself holding his breath as he reached her.

"What are you doing here?"

If only he knew. But he wasn't asking himself that question at the moment because he sure as hell didn't want to have to answer it. He smiled instead and motioned to the box. "You looked like you could use a hand."

"I'm okay." She reached for the box, but he was quicker. His hand brushed hers and a jolt of electricity shot up his arm, into his chest, and fire-balled straight to his groin.

Instant.

Powerful.

Predictable.

He'd had the same reaction to her way back when in the backseat of his pappy's Cadillac and it had scared the hell out of him because he'd never felt that way before. That itchy and tight and out of control.

Then.

He was a full-grown man now and while he still felt the attraction, he could handle it.

Nothing rattled Brett Sawyer. Not a thousand-pound bucking bull or a punch of lust. He just picked himself up, dusted himself off, and pasted on his easiest smile.

"I've got it." He caught the box and lifted it easily. "Where do you want it?"

She frowned and looked as if she wanted to tell him a few choice destinations. The seconds ticked by, but then the expression eased. "Inside." She grabbed another smaller box and started up the front walk. Punching in the key code on the combination lock hooked on the front knob, she opened the door and walked into the shadowy interior. A split-second later, she hit the light switch to the right and light flooded the entryway and illuminated the front porch.

"You can put it right here." She set her own box on a small side table and motioned to the floor next to it.

He bent down and deposited the cardboard on the polished hardwood before turning to admire the front entryway. "What happened to the Bachmans?"

"They retired and moved. Haverty's got the listing."

"So you're working for Les now?"

She shrugged. "It pays the bills." She blew out a deep breath and her chest pushed against the tight confines of her black dress. The buttons strained to stay together and Brett found himself wishing they would just give up the fight.

He stiffened against the thought, determined to keep his mind on something other than getting her naked. "How come you're working tonight of all nights?"

She shrugged. "The world doesn't stop just because something bad happens. The clock keeps ticking and the bills keep piling up."

"I know that feeling."

"So I guess the rumors are true?" She arched an eyebrow at him as she pulled out a stack of fliers and set them on the small table.

"That depends on what the rumors are saying."

"They're saying Bootleg Bayou is in financial trouble."

He frowned. "Nothing I can't handle." At least that's what Brett was desperately telling himself. But after twenty minutes spent convincing the feed store owner to extend his line of credit, he was starting to doubt himself. Things just kept growing and growing, getting heavier by the minute.

In more ways than one, Brett thought as his gaze caught on the shapely curve of Callie's ass beneath the clingy black material and he felt the tightening in his groin. She'd always been curvy, but a few pounds in all the right places made it even harder for him not to look.

Not to want.

"I'll grab the rest of the boxes," he blurted, eager to get a grip before he did something he would truly regret—like push her up against the nearest wall, pop those buttons on her dress, and see if her nipples were still as pink as he remembered. As tasty. He wasn't here for that.

Sure thing, buddy.

The doubt dogged him as he headed back out to the truck. He spent the next five minutes hauling in the two boxes and doing his damnedest to ignore the blonde unpacking the carton of promotional water bottles nearby.

"What next?" he asked when he'd deposited the last of the cardboard onto the floor.

"You can open up that other box with the rest of the water bottles. We're going to stack some here"—she pointed to the table in the foyer—"and the rest are going in the kitchen."

He pulled out his pocket knife, sliced through the packing tape, and opened up the container, grateful to have something to focus on other than the woman moving about in his peripheral vision.

Yep, she'd filled out in all the right places.

She had more curves and damned if her legs weren't longer than he remembered. He slid a glance to the side and caught a glimpse of one delicate ankle, a shapely calf. She wasn't wearing any stockings and the urge to lean over and run his fingertips along her smooth flesh punched him hard and fast in the chest.

He gripped one of the water bottles instead and focused all of his attention on stacking two dozen on the polished table, one after the other, at a record pace until the last one hit the wood and he turned to snatch up the box and head for the kitchen.

The sweet peachy vanilla scent followed him, teasing his nostrils and stirring a whisper of awareness that settled at the back of his neck before creeping down along his spine.

His ears tuned to the soft footsteps as she moved about the house, setting up fliers and distributing promotional products and he couldn't help but wonder which room she was in, and what all he could do to her in each specific spot.

He saw her draped across the sofa, her buttons popping and her lips parting as he leaned over her. Or bent over the staircase, his hands on her thighs as he pumped into her from behind. Or spread across a king-sized bed, her golden hair fanned out around her, her body so lush and open and—

Aw, hell.

He moved faster, emptying out the box and stacking the rest of the bottles. There. Done.

Time to get the hell out of Dodge.

He turned to see her standing in the doorway between the hallway and the kitchen. Her grass-green gaze collided with his for a second and she caught her bottom lip as if thinking of what to say next. Or fighting back what she really wanted to say.

It was a sight that sucked him back in time to all those afternoons spent in the calculus lab, where she'd done her best to keep things strictly business while he'd flirted and talked and done his damnedest to get past the wall she'd built up around herself.

The challenge. That's what he'd told himself. She was a Tucker. The forbidden fruit. And Brett had been more than eager to take a great big bite. She'd turned him down that first time he'd asked her out, but he'd been persistent. He'd asked again. And again. And eventually she'd said yes.

Despite her parents' objection and the fit her grand-daddy had thrown on the front porch when Brett had arrived to pick her up.

Hell, he'd nearly gotten his ass shot off with a sawed-off bootleg special, but Callie had faced James Harlin with a stern look that said she knew what she was doing, and she was doing it whether he liked it or not.

Brett had felt something he'd never felt for any girl at that particular moment—admiration. The feeling had chipped away at his smooth Southern charm and turned him into an awkward, overly excited ball of testosterone. He'd wanted her so bad.

He still did.

The notion struck and he shoved it to the furthest part of his mind. Maybe so, but he wasn't acting on it. That was the difference between the boy he'd been and the man he was now—he wasn't a slave to his basic impulses.

Control. That's what it was all about and he had it in spades.

But back then . . . He'd been desperate that night. Awkward. Overly excited. And so he'd pushed her out of his car and sped away. That first date had turned into their last and he hadn't talked to her since.

He'd meant to. But she'd been too torn up over her parents and he'd been at a loss as to what to say. Hell, he hadn't trusted himself to say anything to her after spouting off like Old Faithful before he'd even gotten his pants off. He'd been embarrassed. Scared. Stupid.

A kid, he reminded himself.

But he was a full-grown man now, and he wasn't losing his head where she was concerned. No ripping off her clothes and burying his face in her breasts. No plundering her mouth with his.

Not ever again.

But there was nothing wrong with being nice. Friendly. He owed her that much. That's why he'd stopped in the first place. To be cordial. Decent.

Drawing a deep breath, he met her steady gaze. "What else can I do for you?"

CHAPTER 8

Take a flying leap.

That's what Callie wanted to say. What she'd been waiting ten years to tell him.

Sure it wasn't the ideal scenario. No killer job or killer heels, but she wasn't going to get caught up in the details. It wasn't as if Brett Sawyer waltzed back into her life every other day. This might be her only chance to blast him and tell him what she really thought of him.

That he was a no-good, unreliable lowlife who'd ruined everything. He'd dumped her and taken the most important thing from her—her parents.

But the truth was, she didn't really want to blast him anymore. And not because she was too tired or because she didn't look her best or because she was coming off one of the worst days of her life. But because, in all honesty, he just didn't deserve it.

Yes, he was no-good and unreliable and a lowlife. And he'd most definitely ruined a lot of things—namely her self-esteem. At least back then. But he hadn't taken her parents from her.

Ten years had taught her that sometimes bad things just happened. To some more than others.

She'd blamed him at first because he'd been an easy

target. She'd been mad and hurt and he'd been such a jerk that night. He'd been the reason she'd had to call her parents in the first place.

Still, he hadn't been the one who'd crashed into them.

He stared at her expectantly. "Are there more boxes?"

"No, I just . . ." Her voice faded and she caught her lip, trying to say something—anything—so she didn't appear a total idiot. His gaze dropped and she could practically feel it slide over the fullness of her bottom lip. "That is, I thought you might want to take a tour of the house."

His mouth crooked at the corner and she saw a hint of the teasing grin that she remembered so well. "You trying to sell me some real estate?"

"Hardly." She had the sudden image of that grin up close and personal a split-second before his mouth pressed against hers and her stomach hollowed out. "I'm not even a licensed Realtor."

Yet.

She steeled herself against the thought, one which had nagged her for the past few years, since the moment Les had urged her to get her Realtor's license. "I'm an office assistant. For now." She wasn't sure why she kept going except that she needed to do something with her mouth that didn't involve kissing him, and rambling seemed like the only thing she could come up with. "As soon as I settle everything with my grandfather's estate, I'm out of here. I've got a stack of resumes ready to send out to the *Dallas Herald,* the *Houston Chronicle,* and a dozen other publications. Everything from a few Texas travel magazines to a local Hill Country tabloid."

"So you still want to be a journalist?"

"An investigative reporter." She shrugged. "At least that's what I'm hoping for eventually. Right now, I'll settle for compiling traffic reports or doing human interest—anything to get my foot in the door. I'm doing a few stories here and there for the *Rebel Yell,* but nothing big. Just enough to keep my feet wet for now."

"I figured you would have taken off after that dream a long time ago."

She remembered how excited she'd been those months leading up to graduation. How hopeful because she'd gotten into one of the best journalism schools in the country. Her hope had died that night as she'd stood in the ER, listening to the doctor deliver the bad news that both her parents had passed away shortly after arriving at the trauma unit. She blinked against the sudden burning behind her eyes and shrugged. "Life doesn't always work out the way we want."

"Tell me about it," he murmured and she noted the weariness around his own eyes.

Something twisted in her chest. "I heard about your grandfather. How's he doing?"

"He's hanging in there." He stiffened, as if fighting some internal battle. "I'm sure he'll be back on his feet in no time."

"But I thought he had Alzheimer's?"

"He does, but he still has good days left. A lot of them." His gaze locked with hers and she saw the glimmer of desperate hope, as if he was still holding on to the idea that everything could be okay. That it *would* be okay.

She recognized the look because she'd told herself the same thing as she'd waited in the ER for news of her parents. Everything would be okay. Life would go on. Dreams would be achieved. "When he's on his feet again and the ranch is in a better position, then I'll hit the circuit again. I landed a new sponsor for this next tour. A big one."

"That's great."

"They just delivered the contracts a few days ago. Once I sign I'll be their spokesperson for the next five years."

"So I'm guessing you're just home temporarily." He nodded and she felt a strange whisper of regret. A crazy reaction because it made little difference if he stuck around. She'd be long gone from Rebel just as soon as she figured a way out of the tax debt. "It's good that you're going back. It would be a shame to give up after that last ride."

"You saw the Vegas run?"

A smile tugged at her lips. "I may have been flipping channels and caught a glimpse of the finals on ESPN." She didn't mean to tell him, but the glimmer that lit his eyes prompted her to keep talking. "You were really great."

His mouth didn't just hint at a grin in that next instant. Instead, she got the real thing as his sensuous lips crooked at the corner. His blue eyes twinkled and her heart stalled. "Sounds like you caught more than just a glimpse."

"Enough to know that you deserved that buckle." And that he'd done not one victory lap around the arena after snagging the title, but three. Instead of basking in the media attention, he'd been fixated on talking to the fans. On thanking them and signing autographs and shaking hands. He'd been the usual smooth-talking charmer that she remembered so well, but there'd been something different about him, as well.

Something humble and achingly close to grateful.

She'd known then that he'd changed from the spoiled, entitled Sawyer who'd always had everything and everyone handed to him.

No one had given him that victory. He'd worked for it.

Fifteen minutes, she reminded herself. She'd watched him all of fifteen minutes, until the show had ended and the latest NASCAR race had taken its place. Not nearly enough time to gauge whether or not Brett Sawyer was still the same self-centered jerk he'd been back in the day.

No one could change that much.

That's what she told herself.

But there was no denying the facts. He'd come home to help his pappy and showed up at the church with a plant and stopped to help her with the boxes and . . .

Motherfudger, he *was* different.

The realization made her want to cross the space between them and see what else had changed about him. Did his lips still feel as soft when pressed against hers? Would he still do that little circle with his thumb at the base of her spine when he pulled her close? Would he make her feel the same dizzying heat she'd felt that night in the backseat of his pappy's fancy car? Would he make her feel all of that and more?

The questions bombarded her, one after the other, making her hands tremble and her body ache and—

Are you freakin' kidding? This is Brett Sawyer. The guy more interested in the chase than the actual prize. You're not throwing yourself at him. You're never throwing yourself at him.

Never, ever again.

She stiffened and glanced at her watch. "I, um, really need to get home."

He arched one eyebrow. "I thought you wanted to give me a tour?"

"I can't. It's, um, against the rules. I'm not a Realtor, so I can't legally show you a house that's on the market." Okay, so it sounded lame, but it was the best she could come up with. "I shouldn't have offered, but my day's been sort of screwy so I'm not really thinking straight. If you come back tomorrow, I'm sure Les would be happy to show you around." She turned and headed for the foyer.

Her heart thundered in her chest for several long seconds before she heard the footsteps behind her.

"Thanks again for stopping to help," she told him as she hauled open the door.

He stopped just a few inches shy and stared at her for a brief moment before he finally shrugged. "My pleasure." His deep, rumbling voice echoed in her ears as he walked out the door and headed down the walkway.

Not a chance, buddy.

She concentrated on locking up the house rather than watching him climb into his truck. There wasn't going to be any pleasure of any kind.

Not his.

Not hers.

No.

His truck grumbled to life and she felt the vibration along her nerve endings. Her heart sped faster but she kept from looking as he shifted the monstrous pile of sleek metal into gear and pulled out of the drive. She'd been down the pleasure highway once before with him, one pitted with dozens of potholes and sharp turns, and she wasn't making the trip again.

No matter how much he'd changed.

She'd changed, as well. She'd learned from her mistakes and experience told her to forget all about Brett, take care of business, and get her life back on track.

That was the smart thing to do. The right thing.

And Callie Tucker always did the right thing.

She just wished the right thing didn't always feel so damned wrong where Brett Sawyer was concerned.

The rumble of his truck faded, thankfully, and she managed to drag in a much-needed breath. A few minutes later, she climbed into her granddad's old truck, fired up the engine, and headed home.

CHAPTER 9

"I tossed the egg salad," Jenna declared when Callie walked into the kitchen twenty minutes later to find her youngest sister standing in front of an open refrigerator.

"Which one?"

"All of them. A whopping twelve." She motioned to a nearby trash can. "In my defense, it wouldn't all fit in the fridge." She indicated the overflowing Frigidaire. The avocado-green monster had seen better days like most everything else in the Tucker household, but with a few creaks and groans it kept churning along.

Thankfully.

Callie had enough to deal with without adding a broken appliance to the list.

"Even Jezebel turned her nose up at it." She indicated the tiny dog yapping at her heels. Jezebel was a Yorkie/poodle/Grade A mutt blend that Jenna had picked up out near the interstate and nursed back to life at the veterinary clinic. She'd brought the tiny dog home until she could find her a permanent place.

That had been over six months ago, during which time they'd also picked up three more dogs, a cat, and a rabbit named Hoppy.

"You have to get that dog out of here."

"I will." Jenna retrieved a Milk-Bone from a nearby container and fed it to the excited animal. "Just as soon as she's back on her feet, she's history."

"She's on her feet." Callie glanced at the dog dancing around the kitchen. "She's on my feet. She's on your feet." She caught Jenna's gaze. "I know you love them, but we can barely look after ourselves. We don't have enough room for so many foster babies." That, and who was going to look after them when Callie was gone? Jenna worked hellacious hours, especially since she'd decided to specialize in equine health. With so many ranches nearby and an overwhelming horse population, Jenna barely made it home before dark on most nights. Ditto for Brandy. And so it was Callie who got stuck looking after all the strays. "You have to get them out of here."

"I'll start looking first thing tomorrow." Jenna crossed her heart before slipping the dog another treat. "I've got immunizations out at the Gerber Horse Farm in the morning, but after that, I'm on it. Swear."

Callie turned her attention back to the counter and the stack of empty egg-salad containers. "You should have saved at least some of this stuff. I could have taken it to the open house tomorrow."

"Trust me, no potential homeowner with even a sliver of taste is going to show up for egg salad. Maybe these pigs in a blanket." She pulled a container from the fridge and popped the lid. "I've got to say, I can't stand to be in the same room with Genevieve Hanson. The woman is old and cranky and the nosiest person I've ever met, but she sure can cook." Jenna pulled a tightly wrapped sausage from the green plastic and took a big bite. "These things are amazing," she said around a mouthful.

The conversation with Les played in Callie's head and

her gaze went to the container in her sister's hand. "Please tell me you didn't eat them all."

"No way." She shoved the last bite into her mouth and reached for a soda. "There's still one left. Say," she motioned to Callie, "why don't you try making some? You could ask Genevieve for her recipe."

But Callie didn't cook. Sure, she'd stepped up to the plate years ago, to make sure the girls had a hot meal every night and she'd even managed to master the basics—eggs, pancakes, meatloaf, a decent roast beef on those rare days when the planets lined up. But she didn't *like* to cook. Not like her sister Brandy, who would gladly spend all day slaving in front of a hot oven. A passion she'd inherited from their mother. The woman had made a mean brownie. She shrugged. "Les will just have to make do with pimento cheese pinwheels."

"Then I'm guessing it won't matter if I finish these off?" Without waiting for a reply, Jenna grabbed the sole survivor and took a bite. "And don't think I'm going to forget about you," she told Jezebel as she pinched off a piece of the goody and fed it to the yapping dog. "I know, I know. It's time to watch our show." She took another bite. "I TiVo'd the season finale of *The Bachelor* and Jez and I just know he's going to pick Lacey. I mean, Bella's nice, too, but she's sort of a slut. His parents definitely like Lacey better. She teaches Sunday school and she has a schnauzer." Jenna winked at the tiny dog. "Jez has a thing for schnauzers."

"You're not seeing Alex tonight?"

Jenna shrugged. "We broke up."

"Does he know that?"

"What's that supposed to mean?"

"That you have a tendency to beat around the bush when you break up with someone."

"It's called letting them down easy."

"It's called being a chicken shit." Callie eyed her sister. "Remember Kevin Rickers? You told him you couldn't breathe and he thought you meant you had asthma. He bought you a humidifier and a case of Primatene."

"I can't help it if he misunderstood me." A smile curved her full lips. "That was sort of sweet, though. Remind me why I cut him loose again?"

"Because he wanted to be your one and only and you're much more into plural arrangements. That's PC for you're a big fat 'fraidy cat when it comes to commitment."

"I can commit. I just don't see the point." She frowned. "Besides, I'm too busy for commitment. I barely have time for fun."

"Again, did you make that clear to Alex? Because we don't need another humidifier."

"Cross my heart I didn't say a thing about not being able to breathe." She shrugged. "I just told him in a nice, it's-not-you-it's-me way, that I was just feeling crowded." She seemed to think. "Or maybe I told him I was feeling over-whelmed." She waved a hand. "Either way, we're done."

"And he realizes this?"

"He got the message loud and clear." She seemed to think. "I'm pretty sure he did. He was definitely standoff-ish at the funeral. He only tried to hold my hand one time."

"Here we go again," Callie mumbled as she turned back to the fridge.

"Where exactly are we going again?" Brandy walked into the kitchen wearing yoga pants and an oversized T-shirt. Her long hair had been pulled up into a ponytail and she wasn't wearing a stitch of makeup, yet she looked every bit as beautiful as if she'd been dressed to the nines. That was the thing about Brandy. She was a natural beauty, unlike Callie, who just looked tired when she wasn't wearing any makeup.

Then again, she *was* tired. Tired of looking out for everyone and carrying the weight of the entire family on her shoulders.

Now, but that would end soon. She would figure a way out of the financial mess, secure the house, and then get those resumes off in the mail.

Callie held tight to the sliver of hope and retrieved a knife from a nearby drawer. "Stalkerville," she told Brandy. "That's where we're going again."

"You broke up with Alex, didn't you?" Brandy shot a glance at Jenna. "Or rather, you didn't break up with Alex. You just think you did."

"Trust me, I did."

"Sure." Brandy shrugged. "I get dibs on the humidifier this time. I want one for the employee break room. Ellie, my new baking assistant, has allergies."

"Very funny," Jenna said. "There won't be another humidifier."

"She was too crowded this time," Callie chimed in, "so he's probably going to get her a few therapy sessions to deal with claustrophobia."

"Wow, you guys are on a roll tonight." Jenna grabbed her chips and soda and whistled at Jezebel. "Later haters. We've got a date with *The Bachelor.*"

"Another date? Isn't that what keeps getting you into this mess?" Brandy called after her. Jenna paused to make a crude hand gesture. Jezebel yapped. And they both disappeared into the living room.

"She has a problem," Brandy remarked. "She's what you call a serial dater. I saw it on *Dr. Phil.* He did a show on addictions and serial dating was right up there with the lady who wipes herself down with antibacterial wipes at least twenty times a day and this guy who ate his own toenails."

"At least she puts herself out there," Callie said, eyeing her sister. "Which is more than I can say for present company."

"Men are a distraction, and I can't afford that right now. I've got everything tied up in this bakery. It has to have my undivided attention."

Jenna loved men. Brandy avoided them. And Callie just didn't have the time.

Unless they showed up unannounced to lift boxes for her, that is.

Brett's image snuck into her brain and she stiffened. "How goes it at Sweet Somethings?"

"I've been open all of one month and I managed to make enough to meet all of my bills. I'd say that's a good start. Next month's projected numbers look even better." She smiled. "I just might pull this off."

"You will. Your cakes are divine and there isn't a better decorator for a hundred miles."

"You know," a serious look pinched her smooth face, "I can't thank you enough for helping me through pastry school."

Callie shrugged. "Family does for family."

"Exactly. Which is why I'm going to pay you back. Every single cent, plus five percent interest. Just as soon as I'm running in the black. Right now, I've got to bring in a second oven if I ever want to up my production . . ."

Brandy went on for the next fifteen minutes about the latest in high-tech baking equipment while Callie finished off a platter of pinwheels and moved on to a mountain of ham and cheese sandwiches. She'd just finished cutting off the last of the crust when Brandy glanced at the clock.

"Wow, would you look at the time? I need to get to bed. I've got to be at the bakery at four a.m. to get the bread in the oven. I'm featuring apple loaves for tomorrow's special." She glanced around. "You about done here?"

"A little Saran wrap"—Callie indicated the overflowing platter of finger sandwiches—"and then I'm off to bed myself."

Unfortunately, twenty minutes turned into an hour before Callie managed to put away the last of tomorrow's snacks.

She'd just shut the refrigerator and killed the kitchen lights when she heard the knock on the back door.

"Are you expecting anyone?" she called out to Jenna, but the girl had already fallen asleep on the sofa, the small dog cuddled on her lap.

"Never mind," Callie murmured as she headed for the back door. A strange tingle of excitement whispered through her as she thought of Brett.

Not that he was knocking on her door now. He had no reason to drive all the way out here.

At the same time, she couldn't deny the whisper of hope as she glanced past the curtains at the dark shadow that stood on her back doorstep.

CHAPTER 10

It wasn't Brett.

Instead Callie opened the door to find Little Jimmy Ham standing on her back doorstep and disappointment ricocheted through her before she reminded herself that she wasn't in any hurry to see Brett Sawyer again.

He made her feel too many things. Too many distracting things.

Jimmy was much better. Safer.

She'd gone to school with Little Jimmy right up until he'd quit during sophomore year to help out at his family's farm. Or what was left of it since it had gone to hell in a handbasket after a drought.

Most people figured he'd been kicked out of school because of bad grades, but Callie knew better. She'd tutored him and while he wasn't the brightest bulb in the tanning bed, he was no dummy, either. He'd just missed out on so much education because of his family's hard luck.

But he'd always been nice and respectful, and so Callie gave him a welcoming smile. "What brings you out here?"

"My momma wanted me to stop by." His brown hair was in desperate need of a cut, but he'd tried to tame the long strands by slicking them back and stuffing them behind his ears. He sported a nearly threadbare blue shirt, the edges frayed, the top button missing near the collar, and an old pair of faded blue jeans. The only thing that wasn't worn were his black sneakers, the laces stiff and tight as if he were wearing them for the first time.

He was tall and lanky like his daddy and his grand-daddy before him, but there was already a Big Jimmy, his dad, and a *Really* Big Jimmy, his granddad, and so *Little* was next in line when it came to distinguishing the men in the family and the name had stuck.

"She wanted me to bring you this," he went on, hold-ing up an apple pie covered in plastic wrap. "She said to tell you how sorry she was."

Delia Ham was just as tall and lanky as her husband and son, and she made the best apple pie in the state. When she wasn't cleaning rooms at the local motel, that is, a job she'd taken among others to help make ends meet since the farm wasn't producing.

"I'm sorry, too," he added.

"Thanks so much." Callie took the offering and stepped back. "You want to come in? I could make some coffee or rustle you up some leftovers." She eyed the goody in her hand and smiled. "We could have a piece of this delicious pie."

"No, no." He shook his head and glanced behind him, as if antsy that someone might catch him on her doorstep. "I need to be getting back. I've got to help my pa with something."

"It's kind of late for a project."

He shrugged. "My pa works a lot of hours."

"I hear that." Callie glanced at the empty gravel drive that curled around the back of the house. "Did you walk all the way here?"

"It's not too far. I cut across down by the river."

"That's two miles away."

He shrugged. "Our truck ain't running so good. It needs a new water pump on account of the old is barely hanging on. Pa says we can only use it for emergencies." He shoved his hands in his pockets and backed up a few steps. "Mister James was always real nice to me," he added. "He didn't deserve what happened to him. You take care now," he added, stepping off the porch.

"I will." She glanced behind her at her keys hanging from a nearby hook. "If you wait up, I could give you a lift home."

"Don't trouble yourself none. The walk is fine." He stuffed his hands even deeper into his pockets and in a matter of seconds, he was gone, disappearing into a cluster of trees near the barn.

Seconds ticked by as Callie eyed the treeline. Finally she closed the door and headed back inside. She ignored the urge to slice into the pie just for herself, slid it into the last empty spot in the refrigerator, and headed into the living room. After tucking a blanket around her sister and a softly snoring Jez, she turned off the TV and headed down the hallway. She stalled in the doorway of the front den and eyed the stack of newspapers sitting next to her grandfather's recliner. She really should bag it all up and toss it.

She would.

Another night when she wasn't so freakin' tired.

But despite the exhaustion she couldn't relax enough to actually catch a few z's when she finally climbed into bed.

She tried to tune out the world, but the past few days kept playing over and over in her head, yanking her back to the slow chug of the ancient window unit and the hum of the lightbulb that flickered every once in a while from the adjoining bathroom.

Recent events rolled through her consciousness—the explosion, the swarm of police, the black-zippered bag disappearing into the coroner's van, the endless stream of old-lady hats passing near the closed casket, the whisper of nosy neighbors, Brett's sudden appearance at the Bachmans'.

She could still smell the intoxicating scent of warm male, cool leather, and just a hint of aftershave. Not the overwhelming, cloying kind that a lot of men wore. No, this was just a splash. A whisper of masculinity that reminded her of strong arms, a solid chest, and the most amazing blue eyes fringed in dark lashes.

For the hundredth time that day, she found herself wondering if he still tasted every bit as good as she remembered.

She drew a deep breath and gave herself a mental shake. She had to get her head back on track. That meant forgetting how helpful he'd been, how *nice,* and focusing on something—anything—else.

She took a shower. She drank hot cocoa. She watched a few episodes of *Orange Is the New Black* on Netflix. She even pulled out her satchel and spent an hour folding and stamping the quarterly newsletters that Les mailed out to his existing customers before moving on to her laptop and the dozens of digital pics she'd taken at the Daughters of the Republic bake sale last week.

The paper was going to run a feature on Julia Carmichael, president of the organization, and they'd asked Callie to supply a few pics from the event.

Where she'd once done most of her work in the makeshift darkroom set up in the back barn with an old camera and some used equipment given to her by her yearbook teacher, she now worked with a cheap digital and an editing program. The pics weren't the best, but they were the best for what she had. And certainly top notch for a small publication like the *Rebel Yell*.

She picked out the most vivid pics, wrote up a few tag descriptions, and sent them via e-mail to Charlotte Mackey, the newspaper's editor, along with an offer to do pics and a story on next week's annual VFW Spaghetti Dinner and Raffle.

It was a little after three a.m. when she finally finished everything and clicked send. Her head ached and her shoulders felt tight, but she still wasn't any closer to falling asleep.

She felt too wired to close her eyes.

Nervous.

Scared.

The truth followed her through the ancient house and out onto the back porch.

Not that she was scared because her granddad was gone and she was all alone. She was used to facing the world all by her lonesome. James had never had her back or helped ease her load. He'd simply sat in his recliner when he wasn't holed up outside, oblivious to the world around him. To the struggle.

She touched her bare toes to the clapboard floor of the back porch and pushed the rickety swing just enough to set it in motion. Hinges creaked and wood groaned, the sounds quickly melting into the buzz of crickets and the snores of the other two foster babies—a mutt named Earl and a Great Dane mix named Susie—that were camped out nearby. There'd been zero comfort in seeing James sprawled in his La-Z-Boy, his snores bouncing off the walls to the point that she'd actually contemplated buying earplugs.

She hadn't because, while annoying, the sound had

always meant that he hadn't drank himself into an early grave just yet.

The notion struck and her gaze shifted to the line of trees that stood at the edge of the massive stretch of grass. Several yards beyond was the spot where James had built his still and met his maker.

Her gaze hooked on the yellow police tape that stretched between two trees that lined the path that led to his old cabin. She'd walked that path just a few days ago.

Run, as a matter of fact. The minute the explosion had hit, she'd been on her feet, heading for the back stretch of woods, her heart pounding, the dread building.

She'd known even before she'd seen the flames slicing through the black night that something bad had happened.

A feeling she would never, ever forget.

One that washed through her all over again as she pushed to her feet and left the rickety swing to walk toward the break in the trees.

CHAPTER 11

The smoke had cleared, but the thick night air still smelled of charred wood. A cloying smell that had nearly suffocated her as she'd run back to the house to call 911 that fateful night.

"There isn't a thing for you to see out there," Sheriff Hunter DeMassi had told her once the smoke had cleared enough and the flames had died. "It's a health hazard and I'll make sure we get a dozer up here to level it and clear off the debris first thing next week. I can't touch anything until the feds have their look-see, but then I'll make sure I help get it all cleaned up. Until then, it's better just to keep your distance."

Better than what? Than seeing James passed out in his own vomit? Callie had seen it all and whatever devastation lay on the other side of those trees wasn't going to shock her. If anything, it would remind her of what an irresponsible old coot her grandfather had been. He hadn't just put himself in danger by doing something so illegal. No, he'd put them all at risk.

Because he was selfish.

Thoughtless.

Mean.

Even if the reverend had said all those nice things about

him. About how he'd been a good man once upon a time and a good husband and a loving father. Callie had never seen any of it. Not one redeeming quality.

Just this, she reminded herself as she reached the end of the path and saw the blackened remains of her grandfather's old trapper's shack. The trees for a hundred-foot radius were scorched down to nothing and the moon cast an eerie glow on what was left of James Harlin's pride and joy cooking site.

Everything was gone except for one of the walls and half of another. Debris littered the inside space and she made out what had once been a table, the burned edges of a transistor radio, the blackened blades of a box fan.

Copper tubing sat here and there, but the main hull of the still—the condenser—had been confiscated by the local authorities and hauled away, along with the few jars of shine that hadn't burst from the heat. The larger gallon containers—all plastic milk jugs James had salvaged over the years—had melted and shriveled while the contents had spit more fuel onto the fire and no doubt helped it spread to the surrounding timber.

Yellow tape spread from limb to limb, surrounding the large area and marking it as a crime scene. The suffocating stench of charred cedar and stale ash cloyed at her nostrils.

Callie ducked under the thin yellow barrier and picked her way around a few fallen limbs and piles of rubble until she reached what had once been the interior of the dwelling.

She'd seen the aftermath of hurricanes that had hit the Texas coast. Amid the piles of rubble would be a calendar or a picture or *something* that had defied the odds of devastation and remained intact.

She eyed the small black-framed bifocals sitting on the

windowsill of the one wall that still stood. A layer of soot covered the plastic and glass, but they were still there, no doubt sitting in the exact spot her grandfather had set them before he'd been blown to smithereens.

Her hand closed around the frames and she noted the yellowed sheet of paper sitting beneath the glasses. It, too, was covered with the same soot. She smeared the greasy covering off and unfolded the paper to see a partial list of ingredients for the infamous Texas Thunder.

The family moonshine had been responsible for every bad thing that had happened in Rebel since its founding. It had also been responsible for every good thing.

The Sawyers had used it as a springboard to their current success. Meanwhile, the Tuckers had let it drag them down so far that Callie had no clue if she could actually climb back up.

Instead, she wondered if maybe, just maybe, it was time to hop into her granddad's truck, hit the road, and never look back.

The notion dangled in front of her like the most decadent seven layer chocolate cake, but Callie wasn't about to reach out. She'd sacrificed ten years of her life to get to this point. To give up now would make all that time a total waste.

It would mean that she'd made all the wrong choices and sacrificed for nothing.

She slid the glasses and the paper into her pocket and eased her way around the rubble.

If only James had managed to pinpoint the final ingredients before he'd blown himself up.

But he hadn't come through with that any more than he'd come through on anything else in his life.

Half-assed. That's the way he'd always done things. The

recipe was no exception. He'd blown himself up, leaving Callie to finish up like he always did.

Ten thousand dollars.

Mark's voice echoed in her head and she entertained the crazy thought that maybe she ought to try her hand at finding the remaining ingredients.

That, or rob a bank. Both would pose a hefty jail sentence . . .

The thought stalled in her brain as she spotted the edge of a tennis shoe sticking up from the debris. Leaning down, she tugged at the toe of the shoe and pulled it free. Rubbing the edge, she revealed a worn leather shoe with a red, white, and blue sole.

She hadn't even realized her gramps had owned a pair of sneakers. He'd lived in boots for as long as she could remember, and then, just two years ago he'd traded the old duct-taped Justins for the camouflage Crocs Jenna had bought him for Christmas. He hadn't taken the comfy sandals off once since. He'd even worn them throughout the winter with socks.

He'd been wearing them, as a matter of fact, when he'd met his maker the other night.

And the shoe?

She leaned down and fingered the edge of the rubber. Old. Shabby. Maybe a leftover from her dad's youth? Lord knew James had had a crap-load of stuff stored out here. Things he'd saved and picked up over the years because he'd never been one to throw anything away if there was even the slimmest possibility that he might need it again.

But a sneaker? It just didn't fit that he would have a pair of sneakers for himself. He wasn't the sneaker type. Not like Little Jimmy with his shiny black pair, probably pulled from the new-shoe bin at the local YMCA.

Unless the sneaker had belonged to someone else?

A bootlegger? A customer? An intruder?

She wasn't sure why the thoughts popped into her head except that it had been a long day filled with tons of people telling her they weren't the least bit surprised about what had happened.

That, and the fact that she'd felt the same unease crawling up her spine the night of the explosion. As she'd stood on the sidelines, waiting for the fire department, she'd had the crazy feeling that something wasn't right.

You play with fire, you eventually get burned.

That's what everyone thought. The thing was, James had been playing with the proverbial fire since he was knee-high. He knew how to make moonshine. Even more, he knew how *not* to blow himself up. Otherwise he never would have made it to the ripe old age of eighty-six. A fire, even a freak accident as the authorities had called it, just hadn't seemed right.

James was a lot of things, but careless had never been one of them. Not when it came to cooking.

She hadn't been able to get him to wear his glasses to drive or to watch TV, or even to heat up his favorite Eggo waffles, but he'd worn them out by the still.

Because he was careful when it came to his shine. Too careful to go out in a blaze of glory because of a dumb mistake like a loose fitting.

"It happens," Sheriff DeMassi had told Callie when he'd given her the findings of his initial investigation just yesterday. "There was a loose gasket on the copper tubing. When the shine heated, the alcohol fumes spilled out and ignited. We've seen it time and time again around these parts. It's a common story."

For a rookie maybe. But James had had eighty years of

experience under his belt. He'd had spills and shoot-outs with the law, and he'd even lost a still to a flood back during the summer storms of 2000, but never a fire.

He'd been too good for that.

That's what her gut told her.

Then again, her gut had also told her to trust him when she'd handed over the money to pay the taxes.

She'd been wrong to put her faith in him and her mistake had cost her, just as he'd obviously been wrong with this last cook and his mistake had cost him. He'd been old, after all. Maybe the years had made him slow and careless.

She thought of Brett and his pappy. The whole town knew the PBR champ was back to salvage the ranch after his sick grandfather had let it go to hell in a handbasket. Pappy Sawyer had made mistake after mistake thanks to his Alzheimer's, and now Brett was paying the price for it.

Callie knew the feeling and damned if it wasn't ironic. They'd been so different back then, on opposite sides of the battlefield, yet here they were walking the same path.

Not that it mattered.

He was still a Sawyer and she was still a Tucker and, as the saying went, never the twain shall meet.

She glanced one last time at the sneaker before pushing it to the furthest corner of her mind. Because as well as she knew her grandfather, she really hadn't known him at all.

Maybe he *had* worn sneakers. Hell, maybe he'd worn them when he'd walked into the nearest Piggly Wiggly instead of the tax office, and handed over her hard-earned money to buy more sweet feed, sugar, and yeast for his damnable research.

No, she hadn't really known him at all, but then that was the story of her life, wasn't it?

She'd been so sure of Brett way back when and he'd disappointed her most of all.

Never again.

No matter how good he looked in a pair of Wranglers.

CHAPTER 12

It was after four in the morning when Brett climbed off the cutting horse and walked the animal into the large barn that stood behind the main house.

Once he'd left Callie at the Bachmans', he'd headed back to the ranch, unloaded the feed from the truck, and taken a horse out to the back forty. He'd spent the hours since combing every inch only to come up empty-handed.

No lost steers moseying around the rocky canyons that edged the far side of the ranch. No telltale remains indicating a scavenger attack or any sort of freak accident. There'd been no tracks. No blood. No bones. Nothing.

As if the cows had vanished into thin air.

Or into somebody's cattle trailer.

The thought struck again and this time he didn't drop-kick it to the curb. He knew his pappy wasn't in the best shape—for now—and the ranch had certainly suffered, but what if there was someone adding to the demise of Bootleg Bayou? What if there really was someone stealing from them?

Pappy may have simply made a mistake when he'd documented the number of cows received last year. Maybe the Alzheimer's had reared its ugly head even then and he'd scribbled in the wrong numbers.

But that wouldn't explain the extra vaccinations used, or the surplus of feed consumed, or the fact that they had ten actual tags unaccounted for.

Those cows had been clipped with their corresponding number at the same time they'd been vaccinated and branded with the ranch's signature double B. They'd then been documented on the master list, and now they were gone.

Vanished into thin air.

The notion echoed in his head as he unsaddled the animal, brushed her down, and walked into the ranch house.

Every light blazed inside and he soon found out why.

"Somebody's burning the midnight oil." The comment came from the young brunette who sat on the leather sofa, a bowl of popcorn in her hands. The TV screen blazed a rerun of MTV's hit show *Catfish,* the sound on low.

"Karen?" Brett stared at his younger sister. She was twenty years old and the spitting image of his mother at that age with her long dark hair, and tall, thin build. Only her Sawyer blue eyes gave any clue that she was Brett's only sibling. "What are you doing here?"

Her smile faded for a heartbeat before she shrugged. "It's Spring Break this coming week and I figured you could use some help around here."

"I've got everything under control." A clatter of pots and pans punctuated the sentence, luring Brett to the kitchen, Karen on his heels.

They found Pappy on his hands and knees, rummaging through a cupboard as if his life depended on it. The old man wore a pair of striped pajama bottoms and a red button-down starched shirt, the buttons mismatched as if he'd been trying to get dressed and given up the task halfway through. Worry tightened the old man's face and narrowed his jaw.

Brett frowned. "What's wrong, Pappy?"

"I need my cup." He waved an arthritic hand. "It was here the last time I saw it. Right here."

"I'll get you a cup—"

"I need *my* cup," Pappy insisted. "It's mine. I need it."

"But—" Brett started, his words dying when he felt the touch on his arm. He turned to see his sister. "Let him be," she mouthed.

"He wants a cup. I can get him a cup."

"That won't help. He needs *his* cup. The cup that Grandmother gave him for their twentieth anniversary," Karen told him. "He's been looking for it ever since I came home last night. He said he needs his coffee and he can't drink it out of any other cup because he promised her he would always use it."

"It's blue with a Texas flag." Pappy paused before moving a Crock-Pot and shoving it off to the side with the stack of dishes he'd already rummaged through. "She bought it last month at the state fair when I wasn't looking and surprised me last week. I gave her a new toaster and she gave me my cup. It's my favorite."

Brett's mind riffled back through his memories and he remembered his grandfather sitting in front of the Christmas tree, a mug of coffee in his hands. A mug that had been shattered when Berle had thrown it at Brett's mother back when Brett had been seven years old.

"You remember, don't you, son?" Pappy lifted cloudy blue eyes. "You were right there. You saw her give it to me."

Brett shook his head. "I don't remember."

"Sure, you do." The old man waved a hand. "You were right there with us, son. It was just the three of us," he told Karen. "Me, Martha, and Berle, here."

"This is Brett," Karen told him gently. "Your grand-son. Berle isn't with us anymore."

"Brett?" Confusion twisted his face and jabbed at Brett's gut. "I ain't got no grandson named Brett. Why, Berle, here, just got married a month ago. Ain't that right, son?"

"Why don't you let me get you some coffee in a different mug?" Karen jumped in before Brett could respond. "Just until we can find yours. Berle, here, can look for it while I take you back to your room. Isn't that right, Berle?" She gave Brett a pointed look.

He fought down a rush of denial and gave a tight nod.

"Good then. Let's get you to your feet." She leaned down and took the old man's hand while Brett helped him to his feet.

"You'll make some fine-looking sons one day," Pappy told him as he stalled, the glimmer of a smile on his old face. "Mighty fine-looking. You just need to remember to control your temper. Mona, here, is a good woman." He pointed to Karen. "She won't stick around if you keep yelling at her all the time. Now I know it's not my business, but these walls are thin."

"I'll be nice," Brett vowed, fighting down the urge to deny Pappy's words. The old man was lost in another time and place and there was no convincing him otherwise.

In Pappy's mind, Brett *was* Berle.

But tomorrow would be a good day. A lucid day and Pappy would realize his mistake.

Brett wasn't Berle. Not now. Not ever.

The truth followed Brett as he headed to his room and sank down on the edge of the large king-sized bed he'd slept in while growing up.

"He's been like this ever since last semester." Karen's

voice drew his attention and he glanced up to see her standing in the doorway. "I was home at Easter and found him digging in the garden out back in the middle of the night. He kept insisting that someone had stolen his tomatoes and trashed his garden."

"He hasn't kept a garden in years."

"I know that and you know that, but he doesn't. Not when he's like this. I talked to Dolly tonight at dinner. She said it's happening more often. She barely gets a full night's sleep these days."

"He's just stressed because things with the ranch aren't adding up. Once I straighten everything out, he'll feel better."

Karen looked as if she wanted to say something, but then she shrugged. "I hope so."

"You don't need to hope. I'll get it all worked out and he'll start feeling better."

She nodded. "It's good to see you home."

Brett grinned. "You, too." The grin faded. "Although I'd rather you head to the beach for your break like every other college student this side of the Rio Grande instead of stressing about all of this."

"I burn too easily. Besides, it looks like you could use a hand." She glanced around. "Don't you think it's high time you cleared out all this crap?"

He followed her gaze to the large shelf filled with rodeo trophies. His first calf rope looped over the edge of the dresser mirror. A half-finished replica of a Model T car sat on the corner of a crowded chest of drawers. In the ninth grade he'd started the model as a class project, but he'd never been able to sit still long enough to finish the engine, never been good at anything that kept him chained to a desk or chair.

Which was why he'd always struggled in school.

He'd managed to creep by, but only after a lot of extra homework and the Rebel High Tutoring Team—a group of smart kids who'd come up with the idea to tutor their not-so-smart peers as a form of community service. An extra accomplishment to round out their already lengthy college applications. Callie had been their ringleader and his tutor.

"Dolly tried to pack up some of this stuff last year, but Pappy had a fit. He always hoped you'd come back one day and he wanted everything to be exactly the same."

Because Pappy had never given up the hope that Brett would turn out to be a better man than his no-good dad.

He thought back to the church that afternoon and the mahogany casket sitting up at the front of the sanctuary. Today had been the first time Brett had been inside the church since the day of his own father's funeral.

He'd been thirteen at the time and his pappy had practically dragged him down the aisle to the front pew. There'd been no cheap plastic daisies for his father.

Only full bloom roses were fancy enough for a Sawyer. With lots of greenery and pinecones spread out across the stained wood. It had been close to Christmas and so the pinecones had made sense.

At least to Brett. No one else had really noticed the pinecones. They'd been too stunned by the fact that at the age of forty-five, Big Berle Sawyer was *dead*.

Splattered all over the interstate by an eighteen wheeler after an all-night drinking binge.

The drinking hadn't come as a shock. No, it had been the fact that another driver would dare take the life of Rebel royalty. The Sawyers owned the town. They lived on the biggest spread and drove the fanciest cars and trucks and had the biggest egos. Especially Berle.

He shouldn't have been behind the wheel at all, but Brett's old man had been too headstrong to admit weakness. He could handle his liquor. Lord knew, he'd had enough practice.

He didn't need anyone taking his keys or telling him what to do. No one stood up to Berle Sawyer.

Even his wife.

Especially his wife.

Mona Sawyer had been pretty headstrong herself, even after living with an overbearing man like Berle. She'd tried to take the keys that night even though she'd known it would lead to a fight. To a beating.

She'd stepped up anyway, and he'd knocked her back down, literally, and the situation had escalated. Berle had yelled. Mona had screamed. Brett had tried to intervene, to lure Berle off Mona, but it had only made the older man angrier. He'd knocked Brett clear across the room and then he'd hit Mona while Karen had crouched in the corner.

Brett had passed out from the blow to his head and by the time he'd opened his eyes, the sheriff had arrived with the news of Berle's accident.

A shock to folks, only because they'd realized that the Sawyers were just people like everyone else. They had their own problems.

But Brett had always known. He'd lived with it. Sure, he'd tried to pretend otherwise. He'd bought into his own hype, just like his old man. He'd been a handful back then. Wild. Volatile. Crazy. A *Sawyer*. He'd done whatever he pleased, always thinking he was above the rules.

That he made the rules.

His father's death should have been a wake-up call, but it had only made matters worse. His mother left, eager to put her abusive marriage behind her, even if it meant leaving her children.

Especially if it meant leaving them.

She'd wanted no reminders of Berle, and Brett had been his spitting image. Likewise for Karen with her Sawyer blue eyes. Mona had left them both with Pappy and moved to Las Vegas.

While Brett spoke to her every now and then and saw her whenever he made it to Nevada for a rodeo, that was the extent of their relationship. She didn't show up for holidays or special occasions. She kept her distance, and Brett couldn't blame her.

His father's death should have been a wake-up call, a push to change his ways before he followed the same tragic path. But it had only made things worse.

He'd been even wilder. More volatile. Living on the edge, pushing his luck. He'd driven his truck too fast. Broken too many rules. Bedded too many women. And drank way too much moonshine.

More. That had been his motto back then.

There wasn't a dare he wouldn't take or a thing he wouldn't do or a woman he couldn't have.

Except Callie Tucker.

She'd been the exact opposite of the girls he'd always taken a shine to. She'd been pretty in a quiet, natural way. No overabundance of makeup or skin-tight jeans or slinky tops. She'd been far too mature to play into society's stereotype. Rather, she'd been fixated on college, on getting the hell out of Rebel and making something of herself and so she hadn't given a lick about pep rallies or parties or football games.

Instead, she'd read and studied and kept her nose to the grindstone. She'd worn plain jeans and shapeless T-shirts, her hair always pulled back into the same lifeless pony-tail. Her parents hadn't had much money and so she'd never worn the latest designers or driven a hot car. But none of that had mattered. She'd still looked at him as if she knew something that he didn't, as if she were better than him.

The notion had snagged his attention faster than any short skirt or low-cut blouse. Because Brett had had his share of both by the age of eighteen, and what he'd really needed was something else. Something different.

Some*one* different.

He'd signed up for tutoring and then he'd spent the next six weeks sitting across from Callie Tucker every day after school. He'd turned on the charm, smiling and flirting and chipping away at the wall she'd fortified between them.

But there had been more than just the cat-and-mouse game between a boy and a girl. They'd actually talked, too. She'd told him about her grandfather's addiction to the shine he brewed up in the woods behind their house, and he'd told her about his dad's abuse and his mom flying the coop, and how Pappy was trying to make up for both.

Of course, it wasn't all the talking that had convinced him to ask her to prom. He would have asked anyway because Callie Tucker was the only girl he'd wanted back then.

He just hadn't realized exactly how much.

Until that night.

Until she'd kissed him and touched him and turned him on to the point that he'd gone over the edge.

He'd grabbed and groped and come right there in his pants.

He'd felt the helplessness deep inside of himself at that moment. The same feeling he'd seen in his dad's eyes that night right before he'd slammed his fist into his thirteen-year-old son's face.

Because he'd been beyond control.

He'd been a slave to the anger roiling inside of him, a slave to the alcohol, a slave to his own damned shortcomings, just as Brett had been a slave to his lust that night with Callie.

He'd known in that instant that if he unfastened his pants and sank deep inside her, he wouldn't be able to stop. There would be no pacing himself, no slowing down to help her accommodate him.

He would have taken her hard and fast, and she would have hated him for it because she'd been so young and innocent. Because he would have hurt her, just as his father had hurt his mother.

And so he'd shoved her out of his pappy's prized Caddy, gunned the engine, and peeled away. Not the most gentlemanly thing to do, but better than rip her clothes off and push her past the point of no return.

That's what he would have done.

What he'd wanted to do.

And why he'd packed his bags and hit the road shortly thereafter.

He'd been too much like Berle and it had been time to turn things around. To change the course of his life before he followed his old man beyond the point of no return.

He'd done just that.

He'd climbed onto the back of each and every bull and fought for control over everything in his life, and while he'd failed miserably at first, he'd eventually started to gain some measure of discipline. He'd held on a little longer each time until finally, he'd done it.

And he intended to keep doing it.

"He was doing okay when I came home," Karen's voice drew him back to the moment. "He remembered where I was going to school and my major. He was even talking about how you used to beat him at Go Fish."

"Yeah, well, he let me win." Pappy had let everyone win. Just as he'd let Berle beat him at cards every Friday night. He'd coddled and spoiled his only son to the point that the man had felt entitled. And he'd done the same with his grandson.

Not that Brett blamed Pappy for his own selfishness. The old man was just doing what he thought was right.

That's all he'd ever done. He'd been a straight shooter. A good man who'd carried on the reputation his own grandfather had established after he'd given up the moonshine business and steered them into a legitimate line of work. Pappy didn't deserve half the shit life had dumped on him, and he sure as hell didn't deserve the Alzheimer's.

Brett couldn't change the hand he'd been dealt, but he could fix the ranch.

If he could figure out what the hell was going on and who might be stealing their cows.

"You know any of the boys Pepper's got working for us?" he asked his sister.

"I know all of them."

"No, I mean personally."

She gave him a sly grin. "Let's see, there's Cade Willet, not the best kisser, but passable. And Danny Monroe. He's a sloppy kisser, but I think with a little practice he could be halfway decent."

"You're not funny."

"Yes, I am. You just don't like the idea of your baby sister kissing anyone." She ran her hands through her long dark hair and pulled the strands over her shoulder. "So what's the sudden interest in the ranch hands?"

Brett thought about mentioning the missing cattle, but he wasn't about to worry his sister. That, and the fewer people who knew his suspicions, the better. He wanted to watch the guys, to see what played out. He didn't want anyone forewarned because Karen might whisper a sweet nothing while lip-locking with one of them. He shrugged. "Just wondering. I haven't been here long enough to get to know any of them, so I thought I'd ask."

"If you want to know about any of the guys, just ask Dolly." She walked over to the bedroom closet and started fingering the old boxes stacked inside. "She feeds them all supper every evening out at the bunkhouse before she comes back here to Pappy." She pulled one of the boxes free. "If anyone could fill you in on them, she might be able to." She held up the familiar hatbox, a smile playing at her lips. "Remember this?"

Brett watched as she opened the box and pulled out the ancient straw Resistol sitting inside.

He stared at the worn Bud Light patch on the front and the various nicks and scratches. He'd worn that hat during every cattle drive back when he'd been a kid.

He'd worn that hat right up until he'd left Rebel, Texas, for good.

"Pappy had Dolly box it up and put it in here in case you ever came back home for more than a day or two. He just knew that someday you would want to hang up your buckles and be a real cowboy right here at the ranch. He always said this hat was more fitting for a cattleman."

"Thanks." Brett put the hat back into the box. "I appreciate it, but I'm no cattleman. I'm going back out on the circuit just as soon as I straighten things out here. I just got a new deal with Wrangler." The biggest, in fact, of his career. He was going to be their spokesman for the next five years.

If he signed the contracts.

The notion struck and he pushed it right back out. *When* he signed, which he would do soon. Maybe tonight, as a matter of fact. All he had to do was pull out the documents and look them over as his lawyer had instructed. Initial a few changes, and bam, the deal would be done.

If Tyler McCall didn't beat him to the punch.

Tyler was his cousin of a cousin of a cousin, who'd been on his ass ever since he'd started riding the circuit a few years ago. The man was young and hungry and hell-bent on catching up to Brett and beating him out for first place.

Not that Tyler was getting his chance anytime soon. Brett was going for buckle number three, and he was signing that deal. The deal of a lifetime.

"Wrangler, huh?" Karen smiled. "Talk about the big time." She shrugged. "No way could you give that up." She plopped the lid on top and set the box on the dresser before heading for the door. "Even if it's only temporary, I'm glad you're home now. Sleep tight, big brother."

If only.

But sleep wouldn't come.

Instead, he heard his pappy's voice from down the hall, followed by Karen's soothing words as she tried to calm the man down.

He had the gut instinct to go to the old man, to *do* something. But that was the thing—there was nothing he could do, not at the moment anyhow. Brett didn't have the first clue how to deal with an irate Pappy. No, better to wait until the man calmed down and then Brett could talk to him, maybe try to figure out if his grandfather could clue him in as to who might be stealing cattle.

Yeah, and I've got some prime pastureland in the middle of the Sahara that you might be interested in.

The voice mocked, but Brett wasn't giving up hope. Tomorrow would be a better day for Pappy.

In the meantime . . .

Brett grabbed a blanket and headed outside for some fresh air. Some freedom. Some blessed distance.

From the past.

The present.

He ended up down by the creek that flowed at the very back of their property, watching the play of moonlight on the mirrorlike surface, listening to the trickle of water and the buzz of insects. The sounds pushed inside his head and shoved aside his grandfather's voice in favor of the soft, sweet whisper of water.

A thin stream of smoke drifted from the trees in the distance and his nostrils flared with the warm, sweet scent of yeast.

Nix the idea that anyone was cooking up a few loaves out in the middle of nowhere. No, the cooking that was going on had nothing to do with bread and everything to do with corn liquor.

Brett had smelled more than his share over the years. Not because Pappy had still been into moonshine, but the ranch hands had always enjoyed cooking up a batch or two for their own personal consumption.

Nothing like his family's infamous Texas Thunder, or so Pepper claimed. He was the only one old enough to have actually sampled some of the original back when he'd been a young boy and his grandpa had been a customer.

Nothing these days compared to the legendary brew.

Brett made a mental note to ask around and see who was cooking on his property, and put a stop to it. He didn't need to add legal troubles to his financial woes.

He stretched out on his back and stared up at the sky, but he didn't see the stars or the moon. He saw her. A halo of golden hair framing the sweetest, warmest woman he'd ever had the pleasure of touching.

Callie had fueled his dreams for so long, made him toss and turn and swell until he was rock-hard and desperate for release. Even when he'd slept with other women, she'd always been there, living in his memories, reminding him of his past.

Calling him back.

But he wasn't going back. Sure, he was here now, but he was different. He'd come too far from that out-of-control, overindulgent asshole he'd been so long ago. He wasn't going back.

Even so, he still wanted her with the same fierceness.

Tonight had proved as much. Every inch of him had ached with the want.

At the same time, he'd realized something very important—namely that he could be within a few feet of her and keep his hands off. No pulling her close, peeling off her clothes, and plunging deep, deep inside.

Not no, but *hell* no. He was keeping his composure and his control.

Even more, he was keeping his distance from Callie Tucker.

CHAPTER 13

"No pigs in a blanket?" Les gave Callie a hopeful stare as she unpacked the food trays and set them out across the granite countertop that separated a custom kitchen from the main living room at the Bachman house. It was early Saturday morning, the day after the funeral and another day into the deadline looming over Callie's head.

Twenty-eight days and counting.

The sun blazed on the horizon, promising a sweltering afternoon. Luckily a cold draft blew through the house's air-conditioning unit, effectively keeping Callie from melting into a puddle at that very moment.

Les, on the other hand, wasn't holding up as well. Even with a short-sleeved royal blue polo and khakis, he had sweat dotting his upper lip. And the bald patch at the back of his head.

"I think you need an iced tea instead of a pig in a blanket."

He touched his forehead. "Cripes, I'm sweating up a storm. Quick, give me one of those imprinted golf towels."

Callie retrieved one of the small towels from the box she'd toted in just that morning. Thankfully, she'd unloaded most everything last night, which had left only the golf towels, the food, and a few miscellaneous items.

Correction—Brett Sawyer had unloaded everything.

The truth echoed through her, stirring a sizzle of awareness that made her stiffen.

Because the last thing—the very last thing—she wanted to feel was a sizzle of anything as far as he was concerned.

No awareness. No attraction. No *like*.

She'd gone that route once before and she'd learned the hard way that *like* was highly overrated.

And downright heartbreaking.

Callie gathered her control and focused on pouring a glass of iced tea from a pitcher. "Here," she said, handing the glass to Les. "Forget about the pigs in a blanket. Jenna got to them before I could stop her, but I've got pimento cheese." Callie indicated a platter. "And I picked up some muffin tops from Brandy's bakery."

"Now these should be a big hit." He grabbed one of the ooey gooey blueberry treats that her sister was fast becoming famous for and took a bite before washing it down with a swig of ice-cold tea. "If I didn't already have a mortgage of my own," he said after another bite, "I'd definitely consider signing up with these as an incentive." Setting his tea glass aside, he rubbed his hands together. "We might land a live one today, after all. Wouldn't that get in Tanner's craw? And speaking of the Sawyer clan, word around town is Bootleg Bayou is just this side of foreclosure." His eyes gleamed as if he'd discovered there was a real Santa Claus. "Which means if Pappy Sawyer has any sense, he'll settle for a short sale and put the property on the market before the bank has a chance to close in." A serious light touched his eyes. "We need that listing."

"Foreclosure? Are you sure?" Okay, she'd heard that things were bad. But *that* bad? An image of Brett from last night pushed into her head. She saw the worry lines around his eyes and the anxiety tugging at his features. "That's a shame."

"For Pappy. For us it's the opportunity of a lifetime."

"But Tanner is a Sawyer. I'm sure Brett and his pappy will give the listing to their own."

"Not if I can provide an interested buyer first. Foreclosure is time sensitive, which means it's every man for himself. I want you to head over there first thing tomorrow and get some good pictures for me. Something to show prospective buyers. Maybe some scenic shots. A few of the outside of the house. A panoramic of the barn and corral. Enough to entice someone."

"Isn't that a tiny bit unethical without getting his permission first?"

"No more so than Tanner taking pictures behind my back and finding a buyer for the Mitchell place before I could even pick up my fliers from the printer. That was low."

"So is this."

"Exactly. Tit for tat." He nailed her with a stare. "I've got a couple in Austin that's contacted me looking for a place like Bootleg Bayou. I need you out there first thing tomorrow so the pics are ready by Monday. Now," he glanced at his watch, "you get all of this food unwrapped and set up while I go outside and put out the Open House sign. Did you pick up the balloons?"

"They're in the cab of my truck."

"Good girl. See, you're detail-oriented, Callie. That's what I like about you, and the main reason you really should consider getting your license. You'd make one hell of a Realtor."

Her real estate license had been a point of contention between them for the past year, since she'd started taking some real estate classes at Les's insistence—to be a good Realtor's assistant, she needed to know the ins and outs of the business. He'd even offered her a small raise to take the classes, which, of course, had been the only reason she'd said yes. She'd needed some way to pull in more money to help with taxes and bills. While folks liked James's moonshine, and he'd made a nice little amount off of it, he hadn't made nearly enough to keep up the property and support a family. He'd barely paid for the gas in his truck and his own supplies.

Callie had been responsible for the rest. And the taxes.

She damned herself again for giving him the money. She should have gone to the bank herself.

She would have but she'd been so busy with a prospective buyer and James had been only five minutes away. And sober at the time. He'd insisted that he would go straight there.

"I don't need a goddamned babysitter, girlie. I'm a grown-ass man. I can handle business myself. Besides, it's my name on the deed. I have to be the one to hand over the money or give you permission to act on my behalf, and I ain't doin' that. I ain't no motherfrickin' invalid."

His name had been on the deed and so she'd caved.

But the grown-ass man part? He'd been lying about that because no mature, responsible adult male would have made the decision to forfeit his family obligations and throw the money away on a pie-in-the-sky dream. But then that had been his plan. He'd known all along that he was going to use the cash to try to remake that damnable Texas Thunder that had ripped the town apart. A recipe divided between two stubborn men who'd no doubt taken the knowledge to their graves.

Ah, but her great-great-grandfather had passed his part

on to James and she had the proof written on the crumpled paper in her purse.

Had Elijah Sawyer handed down his to Pappy? To Brett?

The question stirred in her mind for the hundredth time that morning since she'd woken up with Texas Thunder and ten thousand dollars dancing in her head.

The question kept nagging at her—what if Elijah *had* passed his part of the recipe on to Pappy? And Pappy had handed it over to Brett? What if both Sawyers knew the whereabouts of the missing half? What if the answer to all of her financial problems was simply a matter of asking Brett?

Fat chance.

At the same time, she couldn't help but wonder. And while Brett Sawyer was the last person she wanted to approach for help, she would do it if it meant finding the rest of the recipe and getting on with her life.

He certainly might know.

That's what she told herself when she left the Bachman open house just after lunch and headed through town toward the county road that led to Bootleg Bayou. Les could handle the small stream of potential buyers filtering through the house while she went after more muffin tops, or so she'd said. She needed to talk to Brett while she had her nerve up.

The Sawyers were too smart to throw away the source of their initial wealth. Brett would know and while he might not want to offer up the information under normal circumstances, he was just as hard up for cash as she was.

Desperate.

She held tight to the thought and hung a left at the center of town. She was just about to turn toward the county road when she spotted his truck parked in front of the Law Offices of Creek and Munson.

She put on the brakes and swerved into a parking spot just a few cars away. Taking a deep breath, she retrieved Mark's card from her purse, gathered her courage, and opened the truck door.

Gone was the extra half-hour drive during which she'd planned to map out her exact plan. She had no clue what she was going to say or how, she just knew she had to find out if they were both feeling angst for nothing. The answer to her financial prayers could be just a conversation away.

Her feet hit the pavement and she rounded the bumper and stepped up onto the sidewalk. She stopped near the shiny black four-wheel-drive pick-up truck and peered into the window. The cab was empty.

Another deep breath and she started for the front door of the law office.

She made it two steps before she heard the deep rumble in her ear.

"Looking for me, sugar?"

Electricity sizzled through the air and zapped her at the base of the spine. Her hands tingled and her knees trembled.

"As a matter of fact," she managed after she'd gathered her courage and turned to find Brett standing behind her, "you're just the man I'm looking for."

"How's that?" He arched a dark brow, his gaze drilling into hers.

For a split second, her courage fled and she wanted nothing more than to turn and walk the other way. That or press herself up against him and beg him to finish what they'd started that night so long ago. They'd been so close. He'd had his hands on her thighs and his lips pressed to hers and she'd been so ready to feel him right *there* . . .

But this wasn't about getting physical and detouring from the long road of celibacy. It was about saving her home. Her dreams.

She stiffened, gathering every bit of courage she could muster, and stared him square in the eye. "I really need to talk." She swallowed against a sudden lump and tried to control the quiver in voice. "I've got something that could make us both very, very happy."

CHAPTER 14

Very, *very* happy implied sex.

Lots of bone-melting, breath-stealing, down-and-dirty sex. At least in Brett's mind. So when Callie Tucker murmured the *H* word, it drew his full, undivided attention.

Not that he was going to take her up on such an offer. Callie Tucker was far too dangerous to his peace of mind. Still, he wouldn't mind hearing the proposition. He owed her that much.

"There's a distillery that's interested in the original Texas Thunder recipe," she blurted, killing his hope that maybe she didn't hate him as much as he thought. Maybe she felt the attraction between them every bit as intensely as he did. Maybe she wanted to get him naked just as quickly as he wanted to peel away her skirt and blouse and see all the lush curves beneath.

"Foggy Bottom Distillers," she went on. "I've got the Tucker half, but I still need your half. It's all or nothing."

Her words killed the lustful thoughts—for the moment—and drew his full attention. "Let me get this straight." He ran a hand through his hair and wished like hell he'd gotten a decent night's sleep in a real bed instead of roughing it out by the creek in a sleeping bag. Maybe then he wouldn't be thinking that she was just about the most beautiful woman he'd ever laid eyes on, even with clothes.

She wasn't. He'd gone through dozens of women that could put Callie Tucker to shame. Women with boobs out to here and legs up to there. Buckle bunnies who practically ripped their short-shorts off and begged him to do them.

Yep, he'd seen better-looking women. He'd had better-looking women. And it was just the exhaustion making him think such idiotic thoughts.

He steeled himself and stared down at her, his Costa sunglasses shielding his eyes from the sun and hiding the lustful gleam he knew would give him away. "So what you're saying is that you want my family's half of the Texas Thunder recipe?"

"Technically, it's not me that wants it. It's Foggy Bottom Distillers, and they're willing to pay ten thousand dollars for it. And a royalty once the recipe goes on the shelf for sale." She went on to tell him how James had been working on re-creating the missing half when he'd blown himself to smithereens. How he'd used all of their tax money to buy supplies and now she had exactly twenty-eight days to come up with the money.

What a sonofabitch.

Brett couldn't imagine his own pappy ever doing something so low. Then again, that's exactly what the old man had done, albeit unwillingly. He'd screwed the ranch over by getting sick.

That was the difference between the two men. The two families.

Blood was everything to the Sawyers. No Sawyer would ever intentionally screw over another.

But the Tuckers?

It was every man for himself.

Brett barely resisted the urge to pull Callie into his arms and tell her he would help. That he wanted to help. Because he'd thought about her too often, and regretted their terrible encounter more than anything else in his life. But he wasn't going there with her. Even more, he couldn't help her when he could barely help himself.

He had cows missing and bills piling up and, hell, he was screwed. Completely and totally *screwed*.

No, he couldn't fix her problems any more than he could fix his own. Not without money. And plenty of it.

"Ten thousand dollars?" He eyed her. "Seriously?"

She nodded and pulled the yellowed piece of paper from her pocket. "This is our list of ingredients. There are a few extra on here that James figured were in the original, but there's no real way to know without the other half of this paper." Her green gaze found his again. "Your great-great-grandfather's half."

The tiny slip of yellow paper that he'd seen stuffed between the pages of his great-grandmother's Bible when he'd been a child. She'd recorded every major event in that book, from births to deaths, marriages to divorces. She'd even scribbled a few lines about the time her favorite grandson—Brett's dad—had killed his first deer. She'd been long gone by the time Brett had come along, but he'd seen her careful handwriting in the old book, along with the clippings from various newspapers, and the yellowed half of the infamous recipe.

The last time Brett had seen the Bible, it had been stored away in the safe behind his grandfather's prized picture of a black-and-white drawing depicting the vintage 1920 Oldsmobile that had once belonged to Elijah Sawyer himself. The very car that he'd used to haul shine in during Prohibition.

"You can call the guy yourself if you want to check it out." She handed him a business card.

"They're really willing to pay ten thousand dollars for a recipe?" he asked, eyeing the company's information.

She nodded. "That means five thousand for your half and five thousand for mine." She stared up at him, her eyes reflecting rays of sunshine and gleaming an even brighter shade of iridescent green. "So what do you say? Are you willing to sell your half? I really need this money," she added.

So did he. He was ten cows shy. Short of going into the safe—which is why he'd headed into town in the first place—he had no backup plan to make up the money. He'd come into Rebel to see his grandfather's lawyer, get a copy of the combination, and see about selling his grandmother's bracelet or something equally valuable.

A tough decision that had kept him tossing and turning all night. Among other things, he reminded himself as he stared down at Callie.

She looked so hopeful that he couldn't help himself. He nodded. "I'll see if I can find it."

But first he had to see the lawyer and get the combination to the safe. And then he had to hightail it back to the ranch to meet with the cattle buyer. Short or not, he still had a mess of steers to sell.

"I've got a cattle buy and a few things to do right now, but we could meet out at the ranch later this afternoon," he told her. "Give me your cell and I'll text when I'm done. Then we'll take a look and see what we can find."

"Really?" Something stronger than hope joined the

gleam in her eyes. There was no mistaking the surprise. The delight. The pure gratitude.

His own chest hollowed out and a strange warmth whispered through him. "It's been a long time since I've seen it and I'm not making any promises, but it's definitely worth a look."

Especially when it made her face light up as if she'd just won the lottery.

He just hoped like hell he didn't disappoint them both. He'd done more than enough of that where Callie Tucker was concerned.

"It's not here." Brett stared at the empty interior of the safe located behind the framed black-and-white of Gertie, the infamous 1920 Oldsmobile. He eyed the black interior and disbelief washed through him. "Nothing is here." The safe had been cleaned out. No jewelry. No birth certificates. No family Bible. No mementos from his childhood like his bronzed baby boots and the tiny white child's Bible Karen had held in her hand on her confirmation day.

No recipe.

"Are you sure it was in there?" came Callie's familiar voice from behind him. He'd seen it himself the last time he'd been home, five years ago. He'd stored his first buckle inside the safe, with all of the other family valuables. He'd set the buckle right on top of the Bible.

The buckle was gone, too, just like everything else.

Wiped out.

Stolen?

Hell's bells, there really was a thief at the ranch.

He shook his head. "Sonofabitch."

"Maybe someone moved it." Callie's soft words slid into his ears and he turned to see her standing nearby. She wore a sundress and a pair of flip-flops. Much more casual than her buttoned-up look from earlier that day, and even more dangerous to his peace of mind.

The soft cotton molded to her curves. Her long blond hair was still pulled back in a ponytail, but the edges had come loose and framed her face. Her forehead wrinkled in worry, mirroring the emotion that rushed through him as he turned back to the empty safe.

"Maybe." The thing was, no one had the combination. Pappy had long since forgotten it. The only other person with access was the family lawyer, and he was off the suspect list. Merle had plenty of his own wealth, including a brand new fishing boat he'd christened *The Reel Deal*. Merle didn't need a few pieces of jewelry and an old Bible.

"What about another storage location?"

"The only other place is the attic. There are tons of boxes up there, but nothing of value." At least, there'd never been valuables up there before. But things had changed so much over the past few years that anything was possible.

"It couldn't hurt to look." She looked so disappointed that he had the sudden urge to reach out, pull her close, and tell her everything would be okay.

But everything wouldn't be okay.

Not for either of them.

Brett was short several thousand dollars, he had bills pressing down, and the safe was empty.

Even worse, Callie Tucker was standing there in her white-and-red polka-dotted sundress, the setting sun streaming through the floor length windows behind her, highlighting her long legs through the sheer material. He'd always been a sucker for great legs.

No, everything was far from okay.

Heat firebombed his gut and rushed like a heat-seeking missile straight to his cock. His balls clenched. His muscles all but shook as he fought off the urge to forget everything and reach for her.

She shrugged. "I should have known." She shook her head. "It would have been too easy to just waltz in here and find the recipe, and God knows nothing is ever that easy. At least not for me. Not that you need to hear any of this." She caught her bottom lip and his breathing paused. "I should really get going."

But the thing was, he didn't want her to go. And while he knew there were a dozen reasons why he should let her walk away right now—hell, why he should join in and push her out the door himself—suddenly he couldn't think of a single one.

The only thing that came to mind was how he should have kissed her last night when he'd had the chance. And how he'd be a bona fide idiot to let the opportunity pass him by a second time.

His legs ate up the distance between them and suddenly, he was right there in front of her, so close he could feel the heat coming off her luscious body. And then he did what he'd been dreaming of for far too many nights over the past ten years. He hauled her up against his chest and dipped his head.

One kiss, he promised himself. Just one kiss to see if she tasted as good now as she had back then, and then he was done. End of story. Bye-bye!

He was going to kiss her.

The truth should have sent a bolt of nervousness through

Callie. Instead, anticipation sizzled along her nerve endings. Excitement blossomed in her chest as he lowered his face to hers. His breath brushed her lips a split second before firm, hungry lips slanted so perfectly across her own.

His tongue probed and stroked and tangled with hers. Strong, purposeful fingers came up to cradle her cheeks and tilt her face so that he could deepen the connection.

He smelled of leather and horses and a touch of wildness that teased her nostrils and stirred a rush of memories. But the past didn't pull her back. For all his expertise back then, the way he kissed her now was different.

He'd been a boy back then. Desperate. Impatient.

He was all man now, and he kissed her like he meant it. Like he wasn't a Sawyer and she wasn't a Tucker.

Like he was just a man and she was just a woman, and the weight of the world wasn't pressing down on them.

The thought struck and realization zapped her like a lightning bolt sizzling through the blinding fog.

Because nothing could be further from the truth.

He wasn't just a man, and she wasn't just a woman. And she wasn't setting herself up for another heartbreak where he was concerned. She'd trusted him way back when, so sure that he really and truly wanted her, and she'd been wrong. He'd rejected her when she'd been about to give him her virginity, and while that wasn't at stake now, it was the principle that mattered.

She refused to be disappointed yet again.

She tore her lips from his and stumbled backward, putting some blessed distance between them.

"I really should get going. I've got a ton of things to do tonight and an early morning tomorrow."

"Tomorrow is Sunday."

"Yeah, well, no rest for the weary. I've got a full day. There's the church picnic and then I promised I'd help Les with a few walk-throughs in town. And then he wants me to get a few pictures of your place." She wasn't sure why she told him. She'd taken brochure shots for Les before and never once worried about breaking the rules.

But this was different. This wasn't standing on a public sidewalk, snapping a few harmless pics while she walked by. This was trespassing.

"He said Bootleg Bayou is close to foreclosure and he wants to get the scoop on Tanner Sawyer. He figured if we had some shots of the land, he could get a head start on putting together a brochure."

"No one's foreclosing on my family's ranch. Not while I have something to say about it."

"I'm sorry," she blurted as a dark look passed over his face. "I didn't mean to pick a wound. I just thought you should know." She glanced behind her. "I'll just let myself out."

"You could still snap a few pictures," he said, stalling her in the doorway. "I'm not letting this place fall into foreclosure, but I might consider selling off a few acres up on the east side."

"Really?"

It was his turn to nod. "We need to increase our cash flow and selling a few acres makes the most sense." His gaze caught and held hers. "Put together a brochure. If I like it, you can have the listing."

"It wouldn't be mine personally. I don't have a Realtor's—"

"—license," he finished for her. "You already told me that. Just get everything together and we'll go from there."

A smile played at her lips as she envisioned the possible bonus Les might give her when he heard the news. One she desperately needed since the recipe was still MIA and her chances of finding it now looked slim to none. "You won't regret this. Les is really good at what he does."

"It's not Les I'm thinking about. You're really good, Callie." His gaze darkened and heat whispered across her nipples. "In fact, you're pretty amazing."

If she hadn't known better, she would have sworn his words dripped with innuendo.

If only.

But he'd abandoned her all those years ago, and just when things had been really heating up. She couldn't have been that good, otherwise he never would have turned his back and kicked her out of his pappy's Caddy.

She stiffened at the sudden memory and squared her shoulders. "I can hold my own." She gathered up her purse. "I'll head out tomorrow morning and get a few shots."

"I'm sorry about the safe."

"Me, too." And then she turned and walked away before she gave in to the need churning deep inside and kissed him once more.

Talk about desperate.

But she wasn't letting her emotions get the best of her this time. She wasn't throwing herself at Brett Sawyer.

Never again.

If only that thought didn't depress her almost as much as not finding the recipe.

CHAPTER 15

He had a boner the size of Texas.

Brett shifted, feeling the heavy weight pressing against his zipper as he stood at the window and watched Callie climb into her grandaddy's old blue truck. A soft breeze caught the hem of her sundress and pushed it higher, giving him a tantalizing view of her thigh as she slid onto the seat.

His gut tightened and his cock throbbed.

And all because of a measly *kiss*.

He ran a hand through his hair and tried to ignore the truth that throbbed in his jeans. He wasn't nearly as in control as he wanted to be where she was concerned.

He still wanted her, ached for her, and getting within a mile's radius of her was still dangerous with a capital *D*.

That's what his head told him.

But that damned hard-on chanted an entirely different story.

Damn straight one kiss had turned him inside out. He hadn't had a woman in over four months. Women were a distraction, one he couldn't afford while he was going from rodeo to rodeo during a busy season. Sure, there were lulls when he didn't mind filling his time by getting down and dirty. Hell, there were times when he *needed* to get lost in the moment and forget everything else. But coming off of two of the biggest rodeos of the season—San Antonio and then Houston—before heading straight for Rebel, he hadn't had the chance to breathe, much less burn off some much-needed steam.

It made sense he'd be hard enough to cut diamonds.

Add to that the fact that he'd always had a thing for Callie, and it made even more sense that one kiss would turn him on in a major way.

His damned celibacy was making a less-than-ideal situation that much worse.

He needed to get laid.

Especially if he intended to join forces with Callie and keep looking for his family's half of the recipe.

The safe might have been a bust, but he wasn't giving up. It made sense that the valuables would be missing if there, indeed, was a thief at Bootleg Bayou. But family mementos? The leftover box of cigars from the day he was born? His first pair of baby shoes? His sister's confirmation Bible? Those things had no value to anyone other than the Sawyers, and they'd been stashed right there in the safe along with the jewelry and savings bonds.

The truth echoed in his head over the next half hour as he sank down at his pappy's old desk and finalized the papers for the cattle sale. He was meeting the buyer later that afternoon to exchange paperwork and get his check.

Two thousand short of what he needed, of course, thanks to the missing cattle.

And the missing jewelry.

He'd had every intention of selling something to make ends meet, but letting go of a few acres as he'd told Callie would probably be for the best. The only problem there was that the money wouldn't come quickly enough. Ideally a land sale would take at least a month, but Brett needed to make ends meet *now*.

Frustration rushed through him. He pushed to his feet and eyed the empty safe.

"Where is everything?" The familiar voice sounded behind him and he glanced over his shoulder to see his sister standing in the doorway.

"I wish I knew. I got the combination from Pappy's lawyer and when I opened it up, I found it empty." He slid a glance toward his sister. "I've got ten cattle missing, too."

"How is that possible?"

"Beats the hell out of me. Something's going on."

"Is that why you were asking about the ranch hands? You think one of them has something to do with the missing cattle?"

And the safe.

"I think it's more likely someone outside of the ranch sees us as an easy target, what with Pappy's illness. Things are confusing right now and so it's an opportune chance to make a fast buck. When was the last time you saw the contents of the safe?"

She shrugged. "A year ago. Maybe two. Pappy never opened it up much."

"The last time I saw it was five years ago when Pappy put my first buckle inside with the savings bonds, the jewelry, the Bible."

"Grandma's old Bible?" He nodded and she added, "I didn't even know that was in the safe. The last time I saw that old thing, it was in one of those boxes in the attic. The ones filled with all of Grandma's stuff."

Karen's words sent a bolt of hope through him and he eyed his sister. "So you're telling me it wasn't in the safe?"

She shook her head. "Not since two Christmases ago.

Seeing all those mementos made Pappy upset so Dolly packed everything away and put it up in the attic. It calmed him down. For a little while, anyway." She frowned. "So you really think someone is stealing from us?"

"I don't know, but it's looking more and more likely. Unless Pappy cleaned it out himself."

"He can barely remember who we are, I seriously doubt he opened the safe and moved everything."

"Maybe it was one of his better days." Brett held tight to the hope and glanced toward the open doorway and the whistling that came from down the hall. It was an old Willie Nelson song, his grandmother's favorite as a matter of fact, and his gut tightened.

"He's in his bedroom getting dressed for his date."

"Come again?" Brett arched an eyebrow.

"He told me he's going to call on this really pretty girl he met last week and ask her to the cotillion. I'm pretty sure he's talking about Grandma. He's putting on a red shirt and you know how she liked red."

"When he's feeling better, I'll talk to him."

Karen leveled a stare at him. "You mean *if* he ever feels better."

"I mean *when*." Brett closed the safe. "He's strong, Karen. He'll make it through this." He gathered up the papers sitting atop the desk. "I need to get going. We're finishing up with the cattle sale today." He rounded the polished oak table and headed for the door. "Let me know when you're heading back to school and we'll do something. Lunch or dinner in town maybe."

He left the room, hanging a left toward the front door. The old Willie Nelson tune followed him, reminding him of the past and the Pappy he'd once known. One he intended to hold onto for as long as possible.

Pappy was strong. He could fight this. He would. He just needed a little time.

At least that's what Brett had been telling himself for the past two weeks.

He just wasn't so sure he believed it anymore.

Karen Sawyer stood near the kitchen window and watched her brother mount the multicolored paint in the back corral.

He tossed a leg over, kicked the animal into motion, and raced for the west pasture where Pepper and the others were loading several cattle trucks.

Pappy's whistling echoed in her ears and she blinked against the sudden burning behind her eyes.

While Brett refused to see the truth—that the Pappy they once knew was gone—Karen had accepted it months ago. She'd seen him deteriorating every holiday when she was home from school. At this past year's Christmas when he'd wrapped presents for her grandma, who'd been dead for years. At Easter when he'd hidden eggs for his only son, Berle. On the Fourth of July when he'd dressed in his Sunday best and waited for his beloved wife to come down the stairs so they could head to the annual Red, White & Blue picnic and eat banana pudding.

Each "episode" lasted longer and made him all the more upset when reality set in and he learned that his son was gone and his wife had passed, and the years had turned him into a shadow of the man he'd once been.

A man who was now old and frail and sick.

Those valuable moments of realization were becoming too few and far between, which is why she wasn't heading back to Texas A&M next weekend.

She wasn't just home for the break.

No, Karen Sawyer was home for good.

Pappy needed someone full-time, and while Dolly lived at Bootleg Bayou, she still had a life that existed outside of the ranch. She had a daughter and son-in-law in nearby Austin who'd given her a handful of grandkids to keep her busy during her weekends off. She had bingo on Monday nights and Bible study on Wednesdays. Both of which she'd given up to look after Pappy when Karen was in College Station.

But as dedicated as the old woman was, she wasn't family. It wasn't fair that she should have to sacrifice her life for her employer. Even if she considered that employer a dear friend.

Pappy needed someone who was all-in, every second of every day, and Karen intended to be that someone. Her grandfather had taken care of her ever since her mother had left. Before then, even, because her parents had been too busy fighting to pay much attention to their own kids.

Not Pappy. He'd been the one constant in her life, and now it was Karen's turn to repay the favor.

"You're doing no such thing," Dolly had told her when she'd spilled the news to the woman just yesterday. "You're too young to be taking care of a sick old man. You should be out having fun, living life, falling in love."

Love?

Seriously?

She'd been there and done that, and it had hurt like hell. She'd discovered that firsthand when certified SOB Layton Daniels had two-timed her with some random slut he'd met on Tinder. She'd caught him red-handed a few months ago at a fraternity graffiti party and she'd called it quits that very night.

Men sucked.

The only man she'd ever been able to depend on was her pappy. Sure, her brother was great. She knew she could call him anytime with any problem, but he wasn't *there*. He'd spent the past ten years on the road. Even now, he'd made it perfectly clear that his presence at Bootleg Bayou was just temporary. He had a career. A life.

Karen had neither. School wasn't all she'd hoped it would be, her biology class was kicking her ass, and Layton and his slut seemed to be lurking around every corner, studying in the Student Center, or chowing down in the dining hall, or sucking down beers at the Dixie Chicken.

She needed a break and Pappy needed her, and so she was staying right here where she belonged.

When Callie pulled up in front of the house she shared with her two sisters on Saturday night, the sun had finally set and shadows clustered on the front porch. The light was off, which meant that Jenna was still at the veterinary clinic and Brandy was working late at the bakery.

Like they did most nights.

They were living out their dreams, working hard for the future they'd planned for themselves.

Meanwhile Callie's life was stuck in neutral while she tried to figure out her current mess.

She remembered the burst of hope when Brett had agreed to look for his half of the recipe. For a moment, she'd pictured finding the recipe, calling Mark, walking into the bank to pay off the taxes, and finally sending off the armload of tear sheets that were ready and waiting on the corner of her desk. As if anything in her life had ever been that easy.

A symphony of barking dogs met her when she opened the front door. She spent the next half hour feeding the animals and letting them out to do their business, all the while doing her damnedest to forget Brett and the way he'd tasted.

Better than the past.

Hotter.

Sweeter.

Ugh.

Herding a yapping Jez into the den, she left the dog watching a rerun of *Keeping Up with the Kardashians* while she headed back to the kitchen to drown her own troubles.

Opening the fridge, she pulled out what was left of Nona Munson's prize-winning chocolate meringue pie. The old woman had dropped off two of the rare delicacies after the funeral, the first of which had been devoured in a record five minutes in the church rec hall. Brandy—bless her heart—had managed to hide the second and bring it home so that she could attempt to dissect Miss Nona's recipe and create her own version for the bakery.

That had involved eating nearly half the pie, which left the other half for Callie.

Thankfully.

She fished a fork out of the drawer, sat down at the table, and took her first bite. The decadent taste exploded on her tongue and sent a rush of *ahh* that temporarily distracted her from the all-important fact that Brett Sawyer had kissed her.

Slow and deep and . . .

She shoveled another bite and focused on the sweet meringue and rich chocolate and flaky crust—anything besides the way his lips had slanted over hers and the way his large hand had pressed just so at the base of her spine. There. That was better. No way could Brett hold a candle to Miss Nona's pie.

No matter how tall.

Or sexy.

Or downright yummy.

She ate a few more bites and tried to forget the past

half hour and the way he'd looked at her and the way he'd held her and the way his strong, purposeful mouth had devoured hers.

She kept eating, until she reached the last bite and the only thing she could think of was how much Miss Nona deserved that blue ribbon she'd won last year.

Okay, so that wasn't the only thing she was thinking. Right up there? She was sure to regret pigging out. A girl didn't down half a pie and not pay the price when it came time to get dressed the next morning.

To offset the massive food baby and ease her own guilt, she went on another cleaning binge. She dusted and vacuumed and hauled out the trash. She even grabbed the doggy brush and spent fifteen minutes working through Jez's soft fur.

Not that she liked Jez all that much, or had any intention of getting her own pet once she packed up and left Rebel.

Callie was through being responsible for someone else. Once she had the city limits in her rearview mirror, her only responsibility would be to herself.

Her career.

It was a dream that had gotten her through the tough times in her past, all those long endless nights when she'd worried over James, wondering if he would open his eyes the next morning or if he'd finally drank himself past the point of no return.

A dream that did nothing for her tonight.

Because it wasn't visions of a career in journalism that crawled into bed with her later that night. It was the vivid memory of the hottest kiss of her life and the man who'd given it to her.

And damn if she didn't want another.

CHAPTER 16

It was way too early in the morning.

That was Callie's first thought as she stood on the east side of Bootleg Bayou and stared through a break in the trees at the man who stood near the creek just a few yards away from her, his back to her.

He wore nothing but a pair of snug, faded jeans that molded to the shape of his buttocks, his lean hips, and strong thighs. A rip in the denim bisected his upper left thigh, giving her a peek at silky dark hair and tanned skin.

The first light of day spilled through the trees and sculpted his bare torso. The surrounding foliage cast just the right amount of shadow to accent the corded muscles of his shoulders and arms, the hard planes of his back.

A blanket lay nearby, a pair of worn boots sitting on top next to a pillow.

She sighted through the lens, moved a fraction of an inch this way, a scant distance that way. Zooming in, she searched for just the right angle . . . There. She had him framed perfectly, his shoulders filling up her view. A drop of perspiration slid down his neck, winding a path between his shoulder blades, and her throat went dry.

Her finger stalled just shy of the shutter, her hand tightened on the camera.

Landscape shots, she reminded herself. She was here to knock off a few shots of the rippling creek, the lush trees, the local wildlife.

Sliding her attention past the perfect specimen of man, she fixed her gaze on a whitetail deer that dipped his head and drank from the creek. She zoomed in on the shot, framing the animal perfectly before she snapped off first one picture, then another.

The animal went on about his business, and she did the same. She'd dragged herself out of bed before sunrise on purpose, to capture the first morning light and portray the quiet serenity of a Texas sunrise at Bootleg Bayou. The less she had to use flashes or strobes, the more real the pictures.

She didn't have the fanciest equipment, but a good photographer didn't need the latest bells and whistles. She'd learned that from her yearbook advisor back in high school. Mrs. Brenner had been the best photographer in Rebel at the time. She'd shot every local wedding, captured every major event, and been featured regularly in the local newspaper. She'd graduated from the University of Texas School of Journalism—the school Callie had planned to attend—and she'd been a valuable mentor. Mrs. Brenner had given her her first camera—an old castoff the woman had stopped using in favor of a newer, flashier model—and taught Callie the value of taking care of a camera and treating it as if it were the most expensive piece of equipment available.

"It's not about the camera itself. It's about what you do with it."

She'd taught Callie to do plenty. To play with light and focus. To look deeper into a scene and capture that one element that represented the whole.

That told a story.

One that said she was desperately, undeniably horny.

The truth hit her as she focused on Brett framed in the morning light and tapped the shutter before she could stop herself.

Hello? This is about showing the natural charm of a winding creek lined with cypress and cedar trees, the breathtaking quality of the hills, the strength of the land. You're not here to document the beefcake owner with his broad shoulders and his ripped jeans . . .

The thought stalled as Brett turned, giving her his profile. Muscles rippled. Shadows chased sunlight across his bare torso and the air lodged in her throat.

If a picture told a story, Brett was an award-winning porn star. From the way he lifted his arms in what should have been a casual stretch, to the ever-so-slight thrust of his hips, to the peekaboo rip in his jeans.

She stared at his image in her viewfinder and tried with all of her might not to look.

Come on, Callie. Get it together. Just turn. Walk away. Go back to the truck and get your tripod.

She could march up the nearest hill and take a few panoramic shots. The creek could wait until later, until after Brett was gone and she wasn't so fresh from a night spent tossing and turning and thinking about that kiss.

About him.

Because he was still that pie-in-the-sky fantasy. The unanswered question. The *what if?*

No way would it be as good as she imagined. She knew that firsthand. She'd had a few sexual encounters over the years and they'd all fallen terribly short of her fantasies.

Brett would be the same disappointment.

Or would he?

The question stuck in her brain as he turned toward her.

His gaze powered through the viewfinder and just like that, he was staring straight at her.

The camera slipped from her hands and stalled at her waist thanks to the strap that fastened around her neck. And suddenly there was nothing to hide behind. No barrier between her and the real world.

Sure enough, Brett stared in her direction. A heartbeat later, he wasn't just staring. He stepped toward her and she knew that it was too late to turn tail and run.

"You're up early," he murmured as his legs ate up the distance between them and he came up to her.

"It's the best time for nature shots. The lighting is amazing. Listen, I'm sorry if I bothered you . . ."

"No bother." He touched a hand to his neck and moved his head from side to side. "I was already awake."

"You're sleeping out here?"

"Trying to, and failing miserably." He cast a glance over his shoulder. "There's someone making moonshine farther down the creek."

"I thought I recognized the smell." One she'd caught a whiff of too many times back at home thanks to James and his cooking. "Do you know who it is?"

"No, but when I find out I intend to put a stop to it. I've got enough problems." He shoved a hand through his hair and her gaze hooked on his strong, tanned fingers.

She had the sudden image of those fingers pressed against her skin, trailing down her neck, between her breasts . . .

"We should talk," she blurted before her courage could falter. "About what happened yesterday." She shook her head. "I shouldn't have kissed you back. It's just that you caught me off guard and I've been working so much and, well, it was a weak moment."

He arched an eyebrow. "So you didn't want to kiss me?"

"I'm not saying that."

"So you didn't like kissing me?"

"I'm not saying that, either. It was nice."

"Nice, huh?"

"Okay, it was better than nice. But that's beside the point. I don't have time for kissing." Or anything else.

Especially the *anything else,* she added silently.

"I've got a lot on my plate right now and I think it's better if we just stay focused on business."

He didn't say anything. He just stared at her for a long, silent moment before he reached out and touched the strap hanging around her neck. "This is a sight for sore eyes. I don't think I have one memory of you without a camera hanging around your neck."

It was a sight that Brett remembered all too well. Callie standing on the sidelines at every football game, snapping pictures of the players, the mascot, the cheerleaders. Callie at the Friday night bonfires, the pep rallies, the school dances.

As photographer for the yearbook, she'd been a mainstay at every major event. But while everyone else had been focused on having fun, she'd hung back, drinking in the big picture. Watching, but not participating. She'd never really fit in, a fact that had nothing to do with being a Tucker and everything to do with having big-time dreams in a small, small town.

There was nothing big-time about her now. She wore another sundress like the one she'd had on yesterday. A pale pink number that was sheer enough to make him swallow. The material molded to her full breasts and nipped at her waist. A soft breeze ruffled her long blond hair and teased the hem of her dress, revealing an endless pair of legs. She wasn't decked out like some high-powered journalist, and yet he could still see the hunger in her eyes. The gleam that said she wasn't giving up.

And damn if didn't admire her for it.

Way too much for a man with a strict Hands-Off policy.

Then again, he'd violated said policy last night. And then he'd spent the entire night thinking that maybe it was the policy itself that made him want her that much more.

He'd always been a sucker for what he couldn't have, and while he'd learned that the world didn't owe him shit, he had no problem doing his damnedest to earn what he wanted.

And he wanted her.

Sure, he'd lost his control way back when, but he was a decade older, and a helluva lot wiser. Maybe instead of avoiding trouble, he should head straight for it and prove once and for all that he could handle himself where she was concerned. Then he could stop thinking about Callie, stop wanting her, and get his mind on the business at hand— getting the ranch back on track.

The *maybe* played in his head all of a few seconds before his decision was made.

He wanted Callie, and it was time to stop wanting and start doing.

"I know the safe was a bust yesterday, but I'm not giving up on the recipe." He needed that money every bit as much as she did. And he needed her. And searching through the attic would give him a chance at both. "I talked to Karen and there's a good possibility our half of the recipe might be buried up in the attic somewhere."

A gleam lit her eyes. "Seriously?"

"I can't say for sure, but it's worth a look. We could start going through everything this evening. I've got a long day, but I should be done by about six."

She smiled at him, a full-blown tilt to her lush lips that made his entire body ache. "I'll be there."

CHAPTER 17

"Thank God you're home." Jenna met Callie as soon as she opened the front door that afternoon. "We've got a big problem." The youngest Tucker sister pushed Callie back out onto the front porch and hauled the door shut behind her. "Alex is here."

"How is that *our* problem?

"He brought Arnie McIntyre with him." Jenna glanced behind her as if afraid the two men had followed her out onto the front porch. "Arnie just got his acupuncture certificate online and Alex brought him out here to give me treatments."

"For what?"

"The claustrophobia."

"You don't have claustrophobia."

"I know that and you know that, but when I said I was feeling smothered, he took it a bit literally. He spent all day yesterday Googling treatments. Turns out this one Web site suggested acupuncture, so he called up Arnie and now they're in the living room preparing to stick a crapload of needles in me."

"Again, how is that our problem?"

Jenna glared before the look faltered and desperation

slid into its place. "You have to help me, Cal. I'm afraid of needles."

"You are not."

"Okay, so I'm afraid of Arnie. He's got a lazy eye. Do you know what a lazy eye can do to your aim? I could wind up blind or maimed."

"Just tell Alex you don't have claustrophobia. You have commitment phobia."

"I can't do that." She glanced over her shoulder, her voice lowering a notch. "You didn't see him. He looks so hopeful. You have to do it."

"I'm not breaking up for you. Stand up. Be a woman."

"But I'm no good at destroying people. You're the mean one."

"No, I'm not."

"Yes, you are. Brandy's the focused one. You're the mean one. And I'm the hot one."

"If you're trying to butter me up, you're doing it wrong."

"Don't take it personally. You're just a straight shooter. No beating around the bush. Remember when Jackson Karnes asked you out last year? You told him to take a flying leap."

"I did not. I just said I wouldn't go out with him because it was a conflict of interest. Les was working for him to sell his house, and I work for Les. I couldn't go out with someone that I was technically working for."

Dating, no. Kissing, yes.

Callie's stomach hollowed out and she remembered the purposeful slant of Brett's lips on hers. She cleared her suddenly dry throat. "I had to adhere to a code of conduct."

Then and now.

Even though Brett hadn't actually signed the paperwork

to give Les the listing for the hundred acres, he'd given his word, which was just as binding. Just one more reason to keep her distance.

As if she needed another one.

Yesterday's fall from grace when he'd kissed her and she'd kissed him back had proved beyond a doubt that she was still desperately attracted to him. Attracted and distracted, neither of which she could afford at the moment.

He made her forget what was really important in her life. Paying off the taxes, mailing off her tear sheets, getting out of Rebel. Instead, she found herself thinking about him and how sexy he looked and how great he tasted and how she'd really, really like to taste him again.

This afternoon.

She gave herself a mental kick in the keister. It wasn't as if they had a date. They were joining forces for the money. The recipe. They were going to dig through an old, stuffy attic, not feel each other up.

Not yet.

She shook away the crazy thought. She was not feeling Brett up. Not now. Not ever. Their connection now was strictly business.

"I don't kiss clients," Callie heard herself say before she could think better of it.

Her sister's eyes twinkled suddenly as if she'd just gotten an earful of juicy gossip. "Wait a second. You didn't tell me that Jackson kissed you."

"Because he didn't."

"But you just said—"

"Go." Callie motioned toward the small truck with Rebel Veterinary Clinic blazing across the side. "Get out of here. I'll tell Alex you had an emergency. A calf birthing or something."

"Really?"

"I said so, didn't I?"

Jenna smiled and fished in her pocket for her keys. "You're the best big sister in the entire world."

"And you're still a chicken shit." Her gaze caught Jenna's. "You're going to have to have a real, honest conversation with him sometime soon. You know that, right?"

"I will." Jenna nodded. "I just need some time to find the right words." She started down the steps. "I'll call him later. Oh, and make sure you let Arnie know it's you coming through the door and not me, otherwise he's liable to stick first and ask questions later."

Callie nodded and watched her sister hightail it for the vet mobile. The engine cranked and the motor revved. A heartbeat later, Jenna backed down the dirt drive, swung the vehicle around, and disappeared in a cloud of dust.

"Jenna? Honey?" The voice came from inside the house. "I hate to rush you, but Arnie's all set up. He really needs to get started. He's only got a half hour with us before he needs to head into town and meet with the mayor's wife. She's trying to give up smoking and acupuncture is great for addictions."

The notion stuck as Callie opened the front door and walked inside. Maybe Arnie hadn't made a trip for nothing.

Twenty well-placed needles later (with only one *oops* thanks to Arnie's lazy eye), Callie was ready to head over to Bootleg Bayou.

A mixture of excitement and dread built over the thirty-minute drive. Excitement because she was at least doing something to find the recipe and dread because all the acupuncture in the world couldn't make her forget that kiss or the fact that she wanted another.

Not that she was kissing him again.

Her guarantee?

Distance. She intended to keep three feet between them at all times.

Thankfully the attic was like everything else at the Sawyer spread—huge.

The acreage. The ranch house. Brett himself.

That truth hit home when she leaned up on her tiptoes to pull a large cardboard box off the top shelf of an antique wall unit.

He came up behind her. He leaned in, strong muscular arms coming up on either side to help navigate the cardboard safely to the ground.

His large, dark hands were a stark contrast to the pale creaminess of her own skin and electricity skimmed through her as his thumb brushed the side of her palm. Her fingers trembled. Her heart drummed.

An alarm went off in her head, signaling that he'd breached the three-foot safety zone she'd designated for herself. Too close, but there wasn't a thing she could do about it. He stood directly behind her, surrounding her.

She turned to face him, but he didn't back up. Suddenly, she couldn't get enough air. She drew in a deep breath, the motion pushing her breasts up and out. Her nipples kissed his chest. Electricity rumbled from the point of contact, zigzagging to every erogenous zone in her body.

"Thanks, but I can handle it from here," she managed to say, her voice more breathy than she intended.

"My pleasure."

Mine, too.

The thought slipped into her mind a split second before he touched her. The tip of his callused finger caught a drop of perspiration that slid down her neck. "You're all hot and bothered, sugar."

"Hot, yes." She steeled herself against the purposeful glide of his touch. "Bothered, no. I'd just like to get on with it."

"So would I." Innuendo dripped from the words. His gaze dropped, roaming over her neck and shoulders covered with a fine sheen of sweat, down over the damp material of her T-shirt, the bare skin of her stomach glistening just above the waistband of her shorts.

"The recipe," she croaked, the sound of her own voice effectively breaking the erotic spell that held her captive. "I bet it's in this box." She turned so fast that her shoulder bumped his. Electricity skimmed through her and she stiffened. "Or one of those." She pointed to the stack he'd been working on before he'd abandoned them to help her. "You should get back to work."

He didn't move. Instead, he stood there for a long moment, as if debating whether to reach for her again.

Please, please, please, a small traitorous voice chanted. She steeled herself and wiped at the sweat beading on her forehead. "You'd think the heat would let up once the sun goes down, but I swear it's getting hotter. Not that I'm bothered by the heat. Not at all."

No, she was bothered by him.

Very bothered.

"I'll open another window." He moved then, putting some blessed space between them as he went over to a large dormer window and worked at the opening. Wood creaked and a small breeze whispered into the stuffy room. "There. That's better."

If only. But he was still there. The chemistry between

them was still palpable. And so breathing proved a chore over the next half hour as she went through box after box filled with everything from trinkets to pictures to a hand-carved statue of a male penis.

"Tell me this isn't what I think it is," she murmured as she stared at the smooth lines of the wood, the round globes that looked suspiciously like . . .

"Yep, it's a rocket. At least that's what I was going for when I sat down with Pappy to learn how to whittle. But then I couldn't get the blasters to look like blasters and so I ended up with a replica of Mr. Happy."

"You call your male part Mr. Happy?"

"No, I call mine Rex." His grin was slow and wicked. "Mr. Happy's just a general term that most people recognize."

She wasn't going to ask. That's what she told herself as she set the carving aside and pulled out a handful of pictures. "Rex, huh?" she asked before she could stop herself. "Why Rex?"

"Why not? I mean, I suppose I could have gone with Godzilla or King Kong or something a little more descriptive, but Rex seems more down to earth. Friendly. And that's the real purpose. To get up close and friendly, don't you think?"

"I don't know. I think Rex sounds sort of stuffy. Pretentious even. You should go with something like Buddy. Or maybe Albert. I had a puppy named Albert once. He was super friendly."

"I suppose I could name it after a puppy, but it would have to be a Great Dane pup, or maybe a German shepherd. Something really big."

She glanced up then and caught the twinkle in his eyes. "You don't call it Rex, do you?"

"I suppose I could, but I've never really been the type to call it much of anything. I'm more a man of action."

She blushed, he chuckled, and despite the sexual tension coiling around them, she started to relax.

He'd always been a big flirt, teasing her with his Southern charm and easy smile. He'd always been able to make her laugh and put her at ease even though she knew he posed the biggest threat. He'd been the biggest player in the senior class, and she'd fallen for him anyway because he'd talked to her, teased her, and made her smile.

Then, and now.

CHAPTER 18

Callie and Brett spent the next two hours going through box after box, working from right to left in the large, over-sized attic. They unpacked each box, examining the contents before packing everything back up and marking the outside with a check. The boxes soon gave way to antique dressers, the drawers full, and several old trunks.

Callie reached for the first trunk, but Brett's voice stalled her. "I don't know about you, but I need something to drink. Can I get you anything?"

"Whatever's cold."

He nodded and started down the stairs leading to the second floor. Callie blew out a deep breath and walked toward the open window. Staring out, she drank in the endless stretch of pasture, the rich, lush trees in the distance, the bare glimmer of the creek in the moonlight. She found herself wishing she'd brought her camera, but then the shots were too distant to entice a buyer. This sight was just for the naked eye.

She sank down on the window seat and stared out until she heard footsteps behind her. She turned to see Brett, two beers in his hands. He passed her a bottle dripping with condensation.

"I hope you don't mind Bud Light. It's the only thing

that's really cold. Karen drank the last soda and Dolly doesn't go to the grocery store until tomorrow."

"It's fine." She twisted off the top and took a long pull of the ice-cold beer. She'd never had much of a taste for the stuff, but she had to admit that it certainly hit the spot. Especially when a speck of ice dripped from the glass and fell between her cleavage. The iciness swept a cool path south, over her bare skin, all the way to her waistband, sending a small, welcome shiver through her.

Brett sank down onto the floor, his back to the wall, his elbows propped on his bent knees as he stared at the mound of boxes stacked here and there. He took a long drink of his beer before leaning his head back and closing his eyes.

Silence settled between them for several moments and she took the opportunity to really look at him.

Time had turned the gangly teenage boy into a hard and muscular man. His white T-shirt—soaking wet now thanks to the stuffy attic—clung to his sinewy torso like a second skin, revealing a solid chest, a ridged abdomen. Her gaze lingered at the shadow of a nipple beneath the damp material and a dozen forbidden images rushed through her.

She took a deep breath and moved her attention to the jeans molded to his thighs, his calves. Scuffed black cowboy boots completed the outfit. His entire persona screamed danger. Brett was a womanizer, a use-'em-and-lose-'em type with a taste for sin and a body to back him up. He was the sort of man every mama warned her daughter about.

Trouble.

That's what Callie's own mama had called him, and she'd been right. But for all her objections, she hadn't interfered when Callie had accepted his prom invitation. After an entire year spent sitting across from him in the library, she'd been ready to step out of the role as his tutor and have him see her the way he did every other female at Rebel High.

Her gaze went to Brett's face. He had the trademark Sawyer cheekbones, so strong and defined, as well as a straight, sculpted nose, a firm jaw, and the most kissable lips she'd ever seen on a man. A few days' growth of beard covered his jaw, crept down his neck. His brown hair, as damp as his shirt, curled down around his neck, the edges highlighted the same brownish gold as the aged whiskey that her grandpa had been so fond of.

Her palms burned as she remembered the softness of those dark strands filtering through her fingers, brushing her neck, her collarbone, the sensitive tip of her nipple . . .

She drew a deep breath and noted the tiny lines that fanned out from the corners of his eyes. A scar zigzagged from his right temple and bisected his cheek and she couldn't deny the sudden urge to reach out and trace the puckered skin with her fingertip. To ask him what had happened. A bar fight? An angry bull?

The subtle changes made him seem older than the boy of eighteen who haunted her memories.

This was no boy. He was all man, and he had the hard look of someone who'd seen too much and done even more.

A tiredness pulled at his expression and she stiffened against a rush of sympathy. While they might be facing similar situations now, they were still worlds apart.

If only she didn't keep forgetting that all-important fact.

"I'd hoped we would have found it by now," the deep rumble of his voice drew her from her thoughts.

"The night is still young. We'll find it."

He stared at the bottle of beer and picked at the edge of the label before chancing a glance at her. "And if we don't?" His gaze caught hers. "Do you have a backup plan?"

She shrugged. "I figured I would pay a visit to the bank and ask for an extension. I doubt I'll get it, but it doesn't hurt to ask. Then I'll hit up Les and see if he can give me a loan."

"That means you'll have to stick around to pay it back."

She nodded. "That's usually the way a loan works."

"Why not just let the bank have it? Or do a short sale and split whatever's left with your sisters?"

"We grew up in that house." It was the one place that felt like home. The only place. "My dad and mom worked hard to keep up the bills when James couldn't make it. I can't just let it go. It's all we have. It's all I have left that still reminds me of them."

Silence stretched between them for several long moments before his words echoed in her ears. "I'm really sorry about that night, Callie. I'm sorry it went to hell so fast, and I'm really sorry about your parents."

His sorry didn't matter. She'd told herself that time and time again over the years. It didn't matter what he said. What he thought. None of it mattered.

She'd been right. The words didn't make a bit of difference. They were meaningless, an empty gesture that did little to console or ease the fist tightening inside of her.

Rather it was the gleam of sincerity in his gaze, the glimmer of regret that soothed the fierce ache and helped her next breath come a little easier.

"That broken-down house is my home. It always will be, even when I'm far away from here. I have to hold onto it. My sisters are just starting out. They need a place to stay while they build something solid for the future."

"And what about you? What about your future?"

"It's still there. It's just on pause right now." And for the past ten years. "My time will come once everything else is settled."

He arched an eyebrow. "What if it never settles? What if there's another problem on the heels of this one?"

He voiced the one fear that had niggled at her night after night over the past ten years. The worry that she might never be free of Rebel. That she might find herself stuck, her dreams just that—dreams. Possibilities that existed only in her imagination.

She swallowed against the sudden lump in her throat and squared her shoulders. "Then I'll keep dealing with whatever comes until Fate finally cuts me a break. It'll happen." Her gaze met his. "My time will come. I want to be a photojournalist. It's all I've ever wanted."

"What about settling down someday? Do you want that, too?"

She shrugged. "I've dated a few guys. Kyle Parker and Miles Langtry. They were fun, but it never went anywhere. We're just friends." She watched the satisfied expression that slid over his face and heat whispered through her. "What about you? You think you might settle down someday?"

"I'm sure Tyler McCall would like that."

"Tyler? Your cousin?"

"Fourth cousin, and my biggest competition. He's hot after my spot and he's not too shy about telling any and everyone who will listen. He's gunning for me. One slipup and that's it. He'll sail right past me into first place."

"But you won't slip up," she said, her voice steady with confidence because she knew him. "You passed calculus, remember? She's a meaner bitch than any bull." Her words drew a grin and her heart stalled.

"Yeah, well, I had a secret weapon for that." His gaze held hers and her heart stuttered for the next several beats. "I'm on my own on the circuit."

"Sounds lonely."

He seemed to think. "It shouldn't be. I'm surrounded by a shitload of people on a daily basis, but once the ride ends and the dust settles, it's just me."

"Sounds like you don't like it half as much as you pretend to."

"I don't like it." He shook his head. "I love it. When I hear that buzzer, there's no other feeling. It's just not half as glamorous as people think. It's tough."

"I saw you in the winner's circle in Vegas getting sprayed with a bottle of champagne by two Dallas Cowboys cheerleaders. Talk about torture."

The grin turned to a full-blown smile. "Definitely one of my lowest moments."

"So what about you? You ever thought of ditching the champagne and making it official with one of those cheerleaders?"

He shrugged. "I'm not really into cheerleaders."

"Since when?"

"Since I gave up football practice to sit in the math lab every afternoon with my calculus tutor." His gaze caught and held hers. "I wouldn't have graduated if it hadn't been for you. You were really something, Callie."

Were. The word struck, niggling at her and stirring a rush of insecurity fed by ten years of sacrifice. She had been something. On top of her game. A force ready to take on the world.

Then.

She shook away the disturbing thought and shrugged. "I just helped you study. You were the one in class taking all of the tests. Graduating was all on you. So what about it?" she rushed on, eager to ignore the warmth whispering through her. "Do you see yourself settling down in the future?"

He took another swig of his beer and shook his head. "I'm not the marrying kind. I live out of an RV year-round, going from rodeo to rodeo. It's no kind of life for a wife and kids."

"But you can't ride forever. What about when you retire?"

He shrugged. "I haven't really thought that far ahead. I can't see myself doing anything other than what I'm doing right now."

"I always thought you might come home and take over for your pappy. And now that he's sick—"

"He's still in charge. I'm just helping out until he gets over this rough patch." He wiped a hand over his sweaty forehead, his expression closing as if he didn't want to say another word about the subject. His blue eyes fixated on her like twin laser beams. "You know, Callie, there's never a right time to make something happen. If you really want to get out of here, you just have to go for it. Now. No matter what's happening around you. You can't wait for the planets to line up, otherwise you'll die from old age never having done anything. You don't wait for a chance to leave. You make your own chance."

"Like you?"

"Exactly like me." He nodded. "I wanted a career in bull riding and I knew it wasn't going to happen waiting around here, so I left."

"And you don't have any regrets? You don't wish you had stuck around just a little bit longer? Or come back sooner?"

Or told a stubborn old man that you loved him despite his flaws?

The notion wiggled its way into her head, but she shook it away. James hadn't done one thing to earn her love. He'd never been there. Never cared for her the way a grandfather should have.

No, he didn't deserve her love.

He never had.

"Surely there must be something that keeps you up at night," she added when he shook his head in answer to her questions.

"No," he murmured. "I don't regret a thing."

That's what he said, but Callie didn't miss the stiffening of his shoulders or the tightening of his lips. He hadn't left the past behind, he'd run from it.

From the boy he'd been.

From her.

He was still running, refusing to see the truth, to accept it.

She thought of her grandfather's room stacked with the endless copies of *Reader's Digest,* the empty tubes of Bengay, the crosswords puzzles he'd loved so dearly. Everything was exactly the way he'd left it because she'd yet to go inside, to pack it away, to face her own truth.

Instead, she was making excuses. Stalling.

Hardly. It had been less than a week since his death. She simply hadn't had the time to get the room packed away.

She would. Just as soon as she dealt with everything else.

She glanced around at the enormity of the attic, the boxes stacked here and there, the ancient furniture filled to the brim with mementos and trinkets and possibly—hopefully—the recipe that could save them both. "We really should get back to work." Pushing from the window seat, she started for the first trunk. Sinking down to her knees, she reached for the latch only to feel him beside her.

"I lied."

"About what?"

"I do have one thing that keeps me up at night." He touched her then, pulling her to her feet until they stood toe-to-toe. He didn't say anything for a long moment, just stared down at her, his gaze, dark, intense, stirring. "*You*," he finally murmured. "We never finished what we started that night and that's my own damned fault." He touched a strand of hair that had come loose from her ponytail. His callused thumb brushed her cheek and a shiver ripped through her. His blue eyes darkened to a deep, mesmerizing cobalt, the depths shimmering with a need that mirrored her own. "But that's one regret I don't have to live with."

CHAPTER 19

The moment Brett slid his hands around her waist, Callie's breath caught. Shock jolted through her as he pulled her flush against him, her breasts crushed against his chest, her pelvis cradling the hard bulge of his crotch.

The sudden contact shocked them both.

His gaze darkened.

A gasp caught on her lips.

"I shouldn't have pulled away from you," he murmured, his voice edged with a raw emotion that wrapped around her heart and squeezed tight.

"So why did you?"

"Because I wanted you so much that I got ahead of myself."

"I don't understand—" His lips caught the rest of her sentence as his mouth plundered hers in a kiss that was both deep and desperate.

His tongue slid into her mouth to stroke and tease. Strong hands pressed the small of her back, holding her close. She could feel every inch of his body, from chest to hips to thighs, his desire pressing hard and eager into her belly.

He smelled of leather and fresh air and a touch of wildness that teased her nostrils and made her breathe heavier, desperate to draw more of his essence into her lungs.

She wasn't sure what happened next, she just knew that one minute she was standing in the middle of the attic, her body pressed to his, and the next she was following him down onto the cushioned window seat.

He sat down first. His hand caught her thigh, pulling her down onto his lap until her legs were on either side of his hips and she straddled him.

His lips went to her throat, nibbling and tasting, while his hands slid under her sundress to cup her buttocks and settle her more firmly over the bulge in his jeans.

She gasped and rocked against him, rubbing and stirring while his hands massaged the soft flesh of her bottom.

He slid a hand around, his fingers trailing over the lace triangle of her panties before dipping beneath the edge. One fingertip rasped against her clit and sensation ripped through her. Before she could catch her breath, he slipped a finger into the moist heat between her legs and plunged deep.

A moan burst from her lips as heat slammed over her, pulling her down and sucking the air from her lungs for a long, delicious moment.

"You're so beautiful, Callie. So fucking *perfect.*" The deep rumble of his voice slid through her, slipping along her nerves, stirring them as intensely as the hand between her legs. She shimmied, pressing against his probing hand, clutching at his broad shoulders, her fingers fisting in the material of his soft T-shirt.

The heat burned fierce between them as they kissed and rubbed and worked each other into a frenzy. The air grew hotter, charged with the smell of sweaty bodies and the promise of hot, steamy sex.

She clutched at his shirt, pulling at the material, desperate to feel the warmth of his skin against her own.

"Wait." He caught her hand with his free one, stilling her movements. "Slow down, honey." He took a deep breath and rested his forehead against hers. "We should get out of here. Go downstairs. Find a bed."

He was right.

In the back of her mind, she knew she should put on the brakes. They weren't kids in the backseat of some car, worried about making curfew. They were grown adults. This was going too far, too fast.

The thing was, she didn't want to slow down, to give him time to pull away, to back out, to *think*.

She didn't want history to repeat itself.

"Let's just do it," she murmured, grabbing at his T-shirt, hauling it over his head. She touched her palms to his chest, feeling the hard muscle dusted with silky hair. "Right here. Right now."

The moment she said the words, he stiffened. Her heart pounded once, twice, and then he relaxed and pushed deeper into the wet heat of her body. Sensation drenched her, so sweet and consuming. She caught her bottom lip and her head fell back. This is what she needed. What she'd been waiting for.

He worked her for a few more minutes, making her sigh and gasp as she clutched at the hard muscle of his shoulders. He kissed her again, his tongue pushing deep in a kiss that made the room spin.

And then he pulled away.

"What are you doing?" she stammered, her head still reeling, her body trembling with need.

"I need to be up early tomorrow." His gaze caught and held hers. "And you're not ready for this." He lifted her then, setting her on her feet as he pushed to his.

Her dress fell down around her wobbly legs and she

prayed that the floor didn't give out beneath her. "What's that supposed to mean?"

"You don't have to prove anything." He reached for his T-shirt.

"I don't know what you're talking about."

But she did.

This moment wasn't about sating her lust for him. It was about proving to herself that she was worth his lust. She'd never been the prettiest or the thinnest or the sexiest. Boys had never fallen all over themselves for her, not the way they did for her sister Brandy. It wasn't until Brett Sawyer had stared at her across the top of his calculus book that she'd felt really and truly beautiful.

And when he'd ditched her that night, she'd taken a major blow to her ego. One she'd never fully recovered from.

Because she hadn't just liked him back then. She'd loved him.

She still did.

The truth registered as she watched him pull on his T-shirt, his biceps rippling as he slid the white cotton over his broad shoulders, down his ripped abdomen.

She loved him and if things went fast and furious now, she didn't have to think about the all-important fact that he *didn't* love her.

Not then and certainly not now.

"I shouldn't have pulled away that night, but I'm glad I did. You weren't ready for what was going to happen, any more than you're ready for it now." He stopped just a few inches shy of her, so close she could feel the heat rolling off his hard body. "It's sex, Callie. Just sex."

The minute Brett said the words, he wanted to kick his own ass. A crazy reaction because he knew he spoke the truth.

This *was* sex, pure and simple. That's all it could ever be and so he should just pull her close and get on with it.

He wasn't going to disappoint her now the way he had back then. He wouldn't haul ass the other way before they got to the really good stuff.

But he would haul ass. Eventually. He couldn't stay in Rebel forever and while she knew that, he wanted to be sure she *knew* it.

He would walk away. It was inevitable and he wanted to make sure that she understood as much. That she accepted it. He wouldn't take the decision from her by pushing her too fast. He wanted her to know what she was getting into.

To want him regardless.

Otherwise, she would end up hurt. And angry.

And he wouldn't do that to her.

Not again.

"But I thought . . ." Her words trailed off and he waited. For her to issue the invitation. To make the next move. Instead, she caught her bottom lip and nodded. "I need to be up early, too."

Brett gathered what little control he had left to keep from reaching for her, to saying to hell with right and wrong and simply feeling for the next few moments. Instead, he nodded. "We can keep looking tomorrow evening. Same time."

She nodded and then reached for her purse.

Brett followed her down the attic stairs, watching her as she made her way to the front door.

"See ya," she murmured, and then she walked out onto the front porch, down the steps.

The old truck rumbled in his ears as he slammed the door shut and headed for the kitchen. He was just reaching for a beer when his cell phone rang.

"Long time, no speak, cuz," came the voice on the other end of the line when Brett said hello.

"Tyler?"

"The one and only."

"What do you want?"

"My agent managed to get a sit-down with the Wrangler people. Rumor is that you're not going to sign with them, so they're looking to step up their game with yours truly."

"There is no stepping up with you, McCall. You're sloppy seconds if anything."

"Whatever helps you sleep better at night."

"Did you call just to gloat? Because I'm not in the mood."

"I just thought you should hear it first before the press gets wind of it."

"More like you're trying to psych me out, but it's not going to work. I've already got the contracts in hand. There's no legal way they can change their mind and sign you instead." The power rested in Brett's hands. All he had to do was sign and it was a done deal.

"If they're calling you," Brett went on, "it's strictly because every Lone Ranger needs a Tonto. You're second place, Tyler."

"Maybe, but I'm not giving up without a fight. You're on your way out, Brett. Just make it easy on yourself and call it a day. No one can stay on top forever. Better to go out at the height of your career than to slip up and lose your shit in front of thousands of fans. Besides, you've got enough to keep you busy at home. My momma said she talked to Dolly and Pappy's not doing so good."

"He's fine," Brett snapped. "He just needs a little time."

"Is that so? 'Cause the last I heard, he had Alzheimer's. You do know what that is, don't you?"

"Is there a point to this call?"

"Just wanted to keep in touch and let you know that while you're on pause, I just won first place in Tulsa. Point wise, that pushes me up the board. We're almost dead even now. Another rodeo or two, and you'll be eating my dust."

"This conversation is done."

"Bye, cuz," Tyler's irritating voice called out a split second before Brett hit the off button.

Brett hauled open the refrigerator and reached for a beer. Tyler was a jackass. A mouthy jackass. While the call didn't come as a surprise—the man consistently rubbed every success in Brett's face—the timing did.

What type of cowboy called another cowboy out while he was at home dealing with personal issues?

A cowboy who wanted to win, that's who. Brett knew the game. He'd mouthed off a time or two himself, boasting and bragging to get in the other guy's craw. Personal issues aside.

No, it wasn't the call that bothered Brett so much as what Tyler had said—that Wrangler was starting to doubt Brett's commitment to them.

Then again, he hadn't sent in the contracts or so much as e-mailed to say they were on the way. It had been three weeks and he'd yet to do anything.

Hell, he should just sign them and be done with it.

He would. First thing tomorrow.

Right now, he needed to calm down and cool off.

He popped the top on the beer and took a long swig before heading down the hallway toward his room. On the way, he caught the sound of his sister's voice as she sat by Pappy's bedside and read from an old book from their childhood.

The Little Engine That Could.

Brett had loved that book so much that he'd begged Pappy to read it to him over and over, and the man had obliged every time. He'd never been too busy or too tired.

He'd given the little engine a voice, one that didn't sound as soft, as soothing, as *different* from the familiar grumble that Brett remembered so well.

Everything was so damned different now.

The ranch.

His pappy.

His Callie.

He ditched the thought. She wasn't *his*. She never had been and she never would be. Even if they did have sex. Because sex didn't mean anything. It was one moment in a lifetime of many. Just a blissful escape from all of the problems that weighed them down. Just physical.

If only he could make Callie understand that.

While Brett Sawyer had never been one to shy away from a challenge, he started to wonder if maybe, just maybe he was in over his head this time.

With Callie. With the ranch. With Pappy.

Karen's voice followed him, prompting him to never give up, to keep going and trying, the words feeding the anxiety that skimmed his nerves and wound him tight.

Taking another swig of his beer, he bypassed his bedroom and headed for the back door.

It was time to get the hell out of Dodge.

If only for a little while.

CHAPTER 20

She should text Arnie.

That was Callie's first thought as she drove away from Bootleg Bayou. She should get in touch with him and request an emergency acupuncture session.

At the same time, Arnie called bingo at the VFW on Sunday nights after church, which meant she was out of luck. That, and the first session had failed miserably.

These things take time.

That's what Arnie had told her, but she had the gut feeling that all the needles in the world couldn't fix what ailed her. She wanted Brett Sawyer in the worst way.

She'd been this close to falling at his feet tonight and begging him to make love to her. To finish what he'd started so long ago.

But it wasn't the sex act itself that posed the threat. It was the begging. The need. The last thing Callie wanted was to need Brett Sawyer—or any man for that matter—to crave more than a few moments of carnal bliss to the point that she stopped thinking of her priorities and needed only him. Callie Tucker didn't *need* anyone.

She stood on her own two feet. She always had and she always would.

"You ate my pie." Brandy's voice drifted from the

kitchen doorway and Callie turned to see her sister wearing a pink T-shirt, the Sweet Somethings logo spelled out in white frosting, and a pair of sweats. "I was this close to dissecting Miss Nona's recipe. A few more bites and I would have had it."

"I ran out of cupcakes. It was either Miss Nona's or the apple pie that Little Jimmy dropped off the other night, and I really needed chocolate."

"I figured. What I can't figure out is why you still need the cupcakes. Unless the gossip floating around town is true."

"Gossip?"

"My assistant Ellie said her cousin said that her aunt's brother-in-law saw you talking to Brett Sawyer out in front of the feed store yesterday." Brandy pinned her with a stare. "Since when do you talk to Brett Sawyer?"

"He came home a few weeks ago and I saw him in town the day of James's funeral." She shrugged. "He stopped me to tell me that he was sorry about what happened. So where's Jenna?"

"Vaccinating horses out at the Bensons'. They're so far out of town that she's staying overnight since it's a two-day job."

"Horses, huh?"

"Her favorite. It's a wonder she hasn't brought one home along with the stray dogs. So the whole condolence thing explains the meeting in town," Brandy went on, obviously not about to be distracted, "but it doesn't explain why you went out to Brett's place tonight." Callie's head snapped up and Brandy gave her a pointed stare. "Yeah, I know about that, too."

Callie shrugged and averted her gaze. "He's selling off

some of his property and Les is getting the listing. I just went out to take a few pictures." Not quite the whole truth, but then Brandy didn't have to know about the recipe. Or the taxes. Or the fact that Callie had forgotten both while she'd been grinding on Brett's lap. "So how do you know about tonight?"

"Jimmy Eubanks saw you pass him on the interstate. He saw you turn off on County Road 1450. Everybody knows the only house off that road is the Sawyer spread."

Callie braced herself for the inquisition that was sure to follow.

Did you see Brett?

Do you still like Brett?

Did you get naked with Brett?

"I heard at the bakery today that Karen's home. Haven't seen her myself, but folks in town have. She's got this new haircut and everything. How's she doing?"

O-kay. Callie slid a glance toward her sister, but Brandy had turned away to retrieve a pitcher of iced tea from the refrigerator and Callie sent up a silent thank you. While her sister didn't know the details of that one disastrous night, she knew that Callie had liked Brett and that, for whatever reason, he'd dumped her.

"Karen, huh? I had no idea she was back. I didn't see her. Then again, I wasn't at Bootleg Bayou for a visit. I was busy taking pictures." And busy *getting* busy. "You say she cut her hair?"

Brandy nodded. "Myrtle Sullivan came in for brownies. She said her daughter saw Karen at the Quick Pack and she has this really short bob now. What a shame, right? I mean, she had the prettiest hair back in high school. I can't believe she would cut it . . ." Brandy poured herself a glass of tea and sank down at the table to debate a bob versus a shag while Callie focused all of her energy on making a peanut butter sandwich.

It did little to sate the hunger gnawing inside her. She even chased it with a glass of milk, but no luck. She still felt empty. Needy.

"Here," Brandy said as she pulled out a pink bakery box from the back of the fridge. "After I found the half of a pie missing this morning and Ellie told me about you meeting up with Brett, I figured you could use this." She opened up the box to reveal a jumbo-sized cupcake. "It's my newest s'mores cake with homemade marshmallow frosting." When Callie smiled, Brandy added, "Not that I'm advising you to feed your troubles with a zillion calories, but if you're going to gain a few pounds, it might as well be because of the good stuff instead of that store-bought crap. That, and I took Little Jimmy's apple pie to the bakery. Ellie makes a mean apple pie and I wanted her to taste it. To see if she can figure out what makes Jimmy's mama's pies so darn good."

"Thanks, Brandy."

"I know there's more that you're not telling me, but I'm here if you want to talk." Callie nodded and watched her sister yawn. "I guess I better hit the sack. I'm on bread duty in the morning. That means I'm out of here before sunup."

"I thought you were closed on Mondays?"

"I am, but the chamber of commerce is having a dessert reception after its monthly meeting and I'm providing the goodies. That includes loaves of cinnamon bread for everyone to take home after the event. It's not a huge gig, but I'll take anything I can get right now."

Callie watched her sister head to bed and summoned her

courage. If Brandy could stay focused on what was really important, so could Callie.

That meant no more fooling around with Brett. She needed to find that recipe.

And if she couldn't?

Then it was on to plan B.

"Do I look like I'm made of money?" Les Haverty's voice carried from the open doorway of his office on Monday morning and stalled Callie at her desk. "You might be able to pull the wool over everyone else's eyes, but I keep track of my money. I ordered three boxes of Thin Mints. *Three.* That's it."

"But I've got you down for a box of Tagalongs," came the soft female voice.

"That spiel might work on some other bozo, but I keep track of my money. Now here's my twelve dollars and not a penny more."

A few seconds later, eight-year-old Savannah Sawyer and her ten-year-old sister, Saylor, filed out of the office wearing Girl Scout uniforms and matching frowns.

"What a cheapskate," Savannah huffed.

"A serious tightwad," her sister agreed as they headed for the door.

"Can you believe those girls?" Les demanded a few seconds later when he stormed out of his office. "Why, they tried to scam me. They tried to sneak in an extra box of cookies on my order. As if I would ever willingly buy a box of Tagalongs. Selma hates them. If I brought those cookies home, she would think I ordered them just because I got distracted by Saylor and Savannah's mom, who wears those tight yoga pants to the chamber of commerce meetings. Not that I do get distracted. Even if they are mighty flattering.

So?" Les nailed Callie with a stare. "You left a voice mail last night saying you wanted to talk to me about something?"

She wasn't going to ask. Les had gone off on a pair of Girl Scouts. He would rip her a new one for sure.

At the same time, nothing ventured, nothing gained. "I, um, am having a little financial trouble what with all the funeral expenses and I was thinking that maybe you could give me a loan. I mean, I might not need it. I'm working on a few other things. But if those don't pan out, I was hoping that you might be able to give me a loan."

"How much are we talking?"

"Three thousand dollars. If everything else falls through."

Les shook his head. "I'm afraid there's no way I can do that."

"I know it's a lot of money. You probably don't have that kind of cash."

"I don't. I hand over all the profits to Selma except for a forty-dollar-a-week allowance. She has her dad invest it for us. Last I heard, we own interest in four different RV properties down near Corpus Christi."

"Corpus, huh?"

"I suppose I could ask her," Les went on. "But I don't know if that would be such a good idea. You're not really on Selma's radar—you don't even own a pair of yoga pants—but if she finds out that I want to give you money, she's liable to think there's some ulterior motive. Selma is big on ulterior motives."

"It's fine." Callie shrugged. "I'll come up with something else."

"Have you talked to the bank?"

"They're next on my list."

"I'll put in a good word for you with Howard Toombs. He's the president. Maybe he can work something out."

But the bank had already worked things out. They'd given Callie the extra thirty days when they'd legally been able to foreclose last month. That, coupled with the fact that Callie had no collateral and only a minimum amount of credit, meant that there was probably little Howard could do.

Little amounted to an extra fifteen days.

"I'm afraid that's the best I can do under the current situation," Howard told her later that afternoon when she stopped by the bank on her lunch hour. "I'm really sorry about your grandfather, but we've already floated this as long as possible, Miss Tucker. An extra two weeks is all I can do, and that's stretching it."

"Thanks. I really appreciate everything."

Two extra weeks.

It wasn't much, but it would give her a little more time to find the recipe which, judging by last night, wasn't going to be as easy as she'd originally thought.

If not impossible.

She ignored the doubt and focused on the all-important fact that they'd barely started to look. She'd burned only four days of the six weeks she now had to come up with the money. She could do this.

She *would* do this.

It was just a matter of staying hopeful and focused and *not* begging Brett Sawyer to have sex with her.

If only that weren't easier said than done.

Not that he pressed her lust buttons. If anything, he went out of his way not to touch her when she showed up at Bootleg Bayou later that evening to continue the search.

No brushing up against her or hauling her close, or kissing the common sense right out of her. He barely even glanced her way as they riffled through boxes and went through drawers.

A pattern that repeated itself over the next week as they continued to dig their way through the massive attic.

Even so, she still felt him right there on the fringes, so close all she had to do was reach out.

She wouldn't.

She was already worried and desperate. She wasn't adding stupid to the list. And that's what she would be if she slept with a man she still wanted as much as she wanted her next breath, a man determined to walk away at the earliest possible moment.

Stupid, stupid, *stupid*.

CHAPTER 21

"It's a smart deal," said the man sitting across the massive desk from Brett.

It was Friday afternoon and Brett had come into the house after a long day herding cattle to find the real estate broker waiting for him, along with the stack of pictures that Callie had taken and a leasing agreement.

"I'm willing to take two percent less than the usual commission if you'll sign the papers right now and give me the listing." Les Haverty pulled a pen from his pocket and slid it across the desktop. "You won't get a better deal with anyone else."

Anyone being Tanner Sawyer.

But Brett and Tanner had never really gotten along. Tanner was too greedy. Too self-centered. Too much a typical Sawyer.

That, and Les knew his business. The sales sheet he'd put together looked great, primarily due to Callie's beautiful pictures. Brett couldn't imagine Tanner doing a better job. Even more, Les already had a buyer in mind and time was crucial.

Brett took the pen and scribbled his signature on various sections before handing the agreement back over to the Realtor. "Here you go."

"You won't regret this. I'll move that acreage just like that." Les snapped his fingers before diving into his briefcase to pull out a custom-printed drawstring sack with the Haverty's logo. "Here's your customer appreciation gift. There's a T-shirt and a koozie, as well as a key chain and a gift card for a free lunch at the diner. Just our way of saying welcome to the Haverty family!"

Brett took the sack while Les gathered up his briefcase. "I'll start showing as soon as possible. If you'll let your people know so that they won't think you've got trespassers." Brett nodded and caught the hand Les extended for a shake. "And again, I really appreciate this."

"Just get me my asking price and I'll be the appreciative one."

"Done." Les headed for the door while Brett sank down to file away his copy of the agreement.

"Was that Les Haverty?" The voice sounded and Brett glanced up to see his pappy standing in the doorway.

"Yes, sir, it was." Brett eyed his grandfather. "You know Les?" Last night the man had been convinced he was thirty-five and about to attend his first cattlemen's ball.

"Of course I know Les. He sells real estate." Pappy's gaze met Brett's and for the first time in a long time, Brett saw the familiar glimmer in the man's eyes that said the Alzheimer's hadn't gotten the best of him just yet. "You're selling, aren't you?"

Brett nodded. "Just one hundred acres on the west side. To catch us up on the bills and get us back on our feet."

"That'll help." The old man hobbled into the room and sank down on a nearby sofa. He wore a red-and-white-checkered shirt stuffed into a pair of starched Wranglers and his work boots. "What about the cattle sale? Did you take care of that?"

Brett nodded. "A few days ago, but we were short. Ten head. You wouldn't know anything about that, would you?"

Pappy seemed to think, his gaze intense as he mentally waded through the fogginess that threatened his brain. "I don't know. Did you check the records?"

"The records say we've got ten head missing. I've searched everywhere, but I can't find a trace."

"Did you ask the men?"

Brett nodded. "No one claims to know anything."

"They're good men," Pappy said. "It wasn't their fault. I may not know much here lately, but I do know that. It was probably my mistake. I've made a lot of them lately." He pulled a handkerchief from his pocket and wiped at his suddenly misty eyes. "I don't mean to forget, but it just happens. One second I know what I'm doing and the next, it's like I've never seen my own hands before. Things just don't make sense."

"You're sick that's all."

"But I don't want to be sick." His gaze met his grandson's. "I don't like forgetting stuff."

"It'll be okay. You'll get better. Today's a better day, right?"

Pappy nodded. "It is."

"If you can have one good day, you can have more. You just have to get plenty of sleep and take your medication. The doctor put you on some new stuff. It helps keep the disease from progressing. It's even stopped it in some cases. That'll happen for you. Everything will be okay."

Pappy nodded, but he didn't look convinced. "I think I'd like to take a look out in the barn," the old man finally said. "Did Jewel birth her new calf?"

"Not yet, but it should happen anytime. We're keeping an eye on her."

The old man pushed to his feet. "I'll go look in on her."

"I'll go with you." Brett rounded the desk, but Pappy held up a hand.

"I need to do this by myself." He eyed the ledgers spread out on the desk. "And you need to do this by yourself. I can't do it anymore."

But he could, Brett told himself as he watched the old man walk out the door and head to the barn. If Pappy had another good day like today, and another, he could eventually get back to his old routine.

He would.

It was just a matter of helping out until then.

Until things got better.

"He's in good shape today." Karen's voice drew him around and he turned to find his sister standing in the hallway. "He knew me right away, and he asked about your last ride."

"He looks good."

"For now."

"What's that supposed to mean?" He turned on her.

"That it can't last. You know that, even if you don't want to admit it."

"I know that there's no rhyme or reason to his disease. That things can go north just as fast as they go south. The doctor said as much. Pappy can get better just as easily as he can get worse."

"Just because you want him to get better doesn't mean that he will. We don't always get what we want."

But he already knew that.

He thought of Callie and how badly he wanted her and how she was right there, so close yet she might as well have been a million miles away.

"He isn't gone yet," he told his sister. "Pappy is still

right here even if it doesn't seem like it sometimes. We can't just give up on him."

"I'm not giving up. I'm accepting the truth. And so should you. He's not going to get better." She caught her bottom lip and chewed for a long second as if searching for her nerve. Just like that, she found it and her gaze met his. "I'm not going back to school."

"What are you talking about?"

"I withdrew for the semester." She squared her shoulders and lifted her chin an inch. "I'm not going back to College Station. I'm going to stay here and look after Pappy."

"You can't give up everything you've worked so hard for. You can't give up your life."

"Somebody has to. You won't."

But it wasn't that he wouldn't. He couldn't. He couldn't give up on Pappy. Not when the old man had never given up on him. He'd always believed in Brett. Always kept the faith no matter what boneheaded thing his grandson might have done. He'd loved him when no one else had.

"You might be ready to give up on him, but I'm not," Brett said, stuffing his phone into his pocket and heading for the back door. "He was always there for us. *Always.*"

"It's not about giving up. It's about accepting him the way that he is. The way he's going to be."

But Karen was dead wrong. One good day meant hope for another. And another. Why couldn't she see that?

Brett did and he intended to do everything in his power to help keep Pappy in the here and now.

Slamming the back door, he headed for the barn.

Talk about stubborn.

Karen ignored the urge to storm after her brother and pound some sense into his thick skull. But that wouldn't help. He was in denial and nothing would change until he changed.

And based on this last conversation, that metamorphosis wasn't coming anytime soon.

All the more reason she'd come home for good. For Pappy. To ease his mind and care for him when he lost what little connection he had left to this reality. And for Brett. So that he didn't have to come home to the one place that held so many bad memories.

That's why he'd left in the first place.

To escape the past with their father, and the time after when he'd been following in the man's footsteps. Accepting Pappy's situation would have brought him back home and forced him to face the man he'd been.

The man he was.

He wasn't ready for that. He might never be ready, and that was okay. Karen could handle things here at home.

She headed down the hallway to her room and the laptop sitting on her bed. She was just about to log on to her Facebook page when she heard the front door.

"Can I help you?" she asked the man standing on the doorstep.

He had dark hair, an easy smile, and an air of surprise that said he'd expected someone else to open the door. "I'm looking for Brett Sawyer."

"You just missed him. I'm his sister, Karen. Can I help you with something?"

"You could tell him I stopped by." He pulled a business card from his pocket. "The name's Mark Edwards. I'm with Foggy Bottom Distillers. He called me a few days ago about your family's half of the Texas Thunder recipe. He wanted to know if our offer is serious. I'm here to confirm that it is, indeed, very serious."

"You want to buy our moonshine recipe?"

"Your half. The Tuckers own the other half, but we're ready to purchase theirs, as well, contingent on finding your half, of course. We can't make it without a full recipe."

Which explained why Brett had asked about the family Bible and why he'd been up in the attic every night with Callie Tucker. Karen figured they were just spending time together. It had been no secret that he'd always liked Callie back in the day, and so Karen had come to the conclusion that they'd decided to mend fences and see where things might lead. And she'd certainly never thought to ask him. It wasn't as if Karen and Brett had spent a lifetime confiding in each other. They were seven years apart, and while Brett had always been a good older brother and she'd done her best to be the best little sister, they didn't exactly confide in each other when it came to their sex lives.

Or lack of.

But the meetings with Callie hadn't been about that. They'd been about the old recipe.

The money.

A sliver of disappointment went through her. A crazy reaction for a cynic who'd given up on love completely. So what if Brett and Callie weren't rekindling their romance? All the better. Love sucked. Karen knew that firsthand.

Which explained why she handed the business card back to Mark even though he had the most incredible gray eyes she'd ever seen. And he was cute. In a buttoned-up, three-piece-suit, yuppie sort of way that said he'd never climbed onto the back of a horse or stepped in a pile of steaming manure.

He was one of those pretty boys.

A man exactly like her rat bastard of an ex with his polo

shirts and Citizens of Humanity jeans and Sperry Top-Siders.

"I'll tell him you stopped by." She started to close the door, but he caught the edge with one hand.

"What's the hurry?"

"I've got things to do."

"So do I, but that's no reason to be rude. I'm not finished talking."

She pulled the door back open a few inches and eyed him. "What else is there?"

"Maybe I can come inside and we can sit down. I've got some samples of our current whiskey." His gaze caught hers. "You are twenty-one, right?"

"Sorry. Two months shy."

"I'm twenty-four," he offered, his eyes crinkling at the corners as he smiled.

"I don't recall asking."

He shrugged. "I just thought since we were sharing."

"We aren't sharing. You're sharing and I'm tolerating."

"Are you always so personable or is it just me?"

"Do you really want me to answer that?"

"Ouch. Talk about prickly." He grinned then, a slow slide across his lips, and a balloon expanded in Karen's chest. "But then I like prickly."

Not that she cared what he liked. She didn't. Sure, he had great eyes and a nice smile to go with them, but looks could be deceiving. She knew that firsthand. Just because he seemed harmless enough, didn't mean she was going to let her guard down and talk to him.

Flirt with him.

"Are you going to leave the samples or not?"

"Yeah. Sure." He leaned down and pulled a bottle from a duffel bag at his feet. "Here you go."

His hand brushed hers and a sizzle of heat went through her.

Duh. Karen was on the rebound and Mark was a good-looking guy. It made sense that she would feel flattered. Turned on, even.

She was vulnerable, and he was off-limits.

"Thanks." She started to close the door again and his foot stopped her a second time. She frowned. "What now?"

"Have you had lunch?"

"No."

"Do you want to have lunch?" He held up a hand before she could answer. "Before you say something you'll regret, just think about it. I don't have to head back to Austin for another hour. We could drive into town, pick up something at the diner, and get to know each other along the way."

"Maybe I don't want to get to know you."

"And maybe you're just scared because you do."

And that was it in a nutshell. Karen *was* scared.

Scared because he was too good-looking. Too sexy. And she was far too gullible after her recent breakup.

At the same time, she'd never been the type of person to give up just when things got tough. Sure, her ex had broken her heart, but what she was feeling had nothing to do with her heart and everything to do with good old-fashioned lust.

Mark had great lips and she couldn't help but wonder what those lips would feel like. Taste like.

"It's just lunch," he pressed. "Besides, it's a beautiful day. We should get out and take advantage of it. You know how it is in Texas. It could all go to hell tomorrow and a hurricane could blow through just like that."

He was right.

She thought of her pappy and the smile he'd given her

that morning. A good smile because he'd recognized her. While Brett was way off the mark when it came to the future, he'd been right about one thing.

Today *was* a good day.

Even more, she could relax knowing that everything was okay. For now.

"I'll get my purse."

CHAPTER 22

One good day turned to two. Three to four. A week.

Brett spent every second with his pappy, touring the ranch, going over the existing problems and exploring all the ways to solve them. Selling acreage was the answer. They both knew that, but it didn't make the reality any easier or lessen the shine in the old man's eyes.

Brett spent his days taking care of ranch business and his nights searching for the recipe. He even asked his pappy about it, but the old man only remembered as much as Karen—the recipe had been stuffed in the family Bible, which had been stored somewhere in the attic. As far as the safe, Pappy couldn't remember what had happened to the contents. Not that Brett made a big deal about it. He didn't want worry dragging his grandfather back down into confusion and so he kept Pappy busy with the day-to-day demands of the ranch.

Brett would handle the worry, just as he would find that recipe. Pappy's good days sent a renewed determination through him and he moved faster that night, plowing through boxes so quickly that he almost missed the small Mason jar of gold liquid stashed inside one of them, half-buried beneath a stack of his grandmother's antique quilts.

"You don't think that's actually Texas Thunder, do

you?" Callie voiced the question that raced through his mind the moment he held up the glass container.

"If it is, that would make it over eighty years old." He eyed the clear gold liquid. There wasn't a speck of anything floating in the jar. No cloudy spots. Nothing. Just pure perfection.

"Liquor gets better with age, right?" Callie asked, as if reading his thoughts.

"I'm not so sure that applies to moonshine." His family had been in the cattle business his entire life and while the patriarch of his family had been half of the duo involved in the best liquor to ever come out of the Lone Star state, Brett himself had zero experience with the stuff.

"It could be the real deal, or it could just be what's left of someone's stash." Maybe Pappy's. Maybe his own father's. Berle had been a serious alcoholic and while he never would have bought the mediocre stuff that James had cooked up, he'd gone to great lengths to buy some decent shine, even going as far as driving across state lines, whenever the urge hit him.

"We have to find out."

"We could call that Edwards guy. He might have some connections to help get some answers."

"If he wants the stuff bad enough, I'm sure he'll try." She took the jar from him and stared at the liquid. "Can you believe it? This could really be it."

"Does that mean you're going to head home and start sending out resumes?" He wasn't sure why he brought it up, or why it bothered him so much that she'd put her life on hold.

Maybe because he never had. The first chance he'd had, he'd left Rebel far, far behind.

"I'm not sending out anything until we know for sure

what's in that jar, and then only if it's the real deal." She set the jar to the side and went back to the large trunk she'd been digging through. "In the meantime, we need to keep looking."

"There's no better time than the present," he said after a silent moment.

"For what?"

"The resumes. You keep waiting for a right time, but there isn't one."

"What does it matter to you? It's my business."

He shrugged. "Just thought I'd initiate a conversation. It beats this silence."

"Silence is fine by me." That's what Callie told him, but after twenty minutes going through the chest of drawers, awareness zipping up and down her spine as Brett worked nearby, she was more than ready for a distraction.

"I can't send out resumes yet."

"Not until we get an exact ingredient list for the jar. I know."

"It's not that." She thought of the stack of tear sheets sitting in her bedroom next to her laptop. All she had to do was shove them in an envelope and send them off.

"Then why not?"

"Because the closest I've been to a newspaper in the past ten years are the property listings that I handle for Les. I just started doing a few things for the local newspaper last year. I need more new stuff."

"Why not just send the old stuff?"

"What if it's not good enough? What if I'm not good enough?"

"What if you are?"

His question echoed in her head, prodding a truth she'd done her best to ignore. She'd made so many excuses—she was rusty, she was out of practice, she needed time to get back into the swing of things, but the real worry was that she would get a yes.

The realization hit her as she sat in front of the open trunk and pulled out several old black-and-white photographs of her patriarch Archibald Tucker and his archenemy Elijah Sawyer. Only they weren't enemies way back then. They'd been business partners.

Friends.

Family.

And that was the real trouble of it all. As much as she wanted to get on with her life, her career, she wasn't so sure if she was ready to leave her family.

Or if she would ever be ready.

"With all the bad blood," she blurted, eager to change the subject, "it's hard to believe they were once such good friends." She held up the old black-and-white photo. The two men posed in front of an old Chevrolet, a shotgun in Archibald's hand and a jug of moonshine dangling from Elijah's beefy fingers.

"They were really close," Brett said, letting her shift them onto a different topic. "That's what Pappy always said. He told me that at one time, Archibald was his godfather. Then the shit hit the fan and that was it. The friendship was over."

"What do you think did it? What could have been big enough to kill that kind of a friendship?"

He shook his head. "I wish I knew. Whatever it was, it was enough to divide an entire town. Say, would you look at this?" He pulled the sheet off a nearby table that held an old phonograph and a stack of ancient records. He dusted off the machine and reached for a record. A few cranks of the handle and Roy Acuff's "Wabash Cannonball" carried from the speaker. "My pappy always loved that song. He used to crank up this old machine when I was a kid and dance around the kitchen with my grandma."

"That sounds nice."

He grinned and a faraway light touched his gaze. "I miss those days."

"My parents used to do the Cotton Eyed Joe around the living room on Saturday night. We never had a lot of extra money, so they didn't get to go out much. They would roll up the rug and dance the night away right there at home." Callie fell into her own memories then, seeing her parents in her mind's eye, feeling their giddiness as they twirled around the room.

They'd been so in love that the lack of money had never mattered. Nothing had been able to come between them. Not the stress of raising a family or James and his hateful ways. They'd stuck together through it all, and died together.

Oddly enough, the notion didn't stir the same bitterness she'd felt so many times. There was something strangely comforting about sitting there with Brett so close, listening to the old song, feeling it deep down in her soul. The beat, the excitement, the nostalgia, the loss.

The song played down, ending in a rush of static and Brett picked up another record. A heartbeat later, "The Way You Look Tonight" crackled through the attic.

As if he sensed the melancholy of her thoughts and he wanted to distract her, he smiled and held out his hand. "Care to give it a try?"

"You want me to dance with you?" She glanced around. "Here?"

"Why not?"

Because . . . He was the wrong man and this was the wrong time and certainly the wrong place, but damned if it didn't feel right when he took her hand and pulled her into his arms.

"If memory serves me, you used to like to dance." He slid an arm around her waist. "You weren't very good, but you did get an A for enthusiasm."

"Thanks a lot."

He grinned, a slow, sensuous tilt to his lips that made her tummy tremble and her heart stutter. "That was meant as a compliment."

The past stirred and it was prom night all over again. Moonlight pushed through the large windows, creating a spill of shadows that moved as they moved. She closed her eyes and leaned into him and in her mind's eye, she could see the swirl of colored lights around them. The steady beat of his heart kept tempo with hers. The scent of Old Spice, racing hormones, and spiked fruit punch teased her nostrils.

A dream.

That's what it felt like. As if she were caught up in one of her dreams, reliving their first date, those few precious moments when they'd danced beneath the glitzy Time of Your Life sign and kissed beneath the splatter of neon strobes. She'd been crazy nervous, but then he'd held her, guided her around the dance floor, and she'd relaxed in his arms. He'd made her laugh. He'd made her feel pretty. And then his mouth had been on hers and she'd been swept away on a sea of emotion unlike anything she'd ever felt before.

Or since.

Yep, he was one of a kind. No man had ever measured up to him, and she had the sinking feeling that no man ever would.

Before she could stop herself, she slid her hands up the hard wall of his chest, around his neck. She pressed herself closer. His warm breath sent shivers over her earlobe, the slope of her neck. Large, purposeful hands splayed at the base of her spine. His thumb rubbed lazy circles just above the swell of her bottom.

"Do you know what you do to me, Callie?" His deep voice slid into her ears. "I want you so bad. I always have."

The words, so raw and ragged, shattered the hazy pleasure of her memories and drew her back to reality—to the all-important fact that she was dancing chest to chest with the only man who'd ever broken her heart.

She tore herself away. Putting her back to him, she stared at the spill of moonlight on the windowsill. Just beyond, the rich pastureland stretched endlessly beneath a star-studded sky. In the far distance a few clouds rumbled and she knew the rain was finally coming in.

"What you're feeling is natural." He came up behind her, still a few feet away but close enough that she could feel the heat rolling off of him. "It's chemistry. I want you and you want me. That's all it is, Callie. All it needs to be."

But there was more. Much more. She turned, her gaze going past him to the spot on the floor where she'd set her purse. "I—I really need to get home."

He didn't say a word. He just nodded and turned to take the record off the phonograph. Silence stretched across the distance between them as she snatched up her bag. "I can take the jar and call Mark," she told him.

He nodded as she picked up the container of liquid gold.

She moved past him and true to his word, he didn't reach out and try to stop her. Thankfully. Her control was tentative and she knew one touch would halt her in her tracks.

She walked down the attic steps to the second floor and then headed for the staircase. Down on the first floor, she heard the ancient voice of Pappy Sawyer as he sang along to an old Willie Nelson tune.

He sounded like the man she remembered so well, walking into the general store, whistling "Blue Eyes Crying in the Rain," his shiny alligator boots slapping the floor with each step. Her heart ached for Brett because she knew these good moments were so few and far between. Even so, he wasn't giving up on the old man. He still believed that things would get better. That Pappy would get better. And stay better.

Just the way she still believed she could walk away from Rebel once the taxes were paid and her responsibilities fulfilled.

Could?

Of course she could. She *would*. It's all she'd thought about back in high school, and in all the years since. The one thing that had kept her going through all the crap.

She was leaving, all right.

And so was Brett.

He'd made a life for himself elsewhere. As soon as he settled things here, he would take off again and leave her behind the way he'd done so long ago.

The truth followed her as she descended the front steps and headed for the old blue truck. Climbing behind the wheel, she sat the jar of moonshine on the seat next to her and keyed the engine. Her hand went to the gearshift and she paused.

What in heaven's name was she doing?

Reality hit Callie as she sat in front of the house, the engine idling, her heart pounding. Her headlights sliced through the darkness and she caught sight of Brett standing on the front porch.

He stared at her for a long moment before glancing back at the house. As if debating whether to go back inside.

He didn't.

Instead, he snatched up a rolled sleeping bag that sat on a nearby swing and headed for the side of the house. He disappeared around the corner and she knew he was headed for the solace of the creek. *Leaving,* the way he always did.

He didn't want to go back inside the house, to face his problems, to climb into bed with the memories, the want.

He wanted her and she wanted him.

Want.

He was right. That's all this was about. A physical attraction. The match had been struck way back when, and despite ten years, it was still burning, still feeding a fire that had yet to fizzle out.

It never would.

Instead, it would flame inside of her, feeding off the memories forever unless she turned those memories into reality while she had the chance.

She needed to touch him, taste him, satisfy the lust eating her up from the inside out. Maybe then she could get on with her life, with walking away from Rebel the way she was always meant to.

She could never move forward while her brain was stuck idling in the past.

She killed the lights and the engine, and silence closed in. She sat there for a few moments, listening to the beat of her own heart before she let go of the steering wheel and reached for the door.

Climbing from the seat, she slammed the truck door behind her, headed around the house, and went in search of Brett Sawyer.

It was time to lay the past to rest once and for all.

CHAPTER 23

Callie followed the path through the back pasture to the cluster of trees at the far edge. Ducking beneath a branch, she kept on the worn trail until the trees thinned and she reached a clearing.

Moonlight spilled over the ground, bathing the scene in a celestial light that lent a surreal quality to the moment. The creek trickled nearby, winding its way past the man who stood on the bank, his attention directed at the sparkling water. Moonlight outlined his form, edging his broad shoulders, his strong thighs.

She took a deep breath, gathered her courage, and slid the first button of her blouse free. The material parted and slid down her arms, over her hands. Trembling fingers worked at the catch of her bra, freeing her straining breasts. The scrap of lace landed at her feet. The gauzy material of her skirt joined the growing heap until Callie stood in nothing but her panties and a slick layer of perspiration. Her first instinct was to cover herself. She'd been self-conscious about her weight her entire life, but she was determined to show Brett that she wasn't afraid. That she wanted this.

That she wanted him.

She cleared her throat and he turned to face her. She

focused on the dark shadow that he made surrounded by moonlight and imagined the look in his eyes, the hunger.

The warm night air whispered over her bare shoulders and breasts. Her nipples tightened, throbbed in anticipation of his touch.

But he wasn't reaching out.

He was waiting for her to take the lead, to make the first move, and so she did.

Her breath caught at the first swirl of her fingertips at the aching tips. Her hands moved lower, down the slick, quivering skin of her stomach, to the damp curls at the base of her thighs. The air seemed to stand still around her. Even the crickets faded into the frantic beat of her own heart. Her breath caught, and she touched herself. One fingertip slid along the seam between her legs where the lush lips met. Heat pulsed through her hot body and a shameless moan curled up her throat.

A deep, raw groan rumbled in her ears and then he wasn't standing near the creek. He was moving toward her. Water splashed. Boots crunched rock.

She barely managed to blink before he reached her. He stopped then, his breathing coming harsh and fast as if it took every ounce of strength for him to put on the brakes. But he did. He gave her one last chance to think about what she was doing, to change her mind.

But she wasn't living with another ten years of regret. Been there. Done that.

No more.

The regret stopped tonight.

"Touch me," she murmured. "Please."

And he did.

Strong, muscled arms wrapped around her, drew her close as his mouth captured hers in a deep, thorough kiss that sucked the air from her lungs and made her entire body tremble with need.

She clutched at his shoulders. Denim rasped her sensitive breasts and thighs in a delicious friction that made her quiver and pant and claw at the hard muscles of his arms.

Strong hands slid down her back, cupped her bottom, and urged her legs up on either side of him. Then he lifted her, cradled and kneaded her buttocks as she wrapped her legs around his waist and settled over the straining bulge in his jeans.

"Please," she whimpered, rubbing herself against him. She wanted to get on with it, to move fast and furious so that neither of them had a chance to think about what they were doing.

If he pulled away again . . .

He didn't.

He turned, easing her onto the edge of a large boulder, his pelvis urging her thighs farther apart.

She braced herself as he trailed his tongue over the silk covering her wet heat and pushed the material into her slit until her flesh plumped on either side. He licked, stroking and stirring the sensitive flesh until she squirmed and shoved her fingers into his silky hair.

He gripped the edge of her panties and she lifted her hips to accommodate him. The lacy material slithered down her legs. He caught her ankles and urged her knees over his shoulders. Large hands slid beneath her buttocks as he drew her to the very edge of the rock. At his first long lick, the air bolted from her lungs.

His tongue parted her and he lapped at her sensitive clit. He tasted and savored, stroking, plunging, driving her mindless until her body was wound so tight that she couldn't stand it anymore. A cry vibrated from her throat and shattered the stillness that surrounded them. Her orgasm gripped her and held tight for the next several seconds. Her body trembled and her insides convulsed.

"You're so fucking beautiful." His deep, raw voice pierced the pounding in her ears and she opened her eyes to find him poised above her. He stared down at her, his expression dark and unreadable, and panic rushed through her.

This was it. The moment that he realized she just wasn't enough and pulled away.

Just as he'd done so long ago.

Tension carved his muscles tight, his arms braced on either side. He moved then, but he didn't pull away. Instead, he gathered her close and in an instant, she felt the soft sleeping bag at her back.

He shed his jeans and settled between her legs, his weight pressing her back into the down covering. His erection slid along her damp flesh, making her shudder and moan and arch toward him, but he held tight to his control.

He was going to do this slow. Easy.

He drank in the scent of her—vine-fresh strawberries basking in the summer sunshine—and tried to slow his pounding heart. Strawberries had always been his favorite. He remembered so many warm days picking fruit down by Rebel Creek. There'd been nothing like biting into the sweet flesh, feeling the juice trickle down his throat . . .

Nothing as decadent, as satisfying.

Except her—the woman who haunted his past, his dreams, his now—and her soft-as-moonlight hair that whispered across his bare flesh and made his muscles quiver.

He pressed into her just a fraction and he groaned. "You feel so good," he rasped after a long, shuddering moment.

"Really?" Surprise glittered in her gaze as if she couldn't quite believe him.

She didn't. She didn't trust him any more than he trusted himself, and suddenly more than proving something to himself, he wanted to prove something to her.

That he still wanted her.

That he still needed her.

Now more than ever because he was no longer that spoiled, selfish boy. He was a grown man and she was a grown woman.

His woman.

And it was time she knew it.

A surprised "Oh!" bubbled from her lips before he claimed them in a kiss that was desperate, savage even.

He held her head in his hands, his fingers tangled in her hair, anchoring her to him as he plunged fast and sure and deep, burying himself in one luscious thrust.

The air stalled in his lungs for several fast, furious heartbeats before he slid his hands down her sides to cup her buttocks and tilt her just a fraction so he could slide deeper. Pleasure splintered his brain and sent an echoing shudder through his body. He pulled away then, only to push inside again. And again.

When he finally came, it was like someone zapped his brain with a cattle prod. Heat sizzled across every nerve ending, consumed all rhyme and reason and thought, until he crashed and burned and his entire body went up in flames. He lost it then, but only for a few seconds.

Her moan echoed in his ears as the fire caught and consumed her. He kept moving then, pushing into her until he felt the last quake of her body. Rolling over, he pulled her up against his side.

In the back of his brain, he knew what happened next was a bad idea. Sex was fine, but the details that came after . . . That was the stuff he always steered clear of. He didn't huddle up and whisper sweet nothings, and he sure as hell didn't do the morning after.

No pancakes or bacon or bright ideas about a future together.

He had way too much on his plate to complicate things with an actual relationship.

His future was far away from Rebel, and it had nothing to do with a woman. He'd barely won his second buckle. A man didn't just abandon a pro rodeo career after winning his second buckle. He was at the top of his game. He'd be crazy to walk away.

He was many things, but crazy had never been one of them. His old man had claimed that title.

Brett did the right thing. The logical thing. Like getting the ranch back on track, making arrangements for his granddaddy, and then getting his ass back on the road.

That was the plan, even if he hadn't returned any of his promoter's phone calls.

He hadn't really had the time or the energy, but he would get to it. Just as soon as he found the missing cattle and voiced his suspicions to the sheriff and got a handle on what the hell was going on.

Then he would call his promoter and get back in the game.

He would.

But not just yet.

Right now, he was too tired, too spent, too pleased to

think of anything except slipping an arm around this woman, nuzzling her neck, and getting some much-needed sleep.

But then a shotgun blast cracked open the silence and his first real moment of peace went to hell lickety-split, like the senior ladies' prayer group headed to the all-you-can-eat buffet after one of Pastor Harris's infamous fasts.

CHAPTER 24

Brett watched Callie climb into her truck as he stood on the front porch of the ranch house and answered the endless stream of questions from Sheriff Hunter DeMassi.

He'd wanted to talk to her, but the gunfire had woken up the entire bunkhouse, as well as Pappy and Karen. The house had been wide awake and blazing when they'd walked in, and so he hadn't been able to exchange even a few words with her before the sheriff had given her permission to leave with the others.

At the same time, he had no clue what to say. She'd caught him off guard tonight. And while he'd been damned happy at the surprise, he knew where that left them now.

They'd done it. They'd replayed that night, he'd made up for his biggest regret, and now it was over.

The thing was, he wasn't so sure he wanted it to be over.

Oddly enough, he didn't feel the least bit satisfied. Not like he usually did after a few hours of raw, breath-stealing sex. He felt . . . empty.

Needy.

Hungry.

". . . heard anything like that before?" Sheriff DeMassi's voice pushed into his thoughts. "I talked to the ranch hands and they said they've heard the occasional shot but they just figured it for nearby hunters. Your place backs up to the Walker property on the other side of the creek."

Brett nodded. "But the Walkers don't hunt. Mr. Walker has bad cataracts." At least that's what Karen had said when she'd met them on the porch after the first shot. "And Mrs. Walker is a PETA supporter. She won't even wear a leather belt." Theirs had been the classic country-boy-meets-city-girl romance back when Brett's pappy had been young. The old man had told the story every time they'd seen the couple in town or at church. They were opposites, but then that was the point, Pappy had said. It wasn't about what you had in common when it came to the opposite sex. It's about what you felt.

The way he'd felt about Brett's grandma.

Like he couldn't catch his breath if he didn't see her. Like he was going to die if he didn't catch a whiff of her perfume. Like he was going to climb the walls if he didn't get just one more kiss.

Like Brett himself at the moment.

He ditched the thought and focused on the sheriff and the all-important fact that they had poachers on their land.

"I'll get in touch with the local game warden. Between him and my deputies, we'll get someone out here to keep an eye out the next few nights. See if maybe we can't figure out who's trespassing."

And stealing his cattle.

While Brett had no proof that the gunshot had anything to do with his missing steer, he had a tingling in his gut that told him the two were connected.

Whoever had fired off that gun had something to do with the thousands of dollars Brett had lost out on.

And the missing contents of the safe?

He didn't know, but there was only one way to find out.

"I can post a few of the hands down near the east end where the shot came from."

"I'd rather you let us take care of it. If someone is poaching your land, I'll get to the bottom of it."

Brett wasn't the least bit comfortable sitting around doing nothing, but he respected the sheriff enough to concede. Brett had gone to school with Hunter and his two brothers. They were good men. Upright. If the sheriff said he'd get to the bottom of it, Brett knew he meant it. He nodded. "I'll have Pepper brief the men and let them know you'll be patrolling the area. They'll move what cattle we have left over to the west pasture and steer clear so the east end is all yours."

Hunter nodded and clapped Brett on the shoulder. "It's good to see you home."

"Yeah, well, it's only temporary. Just until Pappy is back to his old self."

Hunter didn't give him the Alzheimer's speech like everyone else did. Instead, he nodded before glancing over his shoulder at the spot where James Harlin's truck had sat only minutes before. A grin tugged at his lips when he turned back around. "So you and Callie pick up where you left off?"

"We're just friends."

Hunter shrugged. "That's what I meant."

"Sure it was."

"Hey, you can't blame a guy for trying to get the gossip straight."

"And what's the gossip saying?"

"That you're just friends. The close encounters kind of friends."

"Well, the gossip is wrong," he heard himself say even though the old Brett would have simply smiled and left his reputation intact. But damned if it didn't bother him that people were talking about Callie. Possessiveness blazed through him and he had the urge to haul ass into town and set the record straight once and for all—Callie Tucker was a good girl. She always had been and she always would be, no matter how many times she did a striptease for him down by the creek.

That had been for his eyes only.

She was for his eyes only.

The notion struck as he watched the sheriff climb into his black SUV and pull down the drive.

Callie *was* his.

Then and now.

And he was the sonofabitch who was going to break her heart again by walking away.

But she knew that this time. She'd come to him with her eyes wide open, with full knowledge that nothing between them would last. Their relationship was temporary, physical, and she was okay with that.

And damned if *that* didn't bother him even more than the fact that there really was someone stealing cattle from Bootleg Bayou.

Callie left a voice mail for Mark Edwards asking to meet as soon as possible and then set her cell phone on her nightstand. She eyed the jar of moonshine she and Brett had uncovered in the attic. A nearby lamp cast a glow through the pale amber liquid and she thought of all the jars just like it she'd seen over the years. A few in the corner of James Harlin's room. Out in the barn. The shed. Under the seat of the pickup. None had ever looked this clear or pure, as if this jar held something a cut above any she'd seen in the past.

The real deal.

Texas Thunder.

Her heart skipped a beat and she tried to remember that it might not be the original shine. There was no way to know without a complete analysis. Until then, she wasn't getting her hopes up.

She sat the jar next to her cell phone and shifted. Her thighs ached with the small movement and awareness rolled through her. The sensitive tips of her nipples rubbed against the soft cotton of her T-shirt and she caught her lip against the sensation. A memory of Brett leaning over her, into her, whispered through her head and she stiffened.

Over and done with.

That's what she tried to tell herself.

Picking up her alarm clock, she set the buzzer for eight a.m.—two hours later than her usual six. But it was already after two in the morning and while she did have to work on Saturdays, it wasn't the usual office hours tomorrow. They had only one open house, which meant she would have a lighter day than usual. Plenty of time to meet with Mark and stop off at the post office.

Her gaze went to the samples of her work stacked near her laptop. Before she could think better of it, she sank down at her desk and reached for the brown manila envelopes she'd picked up ages ago for just this thing. She opened her drawer and reached for the stack of inquiry letters she'd done months ago, on those late nights when James was on a bender and the urge to get the hell out of Rebel had eaten her up from the inside out.

Pressing the button on her phone, she cued an upbeat Luke Bryan song to kill the oppressive silence of her room. She grabbed a letter and a collection of tear sheets.

Over the next half hour, she fed the envelopes one by one until she had thirty. The mailing labels came next.

Over and over, she peeled and stuck until everything was ready to go and there wasn't a single thing left to do but stop at the post office.

Which is what she fully intended to do first thing in the morning because no way was she going to stick around Rebel and waste her life away, regretting the past. The present.

It was time.

That's what she told herself as she killed the music, crawled into bed, and tried to forget Brett Sawyer and the way he'd touched her so tenderly and held her so tightly, as if he never meant to let go.

As if.

He would let her go and then he would walk away, but she didn't care because she was walking away, too. No staying behind, regretting what could have been.

She was through with regrets. She was moving forward.

Even if the notion didn't excite her half as much as it used to.

CHAPTER 25

"I'm afraid she's not here," Callie told Alex when she opened the door the next morning and found him standing on her doorstep, Arnie in tow. "She got stuck on an all-night horse vaccination, but I'll be sure to tell her that you stopped by." When Arnie started to open his mouth, she added, "And I really don't have time for another acupuncture session. I've got an open house in a half hour and a few errands to run before then." Namely a post office stop for the envelopes overflowing her arms. "Sorry."

"Oh, we're not here for acupuncture," Alex said. "Arnie, here," he motioned beside him, "has been working on his hypnosis certificate online, too. Hypnosis is a great way to deter bad behavior."

"That's right," Arnie chimed in. "I usually like to start with the acupuncture first, especially since I actually finished those classes, paid my fifty dollars, and got my certificate, but hypnosis is an even better way to kick addiction. Once I'm through with Jenna, she'll be over her claustrophobia for sure."

"That's right," Alex said. "If you could just let her know that I'm looking for her and I won't stop until I've done everything I can to cure her, I'd really appreciate it."

"Maybe you should just give her some space."

"And give up on the love of my life in her hour of need?" Alex looked horrified. "I could never do any such thing." He squared his shoulders. "I'm going to help her and hypnosis is the way to go."

"We think," Arnie added. "I'm only three classes into the course, but I'm pretty sure I can put her under. That's the real challenge. It can take anywhere from five to fifteen minutes, but once she's there I can get rid of any addiction. It's just a matter of making the right suggestions."

Callie thought of the last few hours she'd spent tossing and turning and lusting after Brett. Even though said lust should have been completely satisfied after last night.

But she still wanted him.

Even more it seemed.

"Fifteen minutes, huh?" She shifted the armload of envelopes.

"At the most, but I'm thinking more like five or ten. I made a perfect score on the section test. Well, near perfect. That last question tripped me up, but I know what I did wrong, so I'm all good."

The *good* stirred a memory of the previous night, of how Callie had felt when Brett had touched her, kissed her, loved her. She stiffened.

There was no love involved. Not then and not now.

Not ever.

"The post office can wait until Monday." She turned and motioned toward the house. "Let's do this."

It had worked.

That's what Callie told herself throughout the rest of the day as she smiled and greeted clients and handed out water bottles, and did her best not to think about Brett.

She succeeded. She was so busy that she didn't spare him a second thought.

Until he walked into her open house and cornered her in the kitchen.

He wore faded jeans, a fitted black PBR 2015 Championship T-shirt, and a hungry look that said he wasn't any more satisfied than she was.

She ignored a sudden rush of excitement and tried to look irritated. "What are you doing here?"

He picked up a water bottle, unscrewed the top, and took a long pull. "I thought we could pick up some lunch," he said when he finally came up for air.

"Why?"

"Because you need to eat and I need to eat and there's nothing wrong with us eating together."

But it wasn't the eating that was the problem. It was the *together*.

She'd meant to find some closure last night, but the only thing she'd managed to do was open another Pandora's box. Where the girl in her had spent all those years pining away for the young boy he'd been, the woman in her was now haunted by the man himself.

She wanted him again. Despite the hour of hypnosis during which Arnie had tried to cure Callie of her addiction to Brett. She'd even had Arnie throw in several suggestions to steer her clear of the cupcakes, which had resulted in quite a mess in the living room that she'd yet to clean up.

Talk about a joke.

Her stomach hollowed out and she found herself longing for a cupcake.

And another kiss.

"I'm really busy." She stared pointedly at a prospective

couple from Austin who walked past the kitchen toward the living room. She grabbed a listing sheet from the counter. "I should really go over the features with them." She started forward but he caught her hand and pulled her in the opposite direction.

"I'd like you to go over the features with me."

"You're not a prospective buyer."

"I might be."

A split second later, he pulled her into the massive pantry off to the side of the kitchen and shut the door behind them. A small light fixture hung overhead, highlighting the floor-to-ceiling shelves and a large wine rack. He pulled her around to face him and stared down at her. "Tell me about this room."

"It's a storage pantry."

"And?"

She eyed him. "You don't really want to know about this room." She busied her lips with the tightest frown she could manage, considering she wanted to kiss him more than she wanted her next breath.

"No, but if it keeps you in here with me, then I'll listen to anything you have to say." He closed the few inches between them. "I've been thinking about you, Callie," he murmured, his lips so close to hers. "Hell, you're all I've thought about since you drove away."

"Shelves," she blurted, turning away and staring at the massive white wall unit. "You could stock a full month of groceries in here."

"I don't care about shelves." He came up directly behind her.

"Maybe even two."

"I don't want to think about you, but I can't stop." His hands slid around her waist, his palms warm through the cotton of her shirt. His fingers caught the hem of her shirt and the rough pad of his thumb rasped against her soft flesh. Heat zapped her.

"I thought this was just sex."

"What makes you think it isn't?" His voice rumbled over her bare neck and she damned herself for pulling her hair up into a ponytail. Goose bumps chased up and down her arms and she came this close to leaning back into him, closing her eyes, and soaking in the heat of his body. Just for a little while.

She stiffened and fought for her precious control. Last night was over and done with.

Temporary.

He'd said so himself.

At the same time, *temporary* didn't have to mean *once*. It just meant that what they had—the physical connection—would come to an end. Soon.

But *soon* wasn't necessarily *now*.

He rubbed the bare flesh of her stomach above the waistband of her favorite black pencil skirt. Her favorite because it was loose enough that she didn't feel like a stuffed sausage, and snug enough in all the right places to make her feel shapely.

Or maybe it was the reverent way Brett touched her that did that.

"You feel so warm." His voice rumbled up her spine.

"I don't think this is a good idea. Not now. Not here." While she wanted Brett, she wasn't supposed to want him. That meant no blushing or trembling or kissing. "There are too many people."

"Sugar, there isn't a soul in sight."

He was right. Her gaze scanned their surroundings, from the closed door to the massive wall unit. A few canisters of various colored pastas sat here and there on the polished white wood, along with bottles of olive oil and a few boxes of gourmet cookies. Bottles of wine had been placed strategically on the hand-crafted rack. A few crystal glasses and a brass corkscrew sat on a nearby shelf. The room had been staged along with the rest of the house to show interested buyers what the place would look like as an actual home.

Maybe even their home.

"We really can't do this." She reached out to wipe away a smudge on one of the shelves. "I've got a lot to do today. I'm meeting Mark Edwards this afternoon to hand over the jar of moonshine. He's got a friend in the chemistry department at the University of Texas who might be able to decipher the ingredients."

"That's great, but that's later this afternoon." Brett's deep voice slid into her ears and sent a jolt of adrenaline through her. "Right now it's just you and me." He pulled her around and she stared up into eyes that glittered with a hungry light.

The air bolted from her lungs and her hands trembled. But then he took them in his. He raised one to his lips, pressing a kiss into her palm that made her heart ache as much as her body.

"I want to be inside of you, Callie. Right now. Right here."

"I . . ." She swallowed and tried to think of something to say, but with his hands so warm around hers, his large body filling up the massive space and drinking up all her precious oxygen, she couldn't seem to find any words. "Les might need me," she finally managed after he nuzzled one of her ears with his lips.

"I need you more."

Need, but what he really meant was *want* because Brett Sawyer didn't need her. Not the way she wanted him to.

The realization should have been enough to zap some common sense into her. But she'd already made up her mind to bury her thoughts of forever when it came to him. He was temporary.

Now.

The sound of muffled voices drifted from the kitchen as someone passed through talking about granite countertops and self-cleaning ovens. Water splashed and rushed as someone flipped on a faucet, reminding her that there were people just beyond the thin walls of the walk-in pantry. People who could walk in at any moment and find Callie Tucker in a compromising position with her most hated enemy.

She stiffened and forced aside the stirring images. "I really don't think this is the right time. Maybe later when we meet to look for the recipe."

"I don't like to wait." He kissed her then, his lips wet and hungry, his tongue greedy as he devoured her.

Lust hit her fast and hard and she realized in that next instant that she didn't like to wait, either. Even more, she didn't want to wait.

Her hands went to the buttons of her blouse as he dropped to his knees in front of her. He trailed his hands down over her buttocks, pausing to knead her bottom through the fitted material of her skirt. Fabric brushed her legs as he slid them down over her thighs, her knees, until they pooled on the floor.

He stood just as her blouse fell open. Air whispered across her nipples as she freed her breasts and let the material slide down her arms.

He bent to drop one kiss onto the tip of her nipple

before pushing her up against the door. One hand caught her thigh, lifting her just enough to wedge his hips between hers and press his denim-covered crotch against her bare flesh.

His gaze drilled into hers as he rocked her, working her into a frenzy with the friction of fabric against her most sensitive parts.

Sensation rippled up her spine.

He urged her higher, his hands holding her tightly as he dipped his head. The first leisurely rasp of his tongue against her ripe nipple wrung a cry from her throat. Her fingers threaded through his hair as he drew the quivering tip deep into his hot, hungry mouth. He suckled her long and hard and she barely caught the moan that burst from her lips.

She clamped down on her bottom lip, swallowing her cries as he licked and suckled and nipped. Her skin grew itchy and tight. Pressure started between her legs, heightened by the way he leaned into her, the hard ridge of his erection prominent beneath his jeans. She spread her legs wider and he settled more deeply between them. Grasping her hips, he rocked into her.

Rubbed against her.

Up and down and side to side and . . .

It was too much and not enough all at the same time. Heat swamped her and she gasped for air. Her hands clutched at him, holding tight as sensation crashed over in a fierce wave that left her trembling in his arms.

From far away, she heard Les's voice. She felt a moment's panic, but then she opened her eyes and Brett was there, filling up her line of vision, blocking out everything except the fire that burned between them.

He eased her to her feet as he pulled a small foil packet

from his back pocket. Tugging at the button of his jeans, he pulled his zipper down and freed his hard length.

She took the initiative then, opening the condom and spreading it on his throbbing penis from tip to root. Her fingers brushed hot skin and silky hair and anticipation coiled inside of her.

He lifted her then, bracing her back against the wall as he pushed between her thighs and pressed the head of his cock into her just a fraction.

Pleasure pierced her brain for a split second, quickly shattering into a swell of sensation as he filled her with one deep, probing thrust.

Her muscles tightened around him, gripping him tight as he held her bottom and braced her for another thrust. He pumped into her, the pressure and the friction so sweet that it took her breath away.

She was vaguely aware of the voices on the other side of the door. But then he touched her nipple and trailed a hand down her stomach. Rough fingertips made contact with the place where they joined and heat splintered her brain. She clutched wildly at his shoulders, bracing herself as she met his thrusts in a wild rhythm that urged him faster and deeper.

Then it seemed as if the room started to shake and spin. The light overhead blazed hotter and brighter and she clamped her eyes shut. But the brilliance was still there, splintering into a fireworks display that shot off and lit up the darkest depths of her mind as she came with an intensity she'd never felt before.

He buried himself deep inside her one last time, anchoring her hips tight around him. A shudder ripped through him and his body quaked as he followed her over the edge.

An odd quiet fell over them then, the sound disrupted

only by her frantic breathing and the furious beat of her heart. She slipped her arms around his shoulders and held him, feeling his heartbeat mimic hers.

He tightened his hold on her, gathering her close, and a strange sense of peace stole through her.

Oddly enough, the fact that she would have to walk out of the pantry with Brett, past whoever might be looking around the kitchen—Les included—didn't bother her nearly as much as it should have.

But then Callie had never worried about what everyone else thought when it came to Brett. She'd snubbed her nose at the world, at all those Tuckers and Sawyers with their preachy judgment and holier-than-thou looks, and she'd set her sights on him anyway. She'd opened herself up to him, to *them*.

And for that one small moment in time, before their disastrous ending, she'd been happy. Content.

Then, and now.

CHAPTER 26

"Speak of the devil," Les said just as Brett was about to make it to the front door.

He stopped dead in his tracks, took a deep breath, and tried to ignore the urge to turn, walk back to the storage closet, and toss Callie over his shoulder, a house full of people be damned.

But she was working, after all, and she didn't want to fuel the gossip that was already spreading around Rebel because Callie Tucker had been seen driving out to the Sawyer spread every night for the past week.

Not that Brett gave a shit what people said, but he didn't want her to look unprofessional and so he'd agreed to a head start. After a deep, thorough kiss on the lips, of course.

Enough to tide him over until he saw her tonight.

As if that were enough.

His body still ached, his muscles bunched tight, and he had the gut feeling that no matter how many times they had sex, it wasn't going to be enough.

He ignored the disturbing thought, pasted on his best smile, and turned toward Les Haverty.

"I was just talking about you," Les said, extending his hand for a shake. "I forwarded Callie's pictures to several more prospects and I've got another buyer interested. He just called and wants to drive down first thing in the morning to take a look at the property. I was going to head out to your place with the good news, but here you are." Les smiled before the expression faded. "Why is that?"

The click of a doorknob punctuated the sentence and Brett glanced over his shoulder in time to see a flushed Callie exit the pantry and head for the first-floor restroom. Her lips were pink and full, her cheeks rosy with desire, her hair slightly mussed and it was all he could do not to go after her. To touch her one more time. Kiss her once more.

More.

"Sawyer?" Les's voice drew Brett's attention and he focused on the Realtor standing in front of him. "Why are you here?"

"I was, um, passing by and I saw your car. I thought I would just stop by and see if you had any more interested buyers and, well, you obviously do. Talk about great news." Brett clapped Les on the shoulder. "Good job."

"Well, I do know my business. Do you remember that old building off of Main and First? That place was condemned last year, but I managed to find an investor who agreed to completely redo it and then donate it to the city to use as a community center. Now that took some talking, but I pulled it off . . ." Les went on about his latest listings and how he was sure to beat Tanner Sawyer out for salesman of the year at the Carson County Board of Realtors annual fish fry and watermelon toss. "I've never actually won, but this is my year. I can just feel it, and it's all because of you. Selling a piece of the legendary Bootleg Bayou will nail it for me. I can't thank you again for giving me the opportunity."

"Let's just hope it happens quick."

Les winked. "You can count on it. Now, I wanted to go over a time frame with you . . ." Les went on about appointment times while Brett tried to forget the woman who walked into the living room and greeted an elderly couple standing in front of the newly renovated stone fireplace.

Sex, he reminded himself. That's all this was. All it could ever be.

He knew that.

So why the hell did he find himself wondering what it would be like to curl up in front of that stone fireplace, Callie in his arms, and simply sit? Talk?

Crazy.

That's what he was. He'd been tossed by too many bulls. Inhaled too much arena dust. Because no way was he thinking that maybe, just maybe, bull riding wasn't all it was cracked up to be and that signing that contract was a move he would surely regret.

That the buckles would tarnish and the fame would eventually fade, and he would be left with nothing to show for his years of hard work.

Yep, he'd hit the dust way too many times.

He was going to be a legend, for Christ's sake. The best of the best. A Cowboy Hall of Fame member for sure.

He was going to be something more than just a spoiled, self-centered, entitled Sawyer like his father. He was on his way. It was just a matter of signing the contract and preserving his winning streak.

Which he would most certainly do.

In his peripheral vision, he caught the flash of a blond ponytail and his heart stalled.

But first he was going to finish things here. That meant finding the recipe and forgetting Callie Tucker.

And if it took another trip to the pantry, or another strip-tease down by the creek, well, he was more than ready for it. He would do whatever it took to work her out of his system and leave Rebel with a clean slate this time.

No unfinished business.

No regret.

No Callie.

No.

He held tight to the notion as he climbed into his truck and hit the dirt road leading to the ranch.

By the time he reached Bootleg Bayou, he actually started to believe it.

Especially when he found his pappy sitting at his desk in the study, his spectacles in place as he read over the ledger that Brett had updated just that morning.

He looked just as Brett remembered him. Thoughtful. Happy. Coherent.

"Hey, Pappy." He ignored the worry that niggled at him. A feeling that slipped away as the old man glanced up and a smile cracked his ancient face. "You look good today."

"I feel pretty good." He glanced down at the ledger and his smile faltered. "We're still not pulling in enough."

"No, but Les Haverty is bringing by a buyer tomorrow. He thinks we'll sell the acreage pretty quick. That should push us into the green for the short-term. I was thinking we might consider out-breeding a couple of our bulls. We've got some prime stock. That might be an option to add to our revenue in addition to the cattle."

"Breeding, huh?"

"Pepper has quite a few contacts who'd pay through the nose for some good semen. We can start with Red and Mack. They're the best of the best. Grade A and registered. One dose of their sperm would surely bring a nice chunk."

Pappy nodded before a melancholy expression slid over his face. "Red was one of Pirate's calves. He was your daddy's first bull. He always said he'd breed the best stock if we ever wanted to open our doors. Seems like he was right."

"I guess there's a first time for everything."

"I know you don't like to talk about your daddy." Pappy pushed the ledger aside and leaned back in his chair. "And you got good reason. He was a hateful SOB sometimes."

"More like all the time."

A sadness touched the old man's expression as he nodded. "Toward the end, he was. But there was a time when he had some goodness in him. Why, I remember when he came home with your first horse. That pretty little filly named Charlotte. You were only two years old at the time and your mama liked to have had a fit, but your daddy just knew you could sit a horse. You were his boy, after all, and he'd been riding since he'd been in diapers." Pappy's gaze held Brett's. "You didn't disappoint. You grabbed hold of the reins with one chubby fist and held tight like you'd been born in the saddle. Your daddy laughed so hard. Why, I don't think I ever seen him that happy."

"Happy? Dad?"

"I know it's hard to believe, but he was a decent father at one time. All of this just got the best of him."

"You mean his pride got the best of him." That's what had motivated Berle. He'd wanted the biggest and the best, and when anyone had threatened that, he'd taken his anger out on his wife. Or his son. "You can defend him until you're blue in the face, Pappy, but it's not going to change my opinion of him."

"I know that. I just want you to know that he never intended to hurt you. It was the liquor. I know 'cause my daddy had it bad for the shine. He managed to kick the addiction thanks to my grandmamma, but some just ain't so lucky. I wish I had seen it getting the best of Berle in time to do something about it, but I was so busy with this place. I know he was a hard man, but he loved you."

"I don't want to talk about this."

"Maybe you don't want to, son, but you need to. You need to remember that this house doesn't hold just bad memories of him. He had his good moments."

"And because of them I'm just supposed to forget all the shitty things he did to Mom? To me and Karen?" Brett shook his head as bitterness welled inside of him. His chest tightened and his throat constricted and it was all he could do to sit still and let his pappy talk.

He wanted to get up, to walk out, to leave.

He needed, to, but the hope in his pappy's eyes held him and so all he managed was to push to his feet. His boots thudded on the hardwood floor as he walked to a nearby bookshelf. He put his back to the old man as the memory of that last night overtook him.

He closed his eyes, hearing his mother's scream, feeling the urgency as he caught his dad's arm and tried to hold the old man back. He could still feel the hard tendons of the man's forearm tight with rage, the crippling pain as the man's fist made contact with his head. The crack echoed in his head and then . . . nothing.

That had been the last time he'd seen his father alive, the last time he'd felt the man's rage, the last chance to say good-bye.

The thought struck and he shook it away. The last thing he'd owed his sorry-ass dad was a decent good-bye. Or a thank you for all those horse shows the man had taken him to when he'd been younger. Or that one Christmas when he'd put on a Santa suit and bounced Brett on his knee. Or the time he'd helped him catch his first fish down at the creek.

All those moments that had faded in the face of so much abuse. Good times all but forgotten.

Or so he'd thought.

But they rolled over him as he stood there, looking at the books, his pappy's voice echoing in his ear, reminding him of the man Berle had once been. Of the father who'd tucked him in at night and tickled him awake every Saturday morning.

Not that it changed anything. Berle had still chosen alcohol over his own family, and while Brett might eventually forgive the man for his sins, he would never forget. Berle had deserted him. He'd deserted them all.

While Pappy had been the one who'd toughed it out, raising his grandkids all by himself, loving them.

For that reason alone Brett forced a smile and turned toward his grandfather. If it eased the man's mind to know that Brett didn't hate Berle, then so be it. "I know it wasn't all bad, Pappy. I remember."

"You do?" Hope fired in the old man's gaze and Brett nodded.

"I remember everything Dad used to do. I also remember everything that you used to do." His gaze locked with the old man's. "I don't know what I would have done without you, Pappy. I never said thank you, but I'm saying it now."

While he still had the chance.

The doubt struck and Brett forced it aside. Things were getting better. Pappy was getting better. And Brett was this close to working Callie out of his system.

Hell, forget better. Things were great.

At least that's what Brett tried to tell himself as he spent the afternoon tending cattle, riding fence, and trying not to count down the hours until Callie Tucker showed up to continue the search for the recipe.

CHAPTER 27

"We need to talk," Brandy said when Callie walked into the kitchen later that afternoon.

Callie dumped her purse on the counter, along with a stack of fliers and a platter of leftover pinwheels from the open house. "If it's about the cupcake apocalypse in the living room, I can explain."

"Actually, it's not about that, but I'd still love to hear your explanation. Especially since I've spent the last two hours trying to get crème filling off the couch cushions."

"Well, see, Alex showed up with Arnie."

"Arnie? That guy's a moron. Why did Alex bring him here?"

"It seems he's recently earned his certification in acupuncture. Alex brought him hoping to help Jenna with her claustrophobia."

"Jenna doesn't have claustrophobia."

"You know that and I know that, but Alex thinks that's why she broke up with him. You know, when she told him she needed her space."

"Okay, that makes sense. In a weird, twisted sort of way, but still. That doesn't explain the cupcakes."

"Well, see, when the acupuncture didn't work, he brought Arnie back to try hypnosis."

"Arnie did acupuncture on Jenna? I saw her yesterday just before she left for the horse vaccinations. She didn't tell me that."

"That's because he didn't do the acupuncture on Jenna. He did it on me."

"Because you're trying to kick the cupcakes." Brandy stated the obvious.

"Sort of. I mean, I did do the acupuncture to kick my addiction, but it didn't work. So when Alex showed up this morning with Arnie again and said he wanted to try hypnosis—on Jenna, not me—I figured I might as well give that a try, too."

"And so he destroyed a bunch of cupcakes in front of you to deter the bad behavior?"

"Not exactly. Apparently, I'm the one who went crazy on the cupcakes. He was just holding up a box and making a suggestion. I took the suggestion and bam, no more cup-cakes."

"That's wild. Understandable, but wild." Brandy eyed her. "So the cupcake thing actually worked?"

"Not really." Callie had scarfed a pack of cupcakes on the way home from the open house. And she'd had sex with Brett at the open house. So clearly the hypnosis hadn't worked. "But it was worth a try."

"Maybe you just need a little time. By tomorrow you might kick the craving completely."

"You really think so?" She latched onto the hope and held tight. "Arnie did say it could take a little while to see results."

"Definitely. But cupcakes aside, we still need to talk." She caught Callie's stare and held tight. "Why didn't you tell me?"

"Tell you what?" Callie averted her gaze and busied herself grabbing a glass from a nearby cabinet.

"That you're trying to sell the Texas Thunder recipe because you desperately need money."

Callie's head snapped up and her gaze met her sister's. "How do you know that?"

Brandy reached beneath the table and pulled out a small drinking glass filled with the telltale gold liquid.

"Where did you get that?"

"From the Mason jar on your nightstand. The one I gave to Mark Edwards when he stopped by looking for you." Brandy swirled the liquid and watched the bubbly funnel that developed. "He said he made it to town early and he was so excited about this stuff that he couldn't wait until your meeting this afternoon." She set the glass down on the table. "He stopped by on the off chance that he might catch you here. He caught me instead and filled me in on what Gramps was doing, and how you've been trying to find the rest of the recipe. He didn't say it, but I'm assuming you're killing yourself working with Brett Sawyer, the one man you hate above all, for a good reason. I just don't know what it is." Her gaze narrowed. "Yet."

"I don't hate Brett." If only, but that ship had sailed long ago and now she was drowning in a sea of desire with no lifeline in sight. "He's an alright guy."

"You're avoiding the issue."

"Which is?"

"Why are you killing yourself?"

She wasn't going to tell Brandy. That was Callie's first thought. She would make something up and keep Brandy in the dark. But her sister looked relentless and Callie had never been a good liar. "We need the money."

"Why?"

"Because James Harlin spent the tax money and now I've got six weeks to come up with it." She tore her gaze from her sister's and busied herself filling a glass with water. "Four now that two have already passed."

"When did you find out?"

"The day before the funeral." She felt the telltale burning behind her eyes, and blinked away the sudden moisture the way she always did. "I guess the bank heard about his death and figured they needed to send an official notification."

"Why didn't you tell me?"

"Because you've got enough on your plate with the bakery. You don't have time to worry about this."

"I'll make time."

"No, you won't, because I'm handling this." Her gaze went to the glass and the few inches of liquid. The scent of apple pie mingled with something much stronger teased her nostrils. "Why did you keep some?"

"Because my new assistant has the palate of a Michelin star pastry chef. With her taste buds and my knowledge of ingredients, we might be able to figure out what's in this stuff."

"You mean if it's even the right stuff. Brett and I found it in his attic. It could be any shine from here to Arkansas. We have no proof it's *the* Texas Thunder."

"You'll know eventually. Edwards said he's handing it off to his guy, but it could take up to four weeks for them to get to the sample. He's trying to move it along, but he's calling in a favor of a friend of a friend, so he's not at the top of the priority list. That means we have to wait. I just figured that maybe Ellie could cut down on the wait time.

If her results match the recipe, there's a good chance this is the real stuff. At least then you can stop worrying and destroying innocent cupcakes."

"I don't want you to worry about this."

"Why? I'm a big girl. I can handle the worry. I learned from the best." Her smile disappeared. "You were always there, Callie. Killing yourself for us. Sacrificing. You don't have to do this alone. I'll do what I can to help. My oven is paid for. So are my mixers. I could try for a secured loan on all of it. I don't know how much that will be, but it's enough to put a small dent in what we owe."

"But you need that money for an extra oven."

"The oven can wait. I'm okay for now. I'd rather hand the money over for this."

"But I don't want—"

"It's not about what you want," Brandy cut in. "I live here, too." A stern expression slid over her face. "And I'm going to help."

"What about Jenna? Did you tell her?"

"She has enough to worry about with stalker Alex. Besides, she's barely making her car payment. She can't help now. But one day . . ." She grinned. "When she has her own veterinary practice and is raking in the cash, we'll call in a return on the favor. Right now, we can handle this. Together."

Callie wanted to believe her sister, but she'd been going it alone for so long that she wasn't so sure she could stop. She still felt the weight of the world on her shoulders, pushing her down, pulling her in a million different directions. Even so, she hugged Brandy, holding her tight for a few long moments and relishing the warmth of her sister's embrace.

And thinking of how she was going to miss it when she finally left Rebel behind for good.

After her talk with Brandy, Callie fed Jez and the other foster animals before jumping into the shower. She meant to wash away the feel of Brett's touch, but it only served to heighten her awareness. Her skin tingled as the water washed over her. Her nerves vibrated with the slick feel of the soap.

She pulled on a T-shirt and jeans and tried to pretend that tonight was just like any other night. Strictly business.

But her body knew better.

The drive out to Bootleg Bayou seemed to take even longer and by the time she rang the doorbell, she all but trembled with anticipation.

A feeling that soon subsided when Brett's sister answered the door.

"He's already up in the attic." Karen pointed toward the staircase and Callie headed up to find Brett smack dab in the middle of unpacking a giant box.

"You're late," he called out. "I've already gone through three boxes."

"I had to drop some things off at the office. I talked to Mark Edwards." She spent the next few minutes filling him in on the plan for getting the shine analyzed. "Bottom line, we still need to find the recipe."

He pointed to a nearby stack. "Have at it."

No kissing. No hugging. No touching of any kind.

Not that they needed to kiss or hug or touch right now. They needed to work first and play later.

If they even played at all.

A doubt that grew with each passing hour as they dug through boxes and searched with renewed vigor.

"Your pappy seems really good today," she finally said, eager to get a conversation going so that she didn't have to think about how good he looked, or how intoxicating he smelled. "I could hear him humming from the den when Karen let me in."

"He's actually having a great week. I think he may have gotten over the worst," Brett said, pulling out a stack of old encyclopedias packed away in a large cardboard box.

"Is he taking some new sort of medication?"

He shook his head and pulled out a thesaurus. "Everything's the same."

"Then it's most likely just temporary." What the hell was she doing? If Brett Sawyer wanted to hide from the truth and pretend that everything was fine, she should just let him be. *Play along and keep her mouth shut.* But at that moment, she sensed the unease that lurked just below the surface. The fear. And she had to say something.

"I know you want to think that everything is going to be fine." She set the doilies she'd found back inside the drawer and pushed it closed. "But it's not. Pappy has Alzheimer's. It's a serious condition that only gets worse. Pretending that it isn't that bad doesn't help anyone, least of all Pappy." And least of all Brett, himself.

It just set him up for a bigger disappointment when the man finally took a turn for the worse, and never came back. And he would. That was inevitable.

"I'm no doctor, but I know there's no cure. I know you don't want to hear that, but it's true. The sooner you admit that to yourself, the better."

"I'm not giving up hope."

"It's not about hope. It's about fear. You're scared." His only reply was a sharp glance that said more than words ever could. "You don't want to accept the truth because you think you're letting your pappy down. That you're giving up on him. You're not."

"Leave it alone, Callie." Warning edged his words and if she'd had an ounce of sense, she would have heeded it.

But she was past the point of backing down. As much as she didn't want to care for Brett, to feel something more than just the lust whispering through her body and licking at her veins, she did.

He was her first love.

Her only love.

The truth hit her as she sat on her knees and reached for the next drawer. She unearthed several photo books filled with pictures of him as a child. Brett riding his first pony. Brett roping his first calf. Brett eating a giant cupcake at his sixth birthday. Brett nailing his first deer.

Happiness radiated from his young face and something squeezed at her heart and stirred a protective urge unlike anything she'd ever felt before.

For the boy he'd been.

The man he'd become.

She didn't want to see him hurt or disappointed or devastated because he refused to see the gravity of Pappy's condition. While he might hate her for pointing out the obvious, she knew she had to try, to pave the way and soften the blow that would eventually come.

She turned on him. "Aren't you tired of running away?"

"What's that supposed to mean?"

"That you've been running your entire life. Away from here. From your past. From your pappy."

"I didn't run from Pappy."

She caught his stare and refused to look away. "You're running right now."

"That's crazy." He motioned at his surroundings. "I'm here."

"Instead of accepting the truth," she went on despite the tight draw of his mouth and the sudden narrowing of his gaze, "you're hauling ass away from it. From him." She could feel the tension that swelled in the room, filling up every nook and cranny. She gathered her determination. "You need to stop. To face it. For your own good."

Talk about the pot calling the kettle black.

The voice whispered through her, reminding her of the stack of *Reader's Digest*s and the tubes of Bengay and the truth sitting in that small den. One that she refused to ac-accept, let alone admit.

That despite James Harlin's bad behavior and his bad decisions and his countless flaws, she'd loved him.

"I miss him." The words were out before she could stop them.

Brett's anger seemed to falter. Surprise lit up his gaze. "Who?"

"My grandfather." She caught her bottom lip for a long moment as the past welled. "He was a sorry SOB, that's for sure, but I actually *miss* him. I never thought I would, but there it is." Her gaze met his. "I've been trying to convince myself otherwise. I didn't want to miss him because he never did one single thing to deserve it. But I know now that denial is even worse than regret. It's not about him. It's about me." She touched a hand to her heart. "My peace of mind. *Me.* I need to miss him, just like you need to accept what's happening to your pappy. Because if you don't, the fear will chew you up now, and the regret will swallow you whole later."

He didn't say anything for a long moment. Instead, he

just stared at her, as if trying to decide something. "There's only one thing I need," he finally said, pushing the box aside. He closed the distance between them until he stood right in front of her, filling up her line of vision and drinking in all of her oxygen. "And it's not peace of mind."

"I think we should keep looking." That's what she said, but she couldn't ignore the gleam in his gaze or the heat that crackled between them. She reached for the next drawer but he stopped her.

"I need this." He took her hand, his strong fingers closing around hers, and pulled her to her feet. His arm slid around her waist and he pulled her flush against his body. "I need you."

CHAPTER 28

"I don't know if this is such a good idea," Callie murmured when Brett led her out to the barn. "What if Karen comes looking for you? Or Dolly?"

"They'll call my cell," Brett told her. He walked past the horse stalls, to the small office that sat at the far end. "The sofa pulls out into a bed," he said once they'd walked inside and he'd shut the door.

Before she could open her mouth and voice another protest, he pulled her close and then he was kissing her again, deeply, desperately. His tongue tangled with hers, exploring every secret and her breath caught.

I need you.

Even if he hadn't already told her as much, she would have felt it. A sense of urgency drove him as he tossed the sofa cushions to the side and pulled out the mattress. Grabbing a blanket from a nearby shelf, he tossed it on the bed and turned toward her.

Another fierce kiss and he backed her up toward the edge of the bed. Her legs hit and she tumbled backward. A split second later, he tossed her boots to the floor and peeled the jeans down her body. He grabbed the edge of her T-shirt and pulled it up and over her head until she sat there wearing nothing but her bra and panties.

He stepped back then and kicked off his boots. Catching the hem of his shirt, he peeled the soft cotton free and tossed it to the side. His hand dove into his pocket and he pulled out a condom. He unbuttoned his jeans then and shoved them down, freeing a massive erection.

Her breath caught and she pushed up onto her feet. Driven by her own need, she reached out and took the latex. Tearing open the package, she eased the contents over the ripe head of his smooth, pulsing shaft, from tip to root.

A growl vibrated from his throat and she glanced up to see him staring down at her, watching, waiting. He pulsed in her hands and she trembled with a renewed hunger.

She wanted to kiss him again, but even more, she wanted to feel him inside, to be so consumed that she didn't have to think. To worry the way she had for the past few hours.

That this might be their last time.

The end would come eventually. They both knew it, and it fueled the heat charging the air.

She spread her legs and waited as he settled between her thighs. The head of his penis pushed a delicious fraction into her and pleasure pierced her brain. Sensation swept along her skin like a fiery tongue that sucked the oxygen from her lungs and left her light-headed.

She lifted her legs and hooked them around his waist, opening her body even more. He answered her silent invitation with a deep, probing thrust.

Her muscles convulsed around him, clutching him as he gripped her buttocks and tilted her a delicious inch so that he could fit more deeply inside.

She lifted her hips, moving her pelvis, riding him until he gasped and started to pump. Deeper. Harder. There.

Right . . . *there*.

Her lips parted. A scream ripped from her lips as the blinding force of her climax crashed over her and yanked her back under. She gasped and clutched at his shoulders, holding tight.

He came right behind her, burying himself one last time. His jaw clenched and the tendons in his neck stretched tight. A moan tumbled from his lips and echoed in her ears.

Brett collapsed on top of her, his face buried in the crook of her neck for the next few moments until he rolled to the side and pulled her back against him, his heart pounding between her shoulder blades. One hand settled on her breast and the other held her tightly around the waist as if he feared she might disappear at any moment.

As if the notion bothered him a hell of a lot more than it should have considering he knew good and well she was leaving Rebel.

The possibility stirred a rush of pure joy, followed by a burst of panic that had her scrambling from the bed and snatching up clothes.

No way was he falling in love with her the way she'd fallen for him. He wouldn't. He couldn't.

She was *this* close to being free of Rebel. The last thing she needed was another reason to stay. Brett falling in love with her, admitting that love, would be like a noose around her neck.

"What's wrong?"

"Nothing. It's just . . . I have to get out of here." She yanked on her clothes and snatched up her boots.

"I'll see you tomorrow," he called after her, but she didn't answer.

Because even more frightening than the notion that

he might have fallen for her, too, was the opposite side of the coin—that he might not care at all.

She'd tried to tell herself that it didn't matter, that she could keep things strictly physical between the two of them, but she couldn't. She loved him and he didn't love her, and it hurt like hell.

And that meant it was time to call it quits.

She would be back.

That's what Brett told himself as he listened to the steady thud of Callie's footsteps. In a matter of seconds, they disappeared and he was left with only the frantic beat of his own heart to kill the oppressive silence.

The deep-seated panic that told him something was wrong and he'd better reach out and hold on tight or she was going to slip right through his fingers.

But then that was the point of it all. To work her out of his system so that he could let her go.

He *would* let her go.

Just not yet.

There was still too much heat between them, not to mention they had a recipe to find. Tomorrow night they would pick up where they'd left off. They would keep searching for the Texas Thunder ingredients, and then when they both grew tired and restless, he would lay her down and work her out of his system once and for all.

That was the plan.

A damned good one, too.

Brett pushed to his feet and pulled on his clothes. He debated heading back inside the main house, but it was still early and he was too worked up to go to bed and much too antsy to sit and have a conversation with his sister. Particularly one that would end with his insistence she go back to school and her stubborn refusal.

She was going back.

Pappy was on the mend and Brett was getting the finances in order and so there was no reason for Karen to forfeit her future.

She was going back to school, all right.

Even if she didn't realize it yet.

Brett led a feisty cutting horse named Sam from her stall and walked the animal down the main corridor to the tack area. Hoisting a nearby saddle, he tossed the rig onto the horse's back and fastened the straps. A few minutes later, he climbed onto the animal's back and walked her out of the barn. The warm night air hit him like a punch to the chest, sucking the air from his lungs and sending a kick of adrenaline through him. He kneed the horse to a gallop.

She bolted, but the sudden movement wasn't nearly as blinding as climbing onto the back of a bull. Instead of fighting him, Sam responded to the sound of his voice and the motion of his body. She played nice the way a good cutting horse should and so there was no battling for control, no worry over hitting the dust. No fear.

No running.

The notion struck as he picked up the pace, but he pushed it aside. He wasn't running.

Hell, no.

He leaned into the ride, urging the animal faster, harder, but not because he was hauling ass away from something. No, he simply had responsibilities. He needed to check things out down near the creek and make sure Sheriff De-Massi had sent someone to keep an eye out.

He surely wasn't trying to clear his head and forget the sweet, sugary scent of Callie Tucker, or the warm feel of her body pressed to his.

And he most certainly wasn't trying to shake the sinking feeling that it really was over between them, and worse, there wasn't a damned thing he could do about it.

CHAPTER 29

Callie stood in the doorway that led to the den and eyed the stack of *Reader's Digest*s that sat on the table next to the old recliner. The newspapers piled next to the chair. The tubes of Bengay stuffed in a pocket that draped over the arm of the recliner. The remote sat on the coffee table where it always did when James wasn't using it. How he'd managed to get it back into the spot when he was roaring drunk was still a mystery. Everything else would be in shambles, but the remote would always be right there, present and accounted for, despite the chaos of the room.

She drew a deep, steady breath and ignored the urge to walk the other way. It was late and she had an early day tomorrow. Now wasn't the time to deal with this.

But she had to deal with it.

She'd preached to Brett about running away, but she'd been doing the same. She was still doing it, she realized, as she stared down and noted that she hadn't actually stepped foot inside the room. She glanced down at the empty cardboard box in her hand. There were a dozen more in the hallway behind her, ready for duty should she put the brakes on and just stop.

Face the fear.

Before she could step forward, however, a knock sounded on the back door.

She sent up a silent thank-you and turned, her legs eating up the distance down the hallway.

She found Little Jimmy standing on her doorstep in his shiny black tennis shoes and worn clothes. He had his hands stuffed in his pocket and a strange look on his face.

"Jimmy? What are you doing here?"

"I don't mean to bother you none." A strange light gleamed in his eyes. "I can come back if you're busy." He looked as if he wanted to turn and run, as if whatever had brought him to her doorstep was as frightening to him as her grandaddy's room was to her.

"It's okay. What's on your mind?"

"I just wanted to see if you needed anything? 'Cause if you do, I'd be happy to help out. I know you and your sisters are on your own now 'cause of what happened." He glanced behind him at the break in the trees.

The yellow tape was gone now and the place beyond dozed clean of the debris that had been left. But the scent of burned cedar still permeated the air and reminded Callie of the tragedy that had turned her life upside down.

Then again, James Harlin had done that years before with his drinking and his gambling and his irresponsibility.

Funny but the thought didn't bring the same bad taste to her mouth and she managed a smile. "Thanks, but I'm good right now."

"Just so you know I'm here." He started to turn, but Callie stopped him.

There was just something about the way he said the words that hinted at something more.

"Why is that, Jimmy?"

"You know. 'Cause your granddaddy was a decent man. At least to me." He stuffed his hands into his pockets and she had the feeling he wanted to say more. "My own pa ain't the patient type, but James Harlin always took his time."

"Doing what?"

He hesitated, glancing behind him yet again before shifting his attention back to Callie.

"It's okay," she told him. "You can tell me."

"He was teaching me how to cook. I'd been helping my daddy for years, but he never thought I was smart enough. He sent me out here to buy some yeast off of James Harlin 'cause we was runnin' short and we had this big order to fill. James was moving slow on account of his arthritis and I offered to help. He started teaching me things then whenever I managed to get away from my pa for a little while."

"It was your shoe I found," Callie mumbled as she remembered the strange tennis shoe amid all the charred remains. "You left a shoe out there."

He nodded. "Sheriff DeMassi came out here one night and James and I had to take off. Ran clear out of my shoe that night."

"Were you there the night of the explosion?"

He shook his head. "No, but I wish I had been. Maybe I could have changed things." He looked so regretful that Callie had the urge to give him a hug.

"You're lucky you weren't there, otherwise there would have been two casualties instead of one."

"Maybe, and maybe I could have stopped it."

But that wasn't how things had worked out.

No one had been with James Harlin that fateful night. He'd been cooking all alone, and he'd died all alone.

"He was a gruff man," Jimmy added, "But he sure knew his moonshine. Cooked up way better stuff than my pa."

His statement stirred her memory and she thought of that night with Brett down by the creek and the tell-tale smell that had filled the air.

"Is your daddy still cooking?"

Jimmy nodded.

"Where at?"

"Down by the creek." The minute the words were out, he seemed to realize what he'd said. "Not the Sawyer creek," he quickly tried to backtrack. "We've got our own water source. On our own land," he blurted. "I'd better get going. My pa will tan my hide if he finds me gone." And with that, he turned and high-tailed it for the trees.

She knew then that it was Jimmy's pa who'd fired off his shotgun that night. He was the one cooking on Sawyer land.

And the missing cattle?

She didn't know. She just knew that she had to call the sheriff and voice her suspicions.

Just as soon as she finished what she'd been about to start.

Heading back inside, she made her way down the hall, into the room that held some of her worst memories.

And some of the best.

Those rare times when she'd found James asleep instead of passed out. So few she could count them on her fingers, but still. They were there, in her head just like all the rest. The smile when she'd nudged him awake and urged him to go to bed. The frown when she'd refused to get him a cinnamon roll because it was way too late and he was already this close to being a diabetic.

"You fuss over me too much."

"Somebody's got to do it."

But the only thing she'd *had* to do was look after her sisters, and even that had been a choice. She'd wanted to take care of them, to watch them grow up safe and sound, just as she'd wanted to help James. To keep him from destroying himself.

She'd failed, but not because she hadn't tried. She'd done everything she could for James. She'd even loved him.

She still did.

She admitted the truth as she packed away his belongings and let the tears flow from her eyes.

Tears that weren't wasted because by the time the last box had been put away and the room cleaned, she felt the precious peace of mind she'd mentioned to Brett. A relief that filled her from the inside out and soothed the hurt in her chest.

Enough for her to call the sheriff.

"And you know the Hams are cooking on Sawyer property how?"

She thought of Little Jimmy and the fear in his eyes. "Just a hunch. Check it out, okay?"

"I'm all for instincts, but I can't believe you don't have any more to go on—"

"Please, Sheriff. I know I'm right about this. Just look into it."

"Will do."

Satisfaction rolled through her as she hung up, bypassed the now clean room that had once belonged to James Harlin, and headed for bed. She shed her clothes, climbed in, and closed her eyes tight, feeling a sense of relief unlike any she'd ever felt before. For a little while, that is.

Until a new day dawned and Callie Tucker had to face the heartbreaking truth that she'd walked away from Brett Sawyer and she wasn't going back.

She wasn't coming.

Brett knew it even before he heard the message Callie left on his voice mail that afternoon saying that Mark Edwards had full confidence that they would decipher the recipe thanks to the sample and that searching for it was futile at this point.

And no search meant no Callie.

Still, Brett found himself up in the attic anyway, going through boxes the next night. And the next.

He'd just finished searching through one of his grandmother's dressers when he heard the commotion.

He headed downstairs to find his pappy on the floor of his closet, searching for a belt that had long since worn out.

"Pappy? Are you okay?"

But he wasn't.

Brett knew it even before the man lifted his head, his blue eyes gleaming with worry and confusion.

"Berle? What did you do with my belt? Your mother bought it for me last week and I swore I loved it. If I don't show up at dinner with it tonight, she'll think I lied."

"It's me, Pappy," Brett told the old man, trying desperately to reach the lucid part of him that had been present all week. He couldn't slide back down, not when he'd just managed to get up. "Brett." He said the name as if it could snap the old man out of his sudden confusion. "Your grandson."

"Brett?" Not a glimmer of recognition lit the old man's gaze. Instead, he shook his head frantically. "This isn't funny, son. I need that belt, otherwise your mama is going to kill me. You have to give it back. If you want a new belt, I'll buy you one. Just not that one."

"I don't want a belt—" Brett started, but Karen's voice cut off the rest of his denial.

"I'll help you look for it," his sister offered the old man. "If Berle didn't take it, it has to be right here." She moved past him, crawling into the closet next to Pappy. "Let's look through these boxes."

"I know I didn't put it there . . . ," the old man began, his attention shifting to the stack of shoe boxes.

"Go," Karen mouthed over her shoulder, and Brett didn't hesitate.

He couldn't breathe as it was. He needed to get out of there. Away from the confusion and the chaos.

He started for the attic, but that would only remind him of Callie and how good she'd felt in his arms, how *right,* and so he headed for the barn.

A short while later, he was riding Sam toward the creek and doing what he did best when it came to trouble— running the other way.

The realization hit him as he hauled ass—determined to outrun the truth that Pappy's good streak had ended and he'd taken a U-turn back toward Alzheimer's hell and, even worse, that Brett had lost the only woman he'd ever cared about.

Callie was right about him.

For so long he'd convinced himself that he'd gone away on purpose. But what he'd really done was run away.

Then from the horrible truth that he was his father's son, with the same raging temper, the same disregard for other people's feelings, the same fierce personality.

And now from his pappy and the Alzheimer's that scared him with its uncertainty and consuming nature.

And from Callie and the feelings that she stirred. Feelings that made him want to forget his career, settle right here in Rebel, and beg her to stay with him.

Yep, he was a runner, all right, and a coward because as much as he wanted to, he couldn't seem to stop.

"You just relax, Pappy, and I'll be right back with some hot chocolate. Then we'll get you back into bed."

The old man sat in the overstuffed chair in his bedroom, a confused look on his face. He still couldn't understand why they hadn't been able to find his belt, but he'd finally accepted Karen's suggestion to get some rest and resume the search tomorrow. She'd promised to help him from sunup until sundown if that's what it took.

Even if Mark did want to take her for a picnic.

She headed for the kitchen and pulled out the cocoa mix. Turning toward the microwave, she nuked some water and then went in search of marshmallows and a mug. Five minutes later, she had a cup of her Pappy's favorite drink. She was just about to head for his room when a text message buzzed on her phone. Pulling it from her shorts pocket, she eyed the words that blazed across the screen.

I know it's late, but I can't sleep. Why don't we meet? Mark.

A smile touched her lips and she started to type in her answer. She was halfway through "Yeah, let's do it," when she heard the yelling outside.

Pappy was up again and headed for the tomato garden.

She swallowed a rush of regret and sent a quick "*Thnx but busy*" before abandoning the cocoa and heading down the hall for the back door.

It was pitch black, but she could see well enough to

make out the old man's form on his hands and knees, digging frantically in the small garden.

She hit the light switch and a warm glow flooded the back porch, pushing out toward the small overgrown area where her grandmother used to grow the biggest, juiciest tomatoes in the county.

"Pappy?" She stepped down off the porch. "It's really late. Why don't we do the gardening tomorrow?"

"Too late," he murmured, working frantically at the dirt. "There won't be anything left. That's what Pawpaw said. We have to do it now. Before they come."

"Who?" Karen asked as she dropped to her knees beside him. "Who's coming?"

"The revenuers. They'll take it all. We have to make sure it's safe."

"Take what?" She glanced down at his dirt-covered hands, at the square piece of silver catching moonlight. He scooped frantically with the flat piece, working his hole deeper.

"All the stuff. But it's ours. They ain't got no right to it. That's what Pawpaw says. That's what my daddy says, too. It ain't theirs. It's ours. We worked for it. It's *ours*."

She touched his shoulder, but it only made him more agitated. "I'm sure there's no hurry. Let's do this tomorrow. I'll help."

"Too late," he murmured. She touched his shoulder and he grew more frantic. "It'll be gone. All gone."

"Then let me help now. I'll dig for a little while and then you can dig." He paused then as she reached for the makeshift spade he was using. "I'll go fast, too. I swear."

He didn't want to let go at first, but finally he nodded. The gardening tool slipped from his hands into Karen's.

She stared down at the piece of metal and a wave of recognition washed over her. She dusted frantically at the dirt, wiping as much away as possible.

Sure enough, it wasn't a broken spade.

It was the coveted PBR belt buckle that Brett had brought home after his first win. The same buckle that had been up in the attic with the Bible that Brett had been frantically searching for these past few weeks.

"Come on," the old man said. "Dig, girl. You have to dig."

"Let me just get something bigger. I've got a spade in the kitchen. It'll do a much better job. In fact, why don't you come with me? I'll get you some hot cocoa and then I'll get right back out here and get to work."

She didn't expect him to cooperate. He was much too manic at the moment. Instead, he shook his head frantically and turned back to his hole. Shoving his hands into the dirt, he started digging with his fingers. "I just have to get it deep enough so that the revenuers can't get to it—"

"I'll help," she cut in. "Just let me get a better shovel and I'll help you."

The offer seemed to ease the tense set of his shoulders and he paused to take a breath. A few seconds passed and he started digging again. Slower this time. As if the frenzied storm of his memories were finally calming down just a little.

Hopefully, Karen pushed to her feet and headed for the kitchen. Rinsing off the buckle, she dried it and set it on the counter where her brother was sure to see it. A quick rummage in the drawer and she pulled out one of Dolly's old gardening spades that she used on the front porch flower pots.

She grabbed the tool just as her phone buzzed again. A wave of excitement rushed through her, followed by a whisper of regret because she didn't have the time to text him back.

Another text and another buzz, and a smile tugged at her lips. He might be just as hooked on her as she was on him.

And while that notion would have scared the miniskirt off her a month ago, suddenly it didn't seem like such a bad thing.

Mark was a nice guy, after all. And seriously cute. A girl could certainly do worse.

"Where did this come from?" Brett asked his sister early the next morning when he found the buckle sitting on top of the microwave.

Karen glanced up from her bowl of cereal and swallowed her mouthful. "Pappy had it. He was using it to dig in the garden. I thought it was a spade at first, until I got a closer look."

He turned the buckle over in his hands. "Where did he get it?"

"I'm assuming upstairs in the attic."

Brett did a mental search of all the boxes that he and Callie had uncovered. If the buckle had been up there, they would have seen it. Unless they'd missed a box or a trunk or *something*. "Where exactly in the attic?"

"I don't know. I just know that he was mumbling about hiding from the revenuers while he was digging in the garden with it." She glanced through the kitchen window at the old man sitting on the front porch in his rocker. An untouched cup of coffee sat next to him. The groan of the rocking chair echoed as he pushed it back and forth, an empty look on his face. "Maybe tomorrow will be better and we can ask him."

Maybe.

Brett grasped at the hope as he left the buckle sitting on the counter and headed for the front door. He could have easily gone out the back and avoided walking clear around the house, but he hated seeing his Pappy with that blank look and so he opted for the long way around.

In the barn, he saddled up his horse and headed for the line of fence that separated the east pasture from the west pasture. They had holes and so he'd sent a handful of men to fix the fence earlier that morning. More than enough to handle the job while he took care of the mountain of paperwork inside the house.

But Brett needed out of the house. To think. To breathe. To run.

The truth beat at him for the rest of the day as he worked his fingers to the bone until he was so tired that he could barely breathe, much less think. By the time he led his horse into the barn, the only thing he wanted was a hot shower and a few blessed hours of sleep.

He was halfway to the house when he spotted the sheriff sitting on the back porch, waiting for him.

"Can we talk?"

"Only if you're here to tell me what the hell is going on down by the creek," Brett said as he stepped up onto the porch. He pulled off his hat and ran a tired hand through his hair. "If you're just going to ask questions, then forget it. I'm beat."

"I found the poachers."

Brett's gaze snapped up. "Who?"

"Big Jimmy Ham. We busted him and his buddies last night. They were cooking a hundred gallons out on the edge of your property. They had a pretty good spot, too. There was a cave cut into the side of that hill about a half mile up. They had everything hidden inside and the entire area around booby-trapped to hell and back. A raccoon came up on them the night you heard the gunshot. They thought they were being raided."

"And instead of running, they shot?"

"It's Big Jimmy. He doesn't have a reputation for being the smartest ax in the toolshed." His gaze grew serious. "It wasn't the first time he shot at what he thought was a poacher. We found the remains of your missing cattle. I'm guessing they were watering by the creek at one time or another and spooked Ham. He shot first and realized his mistake later. Found a freezer of meat after we obtained a search warrant for his property. A mess of cash, too. He'll be going away for a long, long time and you'll be getting compensation for your cattle. Eventually," Hunter added. "It has to go through the court system first, but in the end, the judge is sure to make things right."

The news should have sent a rush of relief through Brett. There'd been no theft. His men were in the clear.

Talk about great news.

It was, but it didn't overshadow the crappy state of everything. His pappy was still sick and life still sucked.

And so he spent his nights avoiding his pappy and his days trying to tie up loose ends at the ranch so that he could get the hell out of town and back to the one thing that was still good—his career.

The one thing that had saved him all those years ago.

And the only thing that would save him now.

He accepted an offer from Les's clients on the acreage, securing the immediate future for Bootleg Bayou, and he made several phone calls to hurry up the chemical analysis on the moonshine sample they'd found in the attic. Where Mark Edwards hadn't managed to pull any strings with his one connection, Brett managed to push things along with his, thanks to the head of the chemistry department, who turned out to be the father of a fellow bull rider and a huge fan.

The sample came back within the next two weeks, but the ingredients didn't match Callie's half and so they knew it wasn't the original Texas Thunder. Still, it was a convincing knockoff that did garner an offer from Mark, but not nearly enough at a thousand dollars to get Callie out of debt.

Even when Brett forfeited his share so that she could have it all.

"You want me to give it all to Callie?" Edwards had asked him. "But you two found it together."

"The money is hers. She needs it more than I do," Brett had told the man.

Still, it wasn't enough.

He knew it and damned if it didn't keep him up at night, along with all of his other problems.

Because he loved her.

He came to that conclusion when he walked into Haverty's Real Estate to sign the final papers for the land sale and saw Callie for the first time since she'd walked out on him.

She wasn't wearing anything special—just a plain navy skirt and a cream-colored blouse—but the sight of her stalled the air in his lungs. His heart skipped a beat and just like that, he knew.

He *loved* her.

He'd always loved her.

Not that it made one bit of difference because Callie Tucker had turned her back on him. She was the one walking away this time, and as much as he wanted to haul her into his arms and kiss her until she did any and everything he wanted, he knew he couldn't.

She'd given up so much for the people that she cared about, put them above and beyond her own dreams, and now it was her turn to make her own decisions. And if that meant leaving Rebel, then so be it. She deserved this chance and he wouldn't try to stop her.

Instead, he smiled and tipped his hat and walked past her into Les's office as if all was right.

As if he hadn't lost everything in the world and his life wasn't going to shit all around him.

CHAPTER 30

She wasn't going to say anything.

That's what Callie told herself as she tried to focus on her computer screen and forget the all-important fact that Brett Sawyer was in the next room and he'd given up his half of the thousand dollars Mark had paid them for the semidecent moonshine they'd found in Brett's attic.

No, she wasn't going to say anything even if she did appreciate the gesture. It wasn't enough in its own right, but coupled with the secured loan they'd managed to get on Brandy's equipment, they would be close to the mark.

Close enough that she could go back to the bank and beg for another two-week extension.

At least that's what she was telling herself.

Another two weeks and she could make up the difference and take the job offer that came in just yesterday from a small entertainment press in Austin.

They needed a good photographer to take pictures of the various Austin bands and her tear sheets had been good enough to land a job. It wasn't even close to an investigative journalist position, but it was a start.

If they were willing to wait for her to wrap things up here.

She ignored the worry that niggled at her and focused

on keying in the last of a new listing that Les was working on. She'd just entered the square-footage specs when Les's door opened and Brett walked out.

Another tip of his hat in her direction and he passed her by. She let loose the breath she'd been holding and congratulated herself. She was home free. Another few steps and he would be out of the office. Out of her life. For good.

"Thank you." The words seemed to come on their own.

He stopped and turned. His blue eyes collided with hers and her breath caught.

So much for not saying anything.

"I really appreciate what you did."

"We wouldn't have found the moonshine if not for you. It was all your idea. I'm just sorry we didn't come up with the actual recipe. I kept looking," he went on, "I even found the Bible, but no recipe. Everything—all the pictures and important documents that I remembered, were gone. It was just the book."

"I'm so sorry."

He shrugged. "Don't be. I'm sure it's all there somewhere. Take care." He started to turn, but she stopped him.

"I heard they found out what happened to your cattle."

He nodded. "They snuck up on the Ham setup and he thought they were feds."

"At least you can have some peace of mind now and Big Jimmy Ham will get what's coming to him." And Little Jimmy won't have to worry about getting the crap beat out of him for every little mistake. Sheriff DeMassi had told her as much when she'd asked about it in town. They'd raided the house and cleared Little Jimmy and his mother of any wrongdoing. "It wasn't your men." She caught her lip for a second as he stared at her, into her, and she fought the urge to press herself close.

"Thankfully not." An awkward silence settled before he added, "I really should get going—"

"I got a job offer," she blurted, the news finally bubbling over.

Surprise lit his eyes, followed by a glimmer of excitement, and something twisted in her chest. "That's great."

"It's just a small paper in Austin, but it's a good starting point."

"Austin, huh? So when do you leave?"

"I don't know. I haven't actually accepted it yet. I'm hoping they'll wait for me to wrap things up here."

"They'll wait," he told her, crossing the few feet between them. "You're that good, Callie." He took her hand and pulled her to her feet until they stood toe to toe. "They would be stupid not to wait for you."

She wanted to say thank you again, to tell him that he was the reason she'd sent out the tear sheets, that he'd given her the courage to do it, the drive, but when she opened her mouth he touched his lips to hers.

Her eyes closed and she relished the soft press of his lips.

And then, just as quickly as he'd kissed her, he pulled away. A wistful smile touched his lips, and then he turned and walked away.

Callie took a step forward, intent on going after him, on saying something—anything—so that she could have one more moment with him. But Les's voice stopped her.

"Can I speak to you a second?"

"About that—" she started, but Les pressed an envelope into her hand and the words fled. "What's this?"

"Pay your taxes, Callie."

"What are you talking about?"

He motioned to the envelope. "It's a check. Pay your taxes."

Confusion tugged at her expression as she stared down at the equivalent of a winning Lotto ticket. The answer to her prayers. And all because of Les.

Her gaze snapped up and collided with his. "But I thought you couldn't do a loan."

"It's not a loan. It's a commission." He motioned to the window. Outside, Brett climbed into his truck and gunned the engine. "From the Sawyer sale," he added. "It was your pictures that sold the place. You deserve the commission. Well, a percentage of it, at least. I have to get paid, too." He nodded toward the check that she pulled free from the envelope. "But based on my talk with the bank president, I think that's just about enough to handle most of your debt."

"What about Selma? Won't she give you a hard time?"

"She knows I couldn't have secured the listing without you. Brett wanted you in on the deal or no deal."

His words echoed in her head and her lips tingled as she remembered the bittersweet kiss from moments before.

A good-bye kiss because Callie Tucker was really and truly finally leaving.

She tried to ignore the sudden whisper of disappointment that went through her. She should be happy. Ecstatic. This was it. The moment she'd been waiting for her entire life. Her one shot at freedom. "You know what this means, don't you?" she said, more for herself than Les.

"That you'll be leaving me?" He shrugged. "I figured. For the record, though, I'm totally opposed to you going anywhere except Realtor's school. But if that can't happen, I want you to go to Austin and knock their socks off."

She cut him a surprised look. "How do you know about Austin?"

"Who do you think gave you a recommendation? I talked to the editor a few days ago. They were hesitant because you have no newspaper experience, but then I told them how you handle all of my listings in the local paper, not to mention a massive newsletter that I send out monthly, and bam, they were willing to give you a chance."

"We don't do a monthly newsletter."

"Not yet, but that's next on my agenda as soon as I win Realtor of the year. Speaking of which, I need to send Tanner a fruit basket congratulating him on my sale. Just so he knows it's a done deal." He turned and headed back into his office. "Take an extra hour at lunch. I'm sure you need to make a trip to the bank."

Relief welled up through her. "Thanks, Les."

"Thank you." He grinned like a child who'd nabbed the last cookie. "Tanner is going to be *pissed*."

Callie reached for her purse, the check tight in her hands, and tried to summon her own excitement.

She should be over the moon. The moment she'd been waiting her entire life for was finally here. Time to pay the taxes and fulfill her last and final duty as caretaker of the Tucker spread, and then she could get on with her life. She could finally make her own dreams come true.

They were right there. Within arm's reach.

If only that notion excited her half as much as the memory of Brett's parting kiss.

She was leaving.

The truth played over and over in Brett's head throughout the rest of the day, but it didn't really sink in until he heard Karen gossiping with Dolly later that evening.

"She got a job at a big-time paper and everything," Karen told the older woman as she reached for a biscuit.

Pappy sat on the opposite side of the table, his gaze fixed on his plate, silence surrounding him, pressing in and isolating him from everyone and everything. He'd been quiet for the past few hours since he'd woken up from his nap. Too quiet for Brett to gauge whether or not he was in this reality or some other from his past.

The *what if* kept him from relaxing. Or so he told himself. No way was he sitting as stiff as a board, his muscles pulled tight to the point that they burned, because the one woman he loved was about to leave town for good.

So what?

Hell, *he* was leaving. He'd pulled out the contracts just that morning. They sat on the desk in the study. All he had to do was sign and call his agent with the good news. And make a phone call to his resident pain-in-the-ass Tyler McCall.

He wanted to deliver the news himself that his distant cousin was going to be stuck in second place a little while longer.

Especially after Tyler's taunting phone call.

And the zillion or so texts since, in which the man had poked and prodded and tried to get in Brett's craw.

No more.

". . . Mark said they paid her a nice amount for some moonshine she found and so I guess she was able to pay the taxes," Karen went on.

"Mark?" His sister's words snagged his attention. "Since when do you know Mark Edwards?"

"Since I've gone to lunch with him a couple of times now."

Brett gave her an incredulous look. "You and Edwards? Having lunch?"

"What's the big deal?" She shrugged. "He came here looking for you one time and found me and, well, he couldn't *not* take me to lunch on account of I'm so charismatic."

Brett frowned. "I doubt he's after your charisma."

"What's that supposed to mean?"

"That he's male, which means that he's got one thing on his brain when it comes to women."

"Which is?"

"He wants to get into your pants." He nailed her with a grim look. "You should stay away from him."

"You really think he wants in my pants?" She looked so hopeful that Brett did a double take.

"And that makes you happy because?"

"Because the child, here, just had a breakup and any woman who's been dumped on by a man likes to know that other men find her attractive," Dolly chimed in. "It's a girl thing."

His gaze swiveled from the old woman to his sister. "You got dumped on?"

"Up at school. He was a jerk and I was too good for him. It's old news." Karen waved him off. "Now about Callie . . . I heard her sister had to mortgage her equipment to help with the taxes, but that she was more than happy to do anything to help."

"That's what family does," Dolly said. "They dig in their heels and help each other."

Any other family besides the one sitting right here at this dinner table, Brett thought.

No, this family ran from trouble. At least half of the family. Karen wasn't running.

She was right here.

Good or bad.

For better or worse.

". . . so then Margie Callaghan told Tracey Reaves who told me that Becky Sue really does want to try to make things work, but Josh is the one who can't get his act together," Karen went on, the talk of families obviously sparking another conversation regarding one of Rebel's wilder clans. It seemed that Becky Sue Callahan had no hope in hell of having a family with her baby daddy Josh Wicker unless he straightened up his act and came crawling back, begging her forgiveness after getting caught with his pants down with a certain cashier at the Piggly Wiggly.

Brett ignored the urge to change the subject back to Callie and ask for more details. Instead, he finished the last bite of his dinner, took a long pull of his iced tea and set his napkin on his empty plate. Pushing to his feet, he picked up his dish and headed for the kitchen.

"You and Edwards?" he asked Karen when she finally followed to help load the dishwasher. "Really?"

"Don't get your boxers in a wad. It's nothing serious." She turned on the faucet and started to rinse a glass. "It just helps distract me from all the drama here." She hauled open the dishwasher and stuffed the glass into the top rack. "Besides, Mark is good for my self-esteem. I doubt it goes anywhere, but then I'm not looking for a relationship. This is just some much-needed fun." Her gaze slid past him to Pappy, who still sat at the kitchen table, a piece of uneaten cake in front of him. "He's getting worse, you know—"

"I've got some paperwork waiting," Brett cut in, sliding a plate into the bottom rack before turning on his heel.

Guilt niggled at him as he started for the door that led to the hall, but he refused to give in. He'd tried to help and everything he said or did just made the situation worse.

There was no reasoning with his pappy when he was feeling bad.

"How long is it going to take you?" Karen's voice stopped him just shy of his escape. "Because I was thinking I might meet Mark at the Dairy Queen and I need someone to stay here with Pappy."

Brett turned and caught his sister's hopeful stare. "Tonight?"

She nodded. "Mark is driving back to Austin for work tomorrow and it's our last night to see each other. Dolly's going to bingo at the church"—she motioned to the woman picking up the leftover roast—"isn't that right, Dolly?"

"Sure is." She hauled open a cabinet and pulled out a plastic storage container. "It's the biggest pot we've seen in six months." She fed the roast into the bowl and popped on the lid. "And I'm itching to buy myself one of those electronic footbaths they sell on the QVC."

"You have to stay with him." Karen gave Brett her widest stare. "Please."

No. It was right there on the tip of his tongue. But damned if he could choke it out. "Fine," he said instead. "Go."

"Really?" Her gaze met his.

Yeah, really?

He tamped down the doubt and squared his shoulders. "I said so, didn't I?"

"Because he's been quiet all day," Karen offered. "You shouldn't have any trouble. I'll get him into bed before I leave." Excitement lit her familiar blue eyes and Brett felt a swirl of guilt. His sister was still so young.

Too young to have to give up her life for an old man.

Even if she was doing so willingly.

"If he gets up and tries to go out to the garden," she went

on, "just let him be. Turn on the light and let him dig for a little while. I'll deal with him when I get back."

But Brett should be the one dealing with his pappy. Taking care of him. Good or bad.

The truth followed him to the study as he left Karen with Pappy and spent the next thirty minutes staring at the contracts.

Reading them, of course, because a man had to read something before he signed it. And if he was going to read the first few pages, he might as well go through the entire thing, page by page, just to be sure everything was in order.

It was an hour after Karen and Dolly had left and he was three-quarters through the stack of documents when he heard the music coming from his pappy's room.

"Blue Eyes Crying in the Rain" by Willie Nelson.

It had been his grandmother's favorite song back in the day. She'd hummed it every night when she'd cooked dinner, or rocked him and his sister to sleep.

For a split second, he thought maybe Pappy was having his own walk down memory lane. Reminiscing. But then he heard the tell-tale shouting, followed by the slamming of a door.

Brett reached the bedroom in a few frantic heartbeats to find his pappy pacing the room. The old man whirled when he heard Brett's voice, his gaze wild and frantic. "I'm supposed to find Martha and ask her to dance." He paced some more. "I promised her we'd dance. I *promised,* but I don't know how." He stared down at his feet as if seeing them for the first time. "I can't remember how."

"It's okay. She's not here," Brett said, but Pappy whirled on him, eyes wild, faraway.

"The dance already started and I promised her I'd

dance!" The old man's frantic voice sent a burst of fear through Brett and the oxygen stuck in his lungs.

He wanted to say something—anything—to make the situation better, but there were no words.

Nothing he could do.

For now.

Pappy just needed time.

Tomorrow he would be back to his old self. The day after that for sure.

But as Brett watched the old man pace, his arthritic hands frantic as he wrung them tightly, his shoulders stiff, his worry profound, Brett knew that time wasn't going to change anything. Time wasn't Pappy's friend. Time was his enemy, whittling away at his memories, killing them off one by one until someday soon there would be nothing left.

"She loves to dance and I promised her we would," Pappy went on. "I knew how. Just a little while ago, I knew, but now I can't remember what to do. I have to remember. I promised her. I *have* to."

Karen was right.

Brett finally admitted as much as he stood there, staring at the one man in the world who'd been both father and mother to him. A strong man who'd faced the world with courage and determination and a strength that had made him one of the most powerful men in the county.

He was a shadow of that man now. Frail. Scared. Tears coursed down his face. Confusion twisted his features. Brett reminded himself that it had been only a week ago that Pappy had been perfectly fine. Sane. *Good.*

That there would surely be another good day.

But at that moment, he just couldn't be sure.

The truth knocked and for the first time, Brett opened the door and faced the one thing he'd done his damnedest to avoid. The undeniable fact that there might never be another good day. This might be it for the rest of his pappy's life.

For the rest of Brett's life.

No heart-to-heart talks.

No words of wisdom from the only man Brett truly trusted.

No guidance.

But Brett was a grown man. It was time for him to lead the way, to give back all that love. It was his turn to step up, to speak words of wisdom, to offer guidance.

Because good or bad, they still had today. Together.

And where Brett had spent all his time running from the truth of his grandfather's illness, he finally put on the brakes and slid to a stop, and surprisingly the world didn't cave in on him.

There were no explosions.

No destruction.

Just the steady whine of Willie's voice and his pappy's frantic footsteps.

"I have to remember," Pappy went on. "I promised her I knew how to dance."

"Then let's do this." Brett stepped forward, slid his arms around his frail pappy, and pulled him close. "I'll teach you."

And then he started to sway.

CHAPTER 31

It was the biggest cupcake Callie had ever seen.

"I know you said you were giving them up, but I thought you might be okay with one last goodie. It's a celebration, after all, and a party's not a party without cake."

Callie smiled at Brandy and tried to imagine not seeing her sister tomorrow. Or the next day. Or the next.

It was a crazy thought, but one she'd been having all too often over the past few weeks since she'd given Les her notice, paid off the taxes, and accepted the Austin job.

It was her last Saturday night in Rebel. Come Monday she would be long gone, headed to Austin to start the next chapter of her life. To send her off, her sisters had surprised her with a going-away party at Brandy's bakery.

She stared at the banner overhead before turning back to the monstrous cupcake sitting center stage amid a zebra-striped tablecloth. Her mouth watered and her stomach hollowed out and she thought of Brett for the countless time.

That's why she'd given up cupcakes.

Because the sweetness, the decadence, the rush of *ahh* reminded her of him, and how they were a poor substitute for the pleasure he'd given her.

She'd gone cold turkey as she'd packed up her room and searched for an apartment and turned in her last volunteer assignment to the local paper.

"That was a great little story you did on the annual spaghetti dinner," Delilah Wickline, the editor-in-chief of the newspaper, had told her just yesterday. "And the pics were great. Why, I should have offered you a job before that Austin paper trumped me."

But you don't know what you've got until it's gone, or so the saying went and Delilah had been proof of that.

Callie had been volunteering for the past few years and the woman hadn't ever thought of hiring her until she'd heard that someone else wanted Callie enough to pay her.

Delilah had made her an offer then, but it had come too late. Callie had given Austin her word, and she wasn't going to break it. How could she pass up a real journalist position to stay here in Rebel and do write-ups on the senior ladies' monthly bake sale or the seventh grade car wash or the yearly chili cook-off?

Rationally, she couldn't and so she was leaving.

Even if she wasn't all that happy about it.

The past few weeks had given her some much needed perspective—namely that she hadn't stalled all these years because she'd been afraid of her own shortcomings. Rather, she'd stalled because Rebel was her home and however silly and nostalgic, she was going to miss it.

She was going to miss her sisters.

She wanted to stay not because they *needed* her to help them succeed, but because she *wanted* to be there to see them do just that all on their own.

That, and she'd gotten attached to Jenna's strays. Just that morning Jezebel had jumped onto her bed and nuzzled her as if the dog knew their time together was about to come to an end.

That small gesture had made Callie weepy for the rest of the day.

Add a surprise party and a giant cupcake and, well, it was no wonder she was wiping at a stray tear when a strange awareness skittered up her spine.

She glanced up to see Brett Sawyer standing near the counter. He wore a pair of jeans, a plain black T-shirt that read *Hooey* in white script, and a straw Resistol that she remembered from their high school days. He'd worn the hat everywhere until trading it in for the fancy hats supplied by his sponsors on the rodeo circuit.

Her heart stalled at the implication of that hat. Or maybe it stalled because he made a beeline straight for her despite the eyes of everyone in the room.

"What are you doing here?"

He shrugged his broad shoulders. "Your sister invited me."

Callie glanced at Brandy, who held up her hands. "I thought he might want to say good-bye," the woman added. Her attention shifted to Brett and she grinned. "Or maybe hello. Listen, if the two of you will excuse me, I need to grab some plates."

Brandy left them to disappear into the back room. The awkward silence that surrounded them soon faded into the sound of music as Jenna switched on the CD player and Jason Aldean started singing about parties and tailgates and dirt roads.

"So what do you want?" She noted the tight lines around his mouth and the shadows beneath his eyes. As if Brett hadn't slept in days. Weeks, even.

As if he'd been as miserable as she had.

"I doubt you came to say good-bye considering we already did that," she added.

"Did we?" He eyed her. "I seem to recall you walking away and not saying much at all."

"There wasn't anything left to say. It was over. You knew it. I knew it. No sense dragging it out."

"You see, that's where you're wrong. It's not over." He stiffened, his shoulders squaring as he stood his ground. "I still want you, Callie, and I'm not letting you go."

"You can't force me to stay."

"I wouldn't try." He shook his dark head. "I just think you need to make a fully informed decision before you pack up and leave."

"I am, you know," she said, more for her own good than his. Because her heart was pounding too fast and her hope was soaring and she was thinking that maybe she wouldn't have to say good-bye to Jezebel, after all. "I already have an apartment."

"I heard."

Her forehead wrinkled. "From who?"

"Hazards of a small town, sugar." His gaze caught and held hers. "I know you're ready to roll out of here, and I want you to go. If"—he emphasized the word—"that's what you really want to do. I would never try to stop you from doing something you really want, Callie. I don't want to be another sacrifice."

"Then what do you want?"

"I want you." His eyes darkened with emotion and the air caught in her chest. "I love you. I always have and I always will. And if leaving here is what you want, then that's fine. You go. I'll just have to get used to Austin."

"What's that supposed to mean?"

"That if you're going to follow your dream, I'm going

to follow mine." His gaze caught and held hers. "You're my dream, Callie. If you want to move, let's move. I've got a suitcase in the truck."

"What about your pappy?"

"Karen can look out for him. She's not going back to school, but I did get her to agree to take some classes locally. She wants to be here and I get it now, so I'm going to wait her out. When the time comes, she'll go back to A&M. Or maybe she won't. Either way, it'll be her decision, not mine. It's her life. Just like this life is mine."

"What about the ranch?"

"Things are stable now thanks to the land sale. Pepper can handle things while I'm gone."

"But what about your career? You're the reigning champ?"

"I've done what I set out to do—I won a buckle. I won more than one, as a matter of fact. It's enough. Tyler Mc-Call's been waiting for a chance to step up, so let him." His gaze brightened. "Bull riding was great. It kept me busy. Too busy to think about everything I was missing, but I'm not missing out any more. I don't want to."

"You can't leave your pappy."

"I can"—he touched her chin then, holding her gaze steady with his—"if I have to. But not because I'm running away. I'll leave because I want to, not because I have to. You were right about me. I *was* running from the ranch, from the idea of turning into my father. But I'm not him. I'll never be him. Even if I stay right here and settle at Bootleg Bayou. Or even if I don't. I'm not running from anything anymore. I'm running to it. I'm running to you." His hands cradled her face, his thumbs smoothing the sudden trembling of her bottom lip. "Wherever you are, that's where I'll be. That is, if you feel the same. You do love me, don't you?"

She nodded and he grinned as if he'd just won that first PBR buckle all over again. "But I don't want you to follow me to Austin. I want to stay here. With my family. With you." Before she could blink, he hauled her against his chest and touched her mouth with his. His tongue slid past her lips to stroke and tease. Strong hands pressed the small of her back, holding her close as if he never meant to let her go.

Not now.

Not ever again.

Pure joy rushed through her, making her heart pound in her ears for a long moment before she became keenly aware of the awkward silence surrounding them, the eager eyes drinking in the scene, the desperate ears hanging on every word.

And she didn't care.

She never had where he was concerned and she wasn't going to start now.

He was a Sawyer and she was a Tucker, and they loved each other. And that was all that mattered.

"Since we're both on the same page," he murmured when he finally pulled away. He dropped to his knee in front of her and stared up through long dark lashes as he pulled an antique ring out of his pocket. "I found this going through the attic. It was my grandmother's ring." He held up the gold band with a heart-shaped diamond. "My pappy bought it for their first anniversary." He seemed to think. "But if you don't like it, I can buy something—"

"I love it," she said, touching a hand to his lips. She smiled through a blurry haze of tears. "I love you and yes, I'll marry you."

He was on his feet in that next instant, pulling her close. "I'm going to make you a very happy woman, Miss Tucker."

"I'm counting on that, Mr. Sawyer." And then she kissed

him, sealing the deal and surrendering herself to whatever the future held for the two of them.

"Well, well." She heard Brandy's voice in the background. "It looks like this going-away party just turned into an engagement party."

"Thank God," Jenna added. "I was afraid that hypnosis had actually worked and I was going to have to let Arnie try it on me."

"Would you stop worrying about yourself and help me out?" came Brandy's irritated voice. "This isn't about you and your fear of commitment. It's Callie's moment."

It was.

Her moment.

Her life.

Her future.

Brett was all three and Callie was going to spend the rest of her life loving him.

"Now stop staring, people," Brandy quipped, "and grab a plate. It's time to eat some cake!"

EPILOGUE

"All done, Mr. Brett."

Brett glanced up from the ledger sheets documenting the latest calf arrivals to see Earl McCauley standing in the doorway of the study. The gray-headed man had been a friend of the family for years and owned McCauley's Seed and Sow—the one and only landscaping service in town. He'd been working for the past few days, weeding and tilling and turning the overgrown patch where Brett's Pappy spent so much time into the viable tomato garden that it had once been.

"The rows are all done, the spikes in place." The man sat a small cardboard box at his feet before pulling a red handkerchief from his pocket and mopping his brow. "We put in the state-of-the-art watering system that you wanted, as well as the six-foot fence to make sure the deer don't get at the seedlings."

"Thanks so much, Mr. McCauley. I know Pappy will be very happy."

The older man nodded. "My pleasure. Your pappy's a good man." He shook his head. "It ain't fair what's happened to him."

It wasn't. Not by a long shot.

At the same time, Brett had stopped regretting the past. Instead, he was focused on making each day forward the best that it could be for his grandfather. Sometimes that meant confusion and chaos. But once in a while, on those rare occasions, it meant a calm peace that stole through the house and reminded Brett of how truly blessed he was to still have the old man in his life.

Like today.

A chair squeaked as the old man rocked on the back porch. Willie Nelson's "On the Road Again" drifted through the screen door.

Life wasn't perfect all the time, but it had its moments.

Brett's gaze shifted to the screensaver on his nearby laptop. It was a selfie that Callie had taken of the two of them down by the creek that night after he'd proposed to her. They held each other close and smiled as she held up the ring he'd slipped on her finger just before asking her to marry him.

After all this time, they were finally together the way they should have been in the first place.

A smile touched his lips as he lifted his attention back to the landscaper. "Just give me a few minutes and I'll write you a check for the invoice."

Brett had sold his touring bus just last month and had made enough to get the ranch back on track for the next few months. In the meantime, he'd followed through on his plan to offer up two of Bootleg's prized bulls for breeding to the highest bidders. The projected income would be just enough to give the ranch an actual profit for the coming year.

His pappy had been right. Brett was every bit the rancher his father had been and then some.

A fact he was no longer ashamed to admit. He was Berle Sawyer's son, and while he had no desire to turn into his old man, he had inherited a few of his better qualities. And that was okay.

Family was family.

Good and bad.

Callie had helped him see that, just as he'd helped her. She was every bit as stubborn as her own grandfather had been—a Tucker through and through—and he loved her for it. He loved the way she stared him down when she thought he was too big for his britches, just as much as he loved the way her eyes darkened when he was deep, deep inside of her.

"Thanks so much," Earl said when Brett handed him a signed check. "If you need anything else, just let me know." Earl turned and Brett went back to the ledger sheet.

"Oh, and by the way," Earl added, drawing Brett's attention once again. "What do you want me to do with this stuff?" The older man lifted the box at his feet.

"What stuff?"

"Just some old coffee cups." Earl rummaged inside. "A few pieces of what looks like some costume jewelry, a couple of faded pictures, and a few other things. We found it all when we dug up the garden. Most of it is covered in dirt and pretty much ruined. I could throw it out if you want—"

"No," Brett cut in, pushing to his feet. He rounded the desk in a matter of seconds as his mind traveled back to the last time he'd seen the inside of his grandfather's safe and its contents before fast-forwarding to the PBR buckle that Karen had recovered from Pappy. The one he'd been digging in the garden with.

Digging?

Or burying?

"The revenuers are coming," his Pappy had said just a few nights ago right before he'd headed out to his garden. *"We have to hide everything."*

It had been the same thing the old man had said to Karen when she'd found him with the buckle.

"Just leave it with me," Brett said, taking the cardboard container from the man.

"You're the boss." Earl signaled good-bye and turned on his heel while Brett's heart beat ninety-to-nothing as he walked back to the desk and set the box on top.

He knew even before he glanced inside what he would find. His gaze shifted and he drank in some of the contents that had once been locked away securely in the safe. His grandmother's bracelet. Her necklace. The bronze baby boots modeled after Brett's first pair. The treasured photographs of his great-grandparents on their wedding day, Pappy in his christening gown, Pappy's first Christmas with his beloved wife, Martha. The small white Bible that Karen had carried during her confirmation sat tucked away amid the dirt-smeared treasures, a yellowed piece of paper sticking out from its dingy folds.

Brett's fingers touched the ancient paper and excitement whispered through him as he slid it free.

And just like that, he found himself staring at the other half of the infamous Texas Thunder recipe.

His muscles went tight and the oxygen snagged in his lungs as reality crashed in on him.

A day late, and several thousand dollars short, but he'd found it.

He'd finally found it.

Read on for an excerpt from the next book
by Kimberly Raye

RED-HOT TEXAS NIGHTS

Coming soon from St. Martin's Paperbacks

CHAPTER 1

It was the moment of truth.

Brandy Tucker switched off the neon pink OPEN sign that hummed in the window of her bakery, Sweet Somethings, and flipped the deadbolt on the front door. Pulling down the hot pink scalloped shades that spanned the storefront windows, she blocked out the rapidly setting sun and a small town full of prying eyes.

The last thing she needed was an audience.

Throwing the deadbolt on the front door, she double checked to make sure the ruffled curtains were pulled to and then walked behind the main display case filled with freshly made cakes and breads.

Her heart beating ninety-to-nothing, she leaned down behind the cash register and pulled out a small pint-sized Mason jar filled with a pale gold liquid.

It wasn't even close to her specialty—chocolate nirvana cake with marshmallow fluff frosting and rich ganache drizzle—but it was just as addictive.

More so if the rumors floating around Rebel, Texas, were even close to the truth.

She could only pray that they were.

Shaking the jar, she watched the bubbles swirl into a tell-tale funnel that, as her late granddaddy used to say, was the sign of a powerful mix. Judging by the speed of the popping and whirling, the alcohol was well over one hundred and sixty proof.

But potency was just the half of it when it came to good moonshine.

Not that Brandy knew all the ins and outs of the stuff. Sure, she was a direct descendent of *the* Archibald Tucker, half of the legendary duo responsible for the infamous Texas Thunder—the best bootleg ever made in the Lone Star State. But Brandy made her living baking cakes and pies. Her claim to fame? Mixing up a light and fluffy butter cream, not stirring together a batch of mash.

Until now.

Her finely tuned taste buds had paid off and she'd done it. She'd supposedly mixed up something better than the original she'd been trying so hard to duplicate. Forget Texas Thunder. This stuff was pure lightning in a jar. A raging tornado.

Texas Tornado.

Her heart pounded at the thought and she drew a deep breath. She was getting way ahead of herself. Yes, she'd tweaked the original recipe, but who knew if it was that much better? All she had was the word of a few bootleggers who'd taken her mash and turned it into an actual brew.

She had no idea if they'd added something to it or altered it during the process. There was no way to be sure that it was one hundred percent hers without seeing the process through—from start to finish.

Which is why she needed to come up with another batch of mash and get it to a professional. Someone who could run the mix in a safe, controlled, *legal* environment. Someone who could tell her if she had, indeed, found her own version of liquid gold.

But first she had to taste this one and see if it truly was all that.

"Don't you think you're going overboard?" Ellie, her baking assistant, asked as she emerged from the storage area. The woman was in her early twenties, tall and thin, with her long red hair pulled back into a ponytail. She wore the tell-tale Sweet Somethings pink apron tied around her waist and a matching T-shirt that read *Go On . . . Whisper Sweet Somethings* to me. "It's not like *we* did anything wrong," she added. "I just handed the mash to a friend who handed it to a friend who handed it to another friend who just so happened to have a still."

"We've still got a jar of illegal moonshine in our possession."

"True, but that's also true for half the people in this town. I'm talking about the processing. We didn't brew anything."

"No, but we might as well have," Brandy paced the length of the counter and fought down a wave of worry. "What if Sheriff DeMassi knocks on that door right now?"

"Sheriff DeMassi is up in Austin at a law enforcement convention. There's just Marty on duty and I've known that boy since he was pulling my hair in Sunday school. He's not the brightest bulb in the tanning bed, so I'm sure he's got his hands full as deputy with the Ladies Rotary Bunko Night going on over at the senior center. You know how those women get when the stakes are high. And hear tell, Laverne Shipley donated a full spa day at the Hair Saloon as a grand prize. I'm sure those old biddies are practically pulling each other's hair out by now. You know Sally Goodwin lost her weave during the last poker tournament they hosted, don't you?"

"Seriously?"

Ellie nodded. "Cara Donnelly pulled it out in one handful after Sally laid down a flush. It wasn't pretty." Ellie's gaze went to the jar sitting on the counter. "Not nearly as pretty as this. I'm telling you, this right here is the mother lode."

Brandy could only hope.

While the original Texas Thunder recipe had finally been found a few days ago, Brandy had no clue if her older sister, Callie, and Callie's fiancé, Brett, were still in the market to sell it. The two had solved most of their own financial problems for the interim, which meant they weren't in any hurry to make a deal.

Perhaps they'd hold onto the recipe. Maybe they'd auction it off. Hell, maybe they'd frame it and keep it for sentimental reasons. Brandy didn't know, and she certainly wasn't asking.

Callie Tucker had given up a scholarship to the University of Texas and forfeited her dreams to stay right here in Rebel and raise her two younger siblings when their parents had passed on. But ten years later, she was finally making her own dreams come true with a job at the local newspaper. Even more, she'd found her own happily-ever-after with the love of her life and once-upon-a-time enemy, Brett Sawyer.

The Sawyers and the Tuckers had been feuding harder and longer than any Hatfield and McCoy, but Callie and Brett were doing their damndest to mend the riff. They were getting married next month, much to the shock and dismay of an entire town still divided, but neither cared about public opinion.

They were in love. Happy.

Brandy certainly wasn't going to fudge that up by dumping a load of problems at Callie's feet.

Big problems.

Namely, Brandy needed to get out from under the loan she'd taken out a few months back to help pay the overdue property taxes left behind after her grandfather's death.

She'd been more than happy to put up her equipment for the secure note to help Callie, who'd been under pressure to save the Tucker family home. But Brandy hadn't counted on the new donut shop that had moved in down the street from her bakery just a few weeks after she'd signed on the dotted line.

A mom and pop endeavor like most places in Rebel, it had taken a bite out of Brandy's early morning rush. Sure, she was the only spot for cakes and pies and other custom-baked goods, but her morning muffin rush had brought in a healthy penny, too. With a fledgling business barely six months old, she had to put every available penny back into her bakery if she wanted it to grow. Chop off a chunk for lost income courtesy of Susie Mae's Habanera jelly-filled donuts—the new *it* breakfast in Rebel—and the substantial loan repayment, and she'd barely broke even this past month. Forget growing and nurturing Sweet Somethings into the go-to destination for all things sugar. Particularly among the special occasion crowd.

At her current size, she could barely produce one wedding cake per week in addition to her regular offerings. To really make a name for herself, she needed to crank out at least three to four custom orders. That meant hiring another cake decorator and bringing in a massive second oven.

And that meant she needed cash.

She reached for the jar. Drawing a deep breath, she willed her hands to steady. Her fingertips caught the edge of the metal and she unscrewed the lid.

In that next instant, the scent of warm strawberries and

something much more potent filled the air and teased her nostrils.

"Go on," Ellie said when Brandy hesitated. "Do it."

"I will. Just keep your shirt on." She tamped down on her reservations, gathered her courage, and touched her lips to the glass.

A quick tilt and the first drop hit her tongue. Slid down her throat. *Shazam!*

Heat rolled through her and firebombed in the pit of her stomach. The floor seemed to tremble. The walls blurred. A ringing echoed in her ears.

Sheesh, the taste packed more of a punch than she'd expected. While she'd never been much of a drinker and she had no intention of becoming one, suddenly she could at least understand why, even in this day and age, there were still men willing to risk life and livelihood to brew up their own hooch.

There was nothing like it.

Like *this*.

Warmth soothed her insides. The sweet, succulent flavor of strawberries danced on her lips. The rich buzz of alcohol filled her head. And dollar signs danced in front of her eyes.

"I think I might be on to something," she gasped, taking another sip just to be sure. Another punch of heat and a full-blown smile split her lips. "It's definitely good. *Really* good."

But was it the best?

She handed over the jar to an eager Ellie and checked the locks on the door again. And then she started for the backroom and the plastic ten gallon tub sitting next to the pile of ingredients she'd assembled for another batch.

Because there was only one way to find out.